THREE WOES

A SUPERNATURAL SURVIVAL STORY

END TIMES BIBLE PROPHECY SERIES
BOOK FOUR

TOBY NEIGHBORS

"Then I looked, and I heard an eagle crying with a loud voice as it flew directly overhead,

"Woe,

woe,

woe

to those who dwell on the earth, at the blasts of the other trumpets that the three angels are about to blow!""

— REVELATION 8:13

1

Some people call me Crazy Hank, and I'm okay with that. If you've lived long enough to read my books, then you know the world seems to have gone completely insane... and I've seen more insanity than most people. You may not believe it, but there is a spiritual dimension that overlays our own. The two dimensions interact in ways I can't really explain, but I've seen into that other place and it's pretty scary, to say the least.

Still, despite a world gone mad and an invisible realm that we can't see, there is hope. Maybe you've seen one of my videos online. I'll admit, I'm not much of a teacher, certainly not as talented as some people I've had the privilege to know. Lorenzo Maltza was my mentor. I went to work for him right out of the United States Air Force, back when there was a United States. Fortunately, I was out before the war, before the "Great Reset", as the powers that be like to call it. But I know what happened to the people that disappeared and I know what's been happening in our crazy world ever since. In fact, I know what's going to happen in the future. Well, not really me, but I know of a book that explains it all. I'm going to tell you all about that, although we're just getting started, so suffice it to say, I'm not like everyone else.

If you've read my other books, you'll understand. If you're just picking this one up and you haven't perused the others, it might seem a little shocking to you. For the past two and a half years, the world has been in a period of time called the Tribulation. Now, before you toss this book into the burn pile, I'll admit that I'm a Christian. I wasn't always, though. I started out as a guy just trying to find some answers. I still am to some extent. You may be, too. You are probably wondering just what happened to our planet. I'm going to tell you, but because it can be a real shock, I'm going to share my story of the last year first.

It starts right after that strange asteroid passed through our atmosphere. Remember the one they called YR4. The scientists claim it was a near miss, but we know there's more to the story. At the time it entered our atmosphere, I was living outside of Mérida on the Yucatan Peninsula. I don't have to tell you about the wars in North America and the earthquake that shook the entire planet. Maybe because I knew what was coming, and maybe because I was supposed to go south, I managed to survive. And not all by myself. I'm married to a wonderful woman who I met in the forests of North Idaho. Mira was known far and wide as a primitive skills teacher and hunter as "Wild Cat". I just call her Cat and thank God every day for her.

My best friend is a former military man named Lester Barski, but everyone calls him LB. He was in charge of security at the Abilene government camp that Cat and I found ourselves in just after the war and before the plague that swept through those encampments like wildfire. He met his better half, Allie Mendolson, there, too, and the four of us managed to survive the trek down to the Yucatan.

To make a long story short, we now live with a group of believers in Jesus Christ in a series of caves only a few miles from the coast and about twice that far to the outskirts of Mérida. We don't have much. We're not survivalists or a militia group, but with the government hunting down anyone who doesn't accept their all-inclusive faith, we have to be careful. At least we did before YK4 went screaming overhead. Since then, the water isn't safe to drink anywhere that we know of except for a spring right outside our main cavern.

I don't have to tell you how it's going with the water systems of the world. People are dying every day and that is no joke. I've seen them. Bellies distended, so sick they can't move and no one to help them. Bottled water has become the most sought-after resource on the planet. And thousands of people in the Yucatan, when they heard about our spring, came to drink, to survive. We welcomed them, helped them, prayed for them and shared the good news with them.

You can probably guess how that went over. A few people listened; the rest turned away or cursed us to our faces. A few even tried to get physical, but LB and I changed their minds about that pretty quickly. We're not violent people, although we are both trained with firearms and we have a few. Cat's an excellent marksman. Most of the believers in our group can handle themselves in a pinch. So, we held out there as long as we could, yet eventually something had to change. We managed to get our hands on an old fishing boat. It had been damaged and repaired many times, but it was still floating and had a working engine.

By the time the NARA (North America Regional Administration) officials showed up at our cave and clean spring, we had the boat loaded with our meager belongings and a lot of clean water. They were ready to fight for control of the spring, but we didn't want trouble. I did warn them that it might dry up after we left. They laughed in my face and we hit the open sea. I can't say I know what happened to the people there, even though we shared the truth with enough of them to feel confident they knew what was coming.

2

"This is beautiful," Cat said as we lay slung in our hammocks on the deck of the fishing boat. Night had fallen and there were over forty people getting ready to go to sleep. LB and Allie were on the night shift. The old boat had a small motor and we weren't in a hurry. We had set out following the coast due east, but were somewhere between Cancún and Cuba. At first, the water had been foul, all bloody and filled with dead fish. But as we moved through the gulf, it cleared up, and the breeze blew fresh air over our ship.

"Ten thousand stars," I said.

"At least," she replied.

"Ever wish we could just stay out here and ride out the rest of the tribulation?"

"Only about a hundred times a day," she said.

We both knew that wasn't going to happen. There was no safe place to hide from what was coming. Even if it had been just the two of us on that fishing boat, we didn't have enough food to last a week. Fortunately, there were only about ninety miles from the Yucatan to Cuba, and once we hit Havana, the Florida coast is only another ninety miles due north. It had taken half a day to reach the open water between Cancún and Cuba. My hope was that we could get to Miami - or what was left of it - in another day or two at the most.

Our friend Allie walked with a limp after getting injured not too long ago. Her leg had healed, but without doctors or surgeons to correct things, it had left her with less function than before. Her limp was exaggerated on the gently rocking boat. She approached us slowly, her hands out. Cat took hold of her hands to steady her friend.

"Everyone is hoping you'll give us an update on what's next," Allie told me.

"I thought we already talked it through," I replied. "There should be plenty of hotels in Miami we can move into. We'll have a fresh start there."

"If they weren't demolished by the earthquake," Cat said. "Or washed away by the tsunami."

"There's only one way to find out," I told them.

"I think they're hoping for more of a Bible update," Allie said. "As in what comes next in the prophetic events."

"Oh," I said, feeling a little foolish. "Sure, I can do that."

"Good," Allie said. "I'll let them know."

I wasn't the official pastor of our group. We weren't a church and I was certainly no theologian. In fact, I was relatively new to Bible prophecy. My mentor, Lorenzo Maltza, had been the expert. Not just on Bible prophecy, but on the supernatural and specifically the UFO phenomenon. I was with him when some of the most respected voices in the Ufology movement were recruited to promote the idea that the rapture was actually a removal of the unenlightened by aliens. Lorenzo had seen through that ploy and tried to warn the others, myself included. But we were all too stupid to see the truth. I could use a kinder word to describe the others, but I was certainly stupid. My mind was all wrapped up in a relationship with a woman who would betray me. When the rapture happened not long after, I was left behind.

Fortunately, God had mercy on me. He's like that, a loving father who doesn't hold our stupidity and stubbornness against us. In fact, he gives us chance after chance to recognize how much we need him. And there's no need to jump through hoops to gain his forgiveness, either. All it takes is simple faith to believe that Jesus Christ was who he said he was, the Son of God. You do that, and you'll find true life and a peace you always dreamed of.

After the rapture, I had poured over the Bible and watched hundreds of hours of Lorenzo's lectures and speeches. It was a crash course in future events. Not everything was spelled out in bold letters about what was coming, but some things certainly were. All you had to do was look for it.

We gathered together in the narrow space between the pilot-house and the area of the deck, where people had made pallets to sleep on or hung hammocks in the rigging. People were sitting on piles of old fishing nets, lobster cages and even the railing of the ship. The pilothouse was small and had no glass in the windows. Allie, Cat, and LB stood inside keeping the ship on course and listening to my talk. I hung a small battery-powered lantern on a nail that was hammered into the wooden wall of the pilothouse, then opened my Bible.

"The fourth angel blew his trumpet, and a third of the sun was struck, and a third of the moon, and a third of the stars, so that a third of their light might be darkened, a third of the day might be kept from shining, and likewise a third of the night," I read. "That's what's coming next, the fourth trumpet judgment."

"What's that mean, Hank?" Someone asked.

"I don't know for certain," I replied honestly. "I just know it will happen."

"When?"

"Next," I said. "There are still four more judgments that take place before the midway point of the tribulation. I'd say that would be in the next twelve months."

"What about the bitter waters?" Someone else asked. "How long will that last?"

"I don't know," I replied honestly. "It could end with the next judgment or it could last until Jesus comes back."

"A third of the sun, moon, and stars," LB said. "That's what, eight hours, say four hours of daylight, four of night?"

"Sounds about right," I said. "And I think we should get settled as soon as we can. The next judgment might be the worst one yet."

3

I'm no prophet. But it seemed to me that every judgment we endured was worse than the last. Fortunately, most of the people in our small group of survivors had managed to find a way through them. The last judgment had been Wormwood that turned the waters bitter. But not all water was tainted and all we had to do was not drink the bad water. Simple, right? And there were other judgments that allowed us to prepare for it beforehand, like the great earthquake. Although I'll admit that one caught me off guard.

So, with the warning from scripture in our minds, we tried to sleep. Some people were seasick, others were too wound up to sleep. For my part, I found the rocking of the boat and the sultry air of the Caribbean to be just what I needed. I slept until dawn, and when I got up, I could see the coast of Cuba behind us.

"Morning, Hank," LB said with a big grin when I joined him in the pilothouse. "Sleep well?"

"I did, actually, thanks for asking," I replied. "We've turned north?"

"Yes indeed," the big man said. "We passed Havana about an hour back, what was left of it anyway."

They were hit hard?"

"Looked like it. The entire city was burned. Nothing left but scorched buildings and piles of ash. I didn't see a soul, but it had to be Havana. It was bigger than any of the other villages we've sailed past."

"Good enough for me," I told him. "How about I take over and you get some sleep?"

"I won't say no," he replied. "But now, you wake me up when we're back along the coast of Florida. All I need is a few winks."

"I promise," I told him. "Thanks for taking the night shift."

"No problem. I sent Allie to get some rest a few hours ago. I better find where she's at."

I opened a bottle of water and took a drink. You might think that water wouldn't be very welcome, but to us, every drop of pure water was as sweet as honey. Especially after seeing what the bitter water did to people and how many poor souls died from dehydration. It was a terrible way to die and I was grateful for every sip of water I got after that.

The little boat was chugging away. We had to refill the engines with fuel every few hours, and she only got about ten miles per hour, but by late afternoon, the Florida coast was in sight. As darkness fell, we caught sight of Miami. There were lights on in the city, yet most of the big coastal hotels were dark.

"Let's weigh anchor," LB suggested. "Tomorrow morning we'll go ashore and find a place."

A few security volunteers stayed up through the night while the rest of us slept. In the dawn, we fired up the engine and made for shore. There were once pristine beaches along the coast of Miami. Those had been filled with the wreckage of ships and refuse from the sea. Just like the waters around the Yucatan, the ocean waters near Miami were more blood than water, a result of what the Bible calls the Second

Trumpet Judgment. Essentially, something from space, probably part of asteroid YK4, hit the oceans and caused a massive die off of fish. The Bible says it turned a third of the oceans to blood, killed a third of the fish, and destroyed a third of the ships on the sea. As someone who just happened to be in a boat when that happened, I can testify that the tsunami that resulted was probably one of the scariest things the world has ever experienced. The result of that judgment was still lingering.

Just like the wrecked ships that littered the beaches, many of the docks had been destroyed, but a few had been rebuilt. We made for one and tied up the fishing boat before climbing out onto solid ground again. It took me a while to regain my land legs. Half of the group stayed with the ship and the rest of us went ashore. We got lucky, too. My plan had been to squat in an abandoned hotel, but instead we found a deserted apartment complex. It was two stories and built well back from the sea shore. We moved in with our meager belongings, including our water. Most of it was in plastic jugs and five-gallon canisters. We were sweating bullets by the time it was hauled up from the ship and safely stored in one of the empty apartments.

There weren't many people in the city, at least not in the section we found ourselves in. Miami had been a thriving, multicultural metropolis before the rapture and the war that followed. We didn't see many people, but there were bodies in various states of decay. Packs of dogs roamed the streets. I was glad to have a weapon in hand as we explored the area.

"What now?" LB asked. "We hunker down, secure this location?"

"What about food?" Preston asked. "We're already getting low."

"That has to be our first priority," I said. "We find food, supplies, maybe even a way to get some power back on in the apartment building."

"What if we're attacked?" Allie asked.

That brought me up short. The last thing I wanted was to get into a shooting match with people. We weren't a military group. Most of the people I was looking after hadn't even handled a weapon before.

They had gathered with Jonathan, our Jewish friend and evangelist, who helped establish the group before moving on to take the good news of God's love and forgiveness further south into Central America.

"We have to protect ourselves," Cat said.

"That's true," I conceded, "but let's not go looking for trouble."

We split up into three groups. One was left at the apartments to guard the water. The other two groups went in opposite directions to look for food. Some people don't believe that God directs his people or cares about the minutiae of our lives. When I first went to work for Lorenzo Maltza, I didn't even believe in God. But in the years since the rapture, I've seen God do incredible things... and we were in store for a miracle in Miami.

4

I led the group that went south of the apartments. I wasn't that familiar with the city of Miami, and most of it was destroyed by the judgments like the great earthquake, but we had found a very good spot among the ruins. Some people might call that luck, I called it God's blessing.

The apartments we discovered were in a section of the city not far from the coast, and close to Matheson Hammock Park. We found that wildlife had taken over the green spaces. There weren't a lot of stores in that area, but most of the homes had been abandoned. We found lots of canned goods and dried foods like pasta and potato chips.

Both teams gathered a haul of food and returned to the apartment building. All the homes had been opened up by a resourceful member of our group who was good at picking locks. The Bible calls believers "saints", but most of the people in our group (including myself) had a very spotty past.

The apartments were small and simple. Cat and I cleaned one out, removing the old clothing and washing bedsheets. That night, we opened a can of Spam and a bag of barbecue potato chips. It wasn't very healthy, but we slept with a full stomach and were grateful for it.

The following day, we met a group of people living in one of the large homes not far from the apartments. They were exhausted and afraid. We had guns, which they expected us to use on them. Instead, we got to share with them, and they, in turn, showed us the warehouse. It was really LB who got the ball rolling. He cooked up a pot of chili and we passed out sleeves of saltine crackers. More importantly, we handed out bottles of water. As the group talked, we discovered they had been rebellious teens. They knew the city and how to get things. It was utilizing those things that held them back.

"What y'all need is some YouTube videos," LB said. "Learn how to do just about anything with them YouTube videos."

"Don't make them wish for something they can't have," Allie warned him.

The leader of the house group was a young man with acne and a bad haircut. They called him Flex.

"I know where there's computers," he said. "That ain't the problem. No power, no way to turn 'em on."

"Just call the power company," LB said. "They'll run right out and fix ya up."

"Stop teasing," Allie said.

"There might be solar power down here," Cat said. "This is the Sunshine State after all."

"Yeah, I know where they've got solar panels, too," Flex said. "This place has all that stuff, but we don't know how to work it."

"A place with computers and solar power equipment?" I asked.

"Yeah, all that stuff," Flex said.

"Can you show us?" Allie asked.

Flex shrugged. "Sure."

And the next day, he did. It was a long trek from where we had taken up residence. There were packs of dogs in the streets and even an alligator near a waterway. It watched us pass without ever moving. I can't say for sure if it was alive or dead, but its eyes were open, and when we came back that same way, it was gone.

After a two-hour hike through the city, the home group led us to what had once been the operational headquarters of Solar Solutions, Inc. Just like the group said, it was just a warehouse; part garage, part storage spaces and part offices.

"It's pretty dark inside," Flex said as he raised one of the overhead doors that led into the garage section of the warehouse.

"What have we here?" LB said. "Baby, this looks right up your alley."

He was referring to a fleet of well-used service vehicles. They were single-cab pickup trucks with frames in the back that held sets of ladders attached to them. In the bed of the trucks were built-in tool storage and space for hauling equipment. Some were even loaded with solar panels, wire spools and batteries for storing the electricity.

"Jackpot," I said.

"I can't believe this is just sitting here," Cat said. "Why hasn't it been looted?"

"No one knows how to use it," Allie said.

Flex wasn't wrong. Even though the sun was bright outside, the interior of the warehouse was gloomy and dark. But that didn't stop Allie. She went in and opened the cab of one of the trucks.

"They don't run," Flex said.

"She ain't gonna take no trip, bud," LB said. "Just watch and learn."

Allie rummaged around for a few minutes, then came out with a tool belt and an LED light attached to an elastic headband.

"There's probably more of these in the other trucks," she said.

We found the lights and explored the building. There was a pair of vending machines in the break room. The group of young people broke them open and feasted on junk food while the rest of us explored the warehouse. It didn't take long to discover the entire facility was powered by solar panels attached to the roof. They had survived the judgments, but the wiring had not, and the battery banks, the big industrial types, were all drained.

"So, what's the plan?" I asked. "Can we get things up and running around here?"

"I don't see why not," Allie said. "But it might take a while."

"We can reconnect the panels, but it might take a few days to pool enough energy to get this place running," LB said.

"We don't need the entire place running," I said. "Just the computers."

"We can do better than that," Allie said. "I'll reconnect to the panels. It won't take too long to charge up one of the truck batteries."

"Oh, yeah. That's the ticket," LB said.

"And there's plenty of equipment here to get power going back at the apartments. We can charge up computers, run some lights."

"What about AC?" LB asked. "I miss some good cool air, that's a fact."

"Not that much power," Allie said. "But maybe enough to get a few of the refrigerators operating."

"That would be a major improvement," Cat said. "There's plenty of game to hunt. We can harvest food from the land, maybe do some foraging too."

"Not me," LB said. "Y'all seen that gator, right? I ain't messing with them, no sir!"

"The point is, we can stock up on real food," Cat said.

I knew we needed to conserve ammunition. The solar warehouse wasn't looted, but I knew every sporting goods and firearm store would be. There was little chance of getting more bullets, and if we ran out, the guns would be worthless. But we had to tackle one problem at a time... and the equipment in the warehouse was a godsend.

"Let's do it," I said. "Get the power flowing. I'll start an inventory on what's in storage that we can use."

Little did I know I was about to make a very important discovery. One that would make all the difference to our little community in the days ahead.

5

Alongside solar panels and hardware for setting them up, Solar Solutions offered a variety of battery bank configurations, including whole-home units, like the Tesla Powerwall. But the real treasure was a pallet full of Starlink internet units.

"What'd you find?" LB asked as I began hauling equipment out of the storage area.

"A chance to find out what's going on in the world," I said.

"How's that?" He asked.

"Look," I said, holding up the Starlink box. "Internet in a box."

"Oh, man, that's slick, Hank. But why do we need it?"

"Are you kidding me? Don't you want to find out what's going on everywhere else?"

"You mean, do I want to know what the anti-Christ and his little green men are up to? Not really, no."

"Well, help me load this equipment up anyway," I said. "You can watch cat videos on YouTube instead of keeping up with world events."

"Very funny," he said.

We loaded one truck with solar equipment, while the young

people stocked up on canned sodas. By late afternoon, Allie had a truck battery charged up. We checked all the electrical connections. Being so close to the ocean made metal oxidize rapidly, including that on battery terminals and inside an engine compartment.

Once we had done all we could to ensure the vehicle would run, including charging the battery, we gave the engine a try. It was sluggish; the fuel pump diaphragm had dried out. Cat removed the fuel line from the fuel injectors on the engine and backfilled it to get the pump working. On the second try, the engine rotated, activating the fuel pump and the truck started.

"Is there anything you can't do, girl?" LB asked.

"I'm not much of a cook," she said.

"That ain't true," LB said.

"Can we get the other vehicles working?" I asked.

"We could try and jump one of the other vehicles, but I wouldn't run them all," Allie said. "We'll run out of fuel soon."

"But we can siphon the other vehicles if we need to," Cat said.

We got a second vehicle running and then started back for the apartments we were calling home. LB drove the supplies and I followed in the second truck. The young people piled into the back. I was tempted to turn on the air conditioning in the cab, but we had lived so long without it that Cat and I decided to keep it off and conserve gas.

It only took half an hour to drive back through the abandoned streets. A few times, we had to stop and go around an obstruction in the road, but it was much easier going than walking. That night, we all slept soundly. Bright and early the next morning, Allie recruited some help and started setting up the solar panels on top of the second-story roof of the apartment building. Wires were run to the Powerwalls. I set up a Starlink device outside the apartment building's office. Soon, we had four of the Solar Solution laptops charging up. They were all password protected, but someone had written the code on the bottom of their laptop with a permanent marker and fortunately the same password unlocked all four of the portable computers. I powered one on and plugged it into the Starlink router. It took less than a minute to get a solid internet connection.

"We're online," I said.

"Food, power, internet," Preston, one of the security members of our group, spoke up. "We have everything we need."

I brought up a news site, and the top story was written all in bold letters:

Water Disaster Averted - Clean Water Available Everywhere

"Is that for real?" Cat asked.

"I guess so," I replied, as I scanned the article. "Looks like the world government is claiming to have solved the problem."

"What a bunch of liars," LB said.

There was a picture of Paul Eon in a hard hat beside a river. Closer to the water was the tall, Nordic-featured alien who called himself Shemi Hazah. I'm pretty sure the being posing as an intelligent alien from another planet was actually one of the fallen angels. He was waist-deep in the water with his hands poised above the surface. The article claimed that the Apkallu, which is what the supposed aliens called themselves, had cleaned the world's water supply.

"This is why I wanted to be online," I said.

"Tell me you don't believe that nonsense," LB said.

"Of course not, but it means one thing we need to get ready for."

"What's that?" Cat asked.

"The Wormwood judgment has passed; that means the fourth trumpet judgment could happen at any time."

To get ready, we gathered more goods from the Solar Solutions warehouse, but also more food, tools, and supplies from wherever we could find them in the city. Vehicles were mined for fuel. Bicycles were used to help search parties gather food and clothing from the abandoned homes.

At night, the members of our group worked together preparing food for everyone. And there were newcomers arriving every day. Most were more interested in food and internet access than the truth about the times we were living in, but the little community was growing and peaceful. I shouldn't have been surprised when some of the new people who had joined our group began to scoff at my teaching.

"You really think this is some kind of judgment on the world?" Flex asked. "I thought all the narrow-minded people were taken away."

That got a chuckle from his friends. A more serious person, Eddy Farning, stood up.

"I didn't know this was a cult," he said angrily, before storming away.

It was hard to deal with rejection, and I'll admit at times I was so angry I had to walk away. People showed up daily who didn't mind taking whatever we were willing to give, even moving into the unoccupied apartments in our building, but most refused to listen to the good news of God's love. I had to remind myself that I was the same way at one time. I had put off what I knew to be true, even after Lorenzo Maltza had saved me from a demon intent on possessing my body and causing me to do things I would never have done willingly.

Perhaps it didn't help that I couldn't explain much about the next judgment we warned people about. A third of the sun, moon, and stars would go dark. That was easy enough to picture, although not the why or what it would mean. But we all found out... and it happened sooner than we expected.

6

It was the next day when we saw the trucks. They were all white EVs with the North American Regional Administration logo on the side.

"What do you think about this?" LB asked.

We were side by side, attaching solar panels to the roof of our two-story apartment building.

"It can't be good," I said.

The trucks were moving through the city. Three stopped in front of our apartment building. My friends, which now included the young people who helped us find the solar equipment, came out to see what was happening. LB and I came down off the roof as an olive-skinned man in a three-piece business suit stepped out of one of the trucks.

"Hello," he said in a friendly voice. "My name is Floyd. Is someone in charge here?"

People turned and looked at me. I would have said that no one was in charge, but apparently, I had been elected by secret committee. The truth was, people in the group thought that I had some type of authority because of what God had shown me. I didn't think that was the case. Yes, I had seen some amazing things. I did have some knowledge of Bible prophecy, but that didn't mean I was in charge of anything. The group wasn't affiliated or obligated to me or anything else. We were just like-minded folks who were trying to survive the most dangerous seven years of human history.

"I guess that would be me," I said. "I'm Hank."

"It's a pleasure to meet you, Hank. Again, my name is Floyd, I'm with NARA and we have good news. Things are changing here in what used to be the States. More areas are opening up. We're connecting people via online and community services. All we ask in return is that you register."

"Oh, hell no," LB mumbled.

Floyd heard him, but chose to ignore the comment.

"Some of us have had unpleasant experiences with the government," I said. "My wife and I were in a FEMA camp that was overrun."

"Yes, there are quite a lot of unfortunate stories like yours," Floyd said. "It's the primary reason why we need everyone to register. There are families trying to find one another."

"What if we don't want to be found?" Pattie, a member of the security team, asked.

"That's... odd," Floyd said. "I suppose that might make some people wonder if you had something to hide... anyway, registration is necessary if you want access to government resources. And trust me, I understand that the United States government did a lot of things wrong before the end. But NARA is different. We are bringing people back together and connecting the world."

"We've got internet," I said. "Working on sustainable power, too."

"I see that. It's very industrious of you," Floyd said. "I'm guessing you appropriated that equipment. We aren't pointing fingers. Since the water crisis, things have been in shambles, but NARA is committed to rectifying that situation. We're going to be collecting reusable goods throughout the city. If you could share with us what you found, and where, it would be a help."

"What types of resources are you giving out?" One of the young people, a girl named Lucern, asked.

"Food, clothing, medicine," Floyd said. "Jobs too. Once you're registered, you can earn digital currency. We'll be helping everyone get housing soon, then transportation. If you have useful skills, we need you. Administrator Nevida will be coming to Miami in a few weeks to check on our progress. It's a pretty big honor. I hope you'll all come out to the registration center very soon."

"Where's it at?" Flex asked.

"Hard Rock Stadium in Miami Gardens."

"That's way up on the north side," Flex said. "Where the Dolphins used to play."

"Correct. We can schedule transportation if you like," Floyd offered.

"That's okay," I told him. "We got a couple of trucks running. We should be okay."

"We already have crews clearing the streets, starting with the Interstates and working our way across the city," Floyd said. "Here's my card. There's new tech coming in soon. Wearables that will keep you connected to the Global Federation. Administrator Nevida says that Administrator Eon is leading the way. Things are looking up. The new golden age is almost upon us."

"Sounds too good to be true," LB said.

"It isn't. We are shaking off the chains of the past and stepping into a bright new future," Floyd said. "Can we count on your support?"

I looked around. Most of the faces I saw were either masks formed to hide emotions or outright hostility. "We're very interested in helping people," I said. "Thank you so much for the information, Mr. Floyd."

We shook hands. Mine was hot, and probably, a little grimy. His was cold, surprisingly so. At the time, I guessed it was because of the air conditioning inside the truck he rode in. But in time, I would learn the truth.

When the trucks left, everyone had questions. They were all looking to me for guidance.

"What are they talking about?" Preston asked. "Is this the mark of the beast?"

"The what?" Flex asked.

I held up a hand to try and calm people down. "I don't think so," I admitted. "But we know it's coming."

"What's coming?" Tua, one of the youngest members of the group, asked.

"Hard times," I said. "Some of you aren't aware of this, but the Bible says we are living in a period of time known as the Tribulation."

"Oh, man, don't even go there," Eddy Farning said.

"You're Bible thumpers?" Lucern asked.

"We're just people," I said. "And you know that what you're hearing from NARA isn't the whole story."

"Don't they execute people like you?" Tua asked.

"I thought all the bigots were taken before the war," Lucern said.

"We aren't bigots," I said. "I didn't want to hear about the truth at first, either. But my mentor helped me to see what's really going on in the world. All I'm going to say about that right now is that everything we've seen and experienced since the disappearances were predicted in the Bible. If you want to know more about that, come see me this evening."

"Count me out," Lucern said.

She, Eddy, and Tua walked away. No one tried to stop them or convince them otherwise. We knew from hard experience that talking about our faith was dangerous.

"If this isn't the mark of the beast," Cat asked, "what do you think it is?"

"A precursor," I said.

"Will you register, Hank?" Gretchen, one of the oldest members of our group, asked.

I shook my head. "No, but I'm certain we'll be persecuted for that resistance."

"Let 'em," LB said. "Won't be the first."

"We're secure in the father's hands," Allie added.

"Who's father?" Flex asked.

"Remember the next judgment," I said. "We need to finish the solar panels and the wiring. We're going to need it."

Pattie and Preston approached. "Should we get the guns?" She asked.

"No," I told her. "The guns are for hunting, not fighting. We don't want to start trouble."

Most of the group was returning to the tasks that had occupied them before Floyd had shown up. There were only a handful of people who weren't elderly in our original group. And the young people we had stumbled upon in Miami weren't much help with the manual labor. LB started back up the ladder, but I waited with Flex and his friend Hannah.

"Tell us what's really going on," Flex said.

"Have a seat," I told them, pointing to some shade under a group of palm trees. "I'll do more than tell you what's going on. I'll show you."

Flex shrugged. Hannah took his hand as they moved off toward the shade. I went into the little apartment and got my Bible. For safety, the cover had been removed and replaced with the hardback cover to *War & Peace*.

"Good luck," Cat said.

"Pray for me," I told her.

"Always," she said, sitting down by our laptop computer and bringing up a news site.

I went outside and approached Flex and Hannah. He looked skeptical. She looked scared.

"Nervous?" I asked.

"Nah," he said.

"Should we be?" Hannah asked.

"Yes, actually," I responded. "I'm going to show you the truth and that's always dangerous, but especially now. It could cost you your life, but better to die in the here and now than to spend an eternity in eternal torment. How familiar are you with the message of God and the gospel of Jesus Christ?"

Flex shrugged, and Hannah shook her head. There were already tears in her eyes. I understood how they felt. I remembered that I had seen things that defied explanation. Fortunately, I had Lorenzo to help me through it. He was kind and patient. I tried to be both as I told Flex and Hannah about what was happening in the world.

"There's a lot to this story," I said. "So I'm going stick to the main points for now, okay?"

They both nodded.

"This book," I said, opening my Bible.

"War and Peace?" Hannah asked.

"No, this is the Bible. I just changed to cover because there are people who would burn it and probably kill me for having it.

Hannah swallowed and Flex glanced over his shoulder nervously.

"Don't worry, you're safe here," I assured them as I ran my hand over the open Bible. "This is what my mentor used to call the guidebook to the supernatural. We've been taught since we were little that what we can see, hear, smell and touch is all there is to the world. But it isn't. There's more, a lot more. The Bible is God's message to us. It not only tells us who he is and who we are, but it tells us what's going to happen in the future so that we know it's all true.

"There were different periods in history when God dealt with humanity differently. Suffice it to say that before the disappearances, we were in what was known as the Church Age. The Bible teaches that we are now in a seven-year period of God's wrath and the final chance for humanity to acknowledge him as the Creator and Savior. We'll get more into that, if you're interested, but first, let me share with you the bona fides of the Bible."

I opened up to Revelations - Chapter 6 - and showed them the scriptures that outlined the Seal Judgments.

"The first is the rider on a white horse," I said. "We didn't know it at the time, but that was Administrator Paul Eon. He made a treaty with Israel, which was predicted in a different part of the Bible. The second seal judgment was war and I don't have to tell you about that."

It's pretty vague," Flex said. "This could be talking about anyone."

"Just keep it in mind," I said. "The third seal judgment was famine. Do you remember when prices went crazy and people were killing each other over a can of soup?"

"Yeah," Flex said.

"It was terrifying," Hannah added.

"It sure was," I agreed. "And then the fourth judgment was death. A quarter of the population died, remember?"

They both nodded. I took a breath and plunged on.

"Fifth judgment was persecution of believers in Christ," I said.

"That was against any narrow-minded religions that proclaimed they had a monopoly on truth," Flex said. "Not just Christianity."

"How many Buddhists did you see beheaded?" I asked. "How many Hindus?"

"This is crazy," Flex snapped.

"But he isn't wrong," Hannah said.

"Sixth judgment was the great earthquake."

"There have always been earthquakes, man," Flex insisted. "Come on, this is getting pretty thin."

"How many worldwide earthquakes have there been?" I asked. "Have you ever heard of a quake that affected the entire world?"

Hannah shook her head and I could see the doubt in Flex's eyes, but his resolve was starting to crumble.

"Look, this book was written almost two thousand years ago," I said. "It predicted all these things, and more." I turned the page to chapter eight. "The last seal judgment is the opening of the trumpet judgments. We're right between the third and fourth one now."

"What were they?" Hannah asked.

"Trumpet one was the hailstorms, with fire and blood."

"Holy shit," Flex said. "That's in the Bible?"

I showed him Revelation chapter eight, verse seven, *"The first angel blew his trumpet, and there followed hail and fire, mixed with blood, and these were thrown upon the earth. And a third of the earth was burned up, and a third of the trees were burned up, and all green grass was burned up."*

"This is the proof," I said. "This is how we know we can trust what the Bible says ... and what it predicts is coming. The second trumpet judgment was the catastrophe on the oceans. Where were you when that happened?"

"My dad's place in Belle Glade," Flex said.

"Hiding in a parking garage in Parkland," Hannah said. "Me, Lucinda, and Tua."

"That one nearly got me," I admitted. "Just because I've got access to the Bible doesn't mean I have all the answers. But God spared me and Cat. We managed to meet back up with our friends, LB and Allie. Eventually, we found the group of believers hiding down near Mérida on the Yucatan Peninsula. We came up here after the third judgment."

"The thing with the water," Flex said.

I nodded. "Pretty smart," I told him. "Did you see Wormwood?"

"What?" Hannah asked.

"The thing that passed through the sky like a comet," I said. "The Bible calls it Wormwood because it made a third of the water bitter. Wormwood means bitter."

"Oh," Hannah said.

"Yeah, we saw it," Flex said. "That was some crazy sh—"

Hannah elbowed him. "Stop cussin', Flex," she warned him."

"Sorry, man," Flex said.

"That's okay. It was crazy. And things are only going to get crazier."

7

"Wait," the young man said and put a hand on the side of his head. "You're saying all the stuff that's happened to the world was written in the Bible?"

I nodded and Hanna leaned forward. She was clearly anxious to know more.

"But if that's true, how come no one expected it? We should have been ready for it."

"People knew, but they didn't believe it," I told him. "I know I didn't. To be honest, I didn't believe anything. I was just doing what I had to do, hardly thinking about anything other than myself."

Flex shook his head. "No, man, this don't make no sense. How could people not know? And how can they still deny it if it really is the way you say?"

"That's a great question," I told him. "You see, the Bible doesn't just tell us about what's going to happen in the world. It also tells us what happened in the past. Not just here, but in the spiritual realms."

"Really?" Hannah asked.

"This is getting a little too trippy," Flex said.

"Just hang with me a moment," I told him. "Where do you think all this came from?"

"What? The world?"

"The world, humanity, everything, even the universe itself. Where did it come from?"

"The big bang or something," Flex said.

"God?" Hannah asked.

"We were taught in school that the universe arose by natural processes. But did you know the very existence of those processes working in conjunction is so unlikely as to be scientifically considered impossible? We were told that life on Earth arose naturally via evolution through natural selection until scientists realized that even in the simplest, singled-celled organism carries too much information in their DNA for life to arise on its own."

"I remember something 'bout it," Flex said quietly.

"I could spend hours going over the ways in which the universe and humans can only exist via the work of a wise creator operating outside of time and space. But, if you'll allow me, let's assume that God exists and that the Bible really is his message to us. Can we do that?"

Flex shrugged and Hannah nodded enthusiastically.

"In the Bible, we have the creation story, and in it, we are told about another created being who tempts Adam and Eve to disobey God."

"The devil," Hannah said.

"Oh, man, I can't believe this," Flex said. He looked down and rubbed the top of his head, but didn't get up.

"The Bible tells us that there was a spiritual creature who once served God and walked in the Garden of Eden. But he chose to rebel against God."

"Why?" Hannah asked.

"Because, in his pride, he wanted to *be* God. He wanted to be worshiped and sit in the place of highest honor. But, he couldn't. And so, he turned his attention to harming what God loves."

"What's that?" Flex asked without looking up.

"People," I told them. "The Bible teaches us that God loves us so much that he sent His Son, Jesus, to die as the payment for all our sins. And that if we believe in Jesus, if we accept that he was who he said he was, that we have forgiveness of all our sins and that we're adopted into God's family."

"Sounds too good to be true," Flex said.

"All we have to do is believe? What about going to church, or getting baptized, and stuff like that?" Hannah asked.

"That stuff was good, but it didn't save you."

"Got to be a good person," Flex said.

"Actually..." I said. "The Bible doesn't say anything about being a good person. In fact, it says we can't be good. That only God is good. We're all sinners. We all sin all the time and we're all falling far short of God's glorious standard. But the good news of Jesus Christ is that he offers us salvation as a free gift. If you believe in Jesus, who claimed to be God the Son, and believe that he died and rose again, you will be saved."

"I don't have to do anything?" Hannah asked incredulously.

It was a hot day. The wind blowing across the small area where we sat in the shade of the tree was warm. I could feel my lips getting chapped. And I was suddenly restless. Part of me wanted to get up and move around. At the same time, I felt foolish. It was like everything I was telling the young couple was absolute nonsense. Had I become a crazy Christian? Worse yet, was I some kind of sadistic cult leader? Maybe Eddy was right, and I was slipping into insanity, and dragging down all the people I loved along with me.

But then, in the back of my mind, I almost heard a voice say, "Keep going." It wasn't audible. Just a thought, sort of a mental nudge. In many ways it was no different than a thought springing up in my mind, but it seemed to come from somewhere, or someone, other than myself.

"That's what makes Christianity unique," I told her. "In every other religion in the world, a person needs to do things to go to heaven when they die. You have to give so much money, obey certain rules, make a pilgrimage, help the poor, the list goes on and on. In those religions, it's all about what you do to earn your reward. But in Christianity, Jesus did it all. We don't have to do anything. We just believe and God does the rest."

Our conversation went on for a while. They both had questions, and I did my best to answer them. But then God did something I couldn't do. No one heard the fourth trumpet blast, but suddenly, without warning, everything went dark.

"What's happening?" Hannah said, her voice brimming with fear.

"Holy shit!" Flex declared. "Oh, no! Oh, no!"

"Hang on," I said.

"I'm blind!" Hannah shouted.

"No, you're not blind," I tried to reassure her.

But in reality, there wasn't much confidence in my voice. It wasn't just dark out; it was pitch black. It was like we had all been dropped into a deep underground cave where no light can reach you. The sun didn't just stop shining. There were no stars, no moon, just inky black darkness.

From the rooftop behind me, I heard JD say, "Well, this ain't good."

"What is happening?" Flex demanded to know.

"It's the fourth trumpet judgment," I told him. "Remember, I warned you all that this would happen. A third of the sun and a third of the stars will stop shining."

"That's impossible, man!" Flex shouted. "You're talking crazy. This is all crazy!"

"Just stay calm," I told him. "We've been preparing for this."

At that moment, the breeze picked up slightly and it was cooler than before. It felt refreshing at first, almost like I had stepped in front of an electric fan. Behind me, Cat stepped to the door of the apartment building's tiny office. "Electronics are all down," she said. "Flashlights too."

I reached into my pocket and pulled out the small butane lighter I carried with me. I flipped back to the top and spun the wheel, which created a spark. The flame rose to life and cast a small ring of golden light around me.

"Candles," I said. "Light the candles and let's check on everyone."

Hannah and Flex went with me back to the office, where, to their relief, Cat had already lit them a candle. We had collected all the candles we could find since arriving in Miami. But we had no idea how long the fourth trumpet judgment would last. Maybe it would be short, or maybe it would go on and on. We had no way of knowing.

"Try not to burn more than one at a time," I said. "A third of the day and a third of the night is eight hours. We'll run out of candles if we aren't careful."

"I believe," Hannah said, putting her hand on my arm. "I believe in Jesus!"

"That's wonderful," I told her. "We'll all help you learn as much about him as we can."

"We have a few extra Bibles," Cat said. "Tomorrow I'll find one for you."

"Flex?" Hannah said.

"I don't know, babe. This... this is heavy shi... I mean heavy stuff."

"We won't push you," I said. "But don't wait too long. None of us are promised tomorrow."

"Yeah, I get that," Flex said. "Let's go find the others. They're probably flipping out about now."

The young couple went off with a candle to find their friends. I went around to the ladder. Climbing a ladder up twenty-five feet into the air while holding a candle isn't easy. With every step I took, the flame flickered. I was afraid that it would go out. The wind hadn't let up either. Most days and nights, there was a steady breeze coming off the ocean. I tried to shield the candle with my body, but it wasn't easy. When I reached the top, the candle shone just bright enough that I could see LB sitting on the roof.

"Man, I thought I was stuck up here," he said.

"Just be careful getting to the ladder," I told him. "This candle could go out any minute."

And it wasn't just the fragility of the candle flame that was worrisome. The darkness was thick and heavy. It's a little odd to describe it in such terms. Normally, darkness is just the absence of light. But what we found ourselves in was different from that. It was almost like the darkness was alive. All my life, I've heard people say that darkness can't extinguish light, yet it seemed that after the fourth trumpet judgment, that axiom was no longer true. The light from my candle was small and weak. In fact, it seemed to be getting weaker every minute. Fortunately, it was enough light for LB to find the ladder and get safely down from the roof.

We took our candles and went to check on the members of our group. Most had been in their apartments or close by when the judgment took place. They were grateful to get a candle lit, and no one was hurt, but by the time we had checked on everyone, the temperature had fallen dramatically.

"Got to be twenty degrees cooler," LB said as he and Allie joined Cat and me in our apartment.

"And it's going to get colder," Allie said. "We don't have heaters."

"There's a lot we don't have," Cat said. "And we were expecting this."

"Tomorrow we should go and find as much as we can," I said. "Forget the solar setup for now."

"It don't do us much good," LB said. "Even when the sun was shining all day, we weren't gaining much electricity."

"We'll have to cut back on everything that uses electricity," Allie said.

She was right, but we were indoors, and we had candles. LB and Allie returned to their own apartment. There was nothing more to do. I kept my lighter handy, but we blew out the candle. Since the water was no longer bitter, we were able to pump enough to bathe with. I washed off in the dark and felt a shiver of cold, which was a sensation I hadn't felt in a long time. The Yucatan was hot, although it had been a little cooler in the caves we sheltered in. And Miami was both hot and incredibly humid. Although, after cleaning myself up, I felt chilly.

"We should close the windows," I said.

"Already did," Cat said. "And there's an extra blanket on the bed."

"You are a saint," I said. "My very own angel."

I felt my way to the bed and pulled back the covers. That's when the first image flashed in my mind. We had extinguished our candle, so the room was completely black. I couldn't see my hand in front of my face, much less anything else. But I had lived in the small apartment long enough to know my way from the little bathroom to the bed. But when I pulled back the covers, it was like I saw the mattress. The sudden vision was similar to the flash from a bolt of lightning in the dark. For just a split second, it was as if I could see. Only what I saw horrified me.

I screamed. Which frightened Cat, who screamed in response. The walls of our little domicile weren't thick or well-insulated. I heard the woman in the next unit over scream as well, and there was rustling movement in the apartment above us.

"What is it? What happened, Hank?" Cat asked. "Are you hurt?"

I felt cold, not from the temperature but from fear. In that moment, I had seen my bed covered in blood and writhing with large, white maggots. Nestled on top of them was Cat's lifeless body. Her eyes had been open and glassy. I dropped to my knees.

"I'm not hurt," I said, leaning against the bed. "I'm okay."

"What happened?"

"I don't know," I said, while silently praying, *Oh, God, please don't let it be a vision of what's to come. Please don't let her die.*

"Hank, you're scaring me," she said.

"I saw something," I told her.

And I wasn't the only one. From another apartment, there was another piercing scream.

"What is going on?" Cat said.

In that moment, I knew. I can't say how I knew; the explanation just popped into my head and I was absolutely certain of it. As we struggled to survive the judgments of the tribulation, most of our study of the Bible had centered on the prophetic texts. But I remembered in that moment something that Lorenzo Maltza had taught me. He always seemed to know what to say and do, no matter what happened to him or what he was being presented with. He told me that one of his spiritual gifts was the word of knowledge. I didn't know what a spiritual gift was, much less a word of knowledge, but it turns out that the Holy Spirit enabled the Christians in the church age to do things. Sometimes they had the wisdom to know what to do in a given situation, at other times they were shown prophecies, or even able to heal the sick. Since the end of the church age, the Holy Spirit didn't dwell within believers, but I never felt abandoned. It always seemed like, during the most trying circumstances that God helped me.

I believe I received a word of knowledge about the darkness of the fourth trumpet judgment in that very moment.

"Fear," I said out loud. "It's not just darkness, Cat. There are beings that dwell in darkness and hate the light. They've got free rein now."

"What does that mean? Are we in danger?"

"No," I said. "They can't hurt us, but they have the power to frighten us. Maybe it is worse for the people who don't believe in Jesus. Come on, we have to help."

I flicked on my lighter and saw Cat across from me. She was in the bed with the covers pulled up to her chin. She looked at me, and I felt a shiver of relief. Her eyes were clear and bright with life. But she also looked pale and terrified.

"I thought it was better to just wait this out," I told Cat. "But we need to warn everyone about the demonic activity in the darkness."

"I don't want to move," Cat said.

"You can stay here, if you want to."

"Not alone," she demanded.

"I think God showed me what's happening, sweetheart. He wants me to tell the group."

Cat sighed, and who could blame her? We loved our fellow believers and many more people who were part of our apartment community, even those who didn't believe. But we had done a lot for them, and there were times when Cat and I both wanted to simply take care of ourselves. But I couldn't deny what God had done. It was highly likely that all across the ruins of Miami, people would be going mad from fear in the oppressive darkness.

I helped her up and we got dressed. It was colder outside than it had been since we arrived in Miami. The fourth trumpet judgment was nothing to scoff at... and it was just getting started.

8

I t wasn't easy getting to everyone. The people in our apartment complex all had candles, but like us, many had extinguished them. We had all been in survival mode for a long time and the first rule of survival is to conserve your resources. None of us expected the demonic attack.

You might be the kind of person who doesn't believe in the supernatural. I don't blame you. I used to be the same way. I thought everything could be explained via science with naturalistic cause and effect. But the truth is just what I told Flex and Hannah. There is a war going on and we're caught in the middle of it. Yet it's not a war with bullets and bombs, but a spiritual war against very powerful beings in a parallel dimension. We don't see the enemy, and yet, because we are loved by God, we are a target. The devil has no rules he won't break and there is no honor in him. Which is why his demons were given free rein to terrorize humanity.

We would find out just how bad things were later, but that first night, we managed to get everyone together. The believers in our community were shaken. The non-believers were absolutely terrified. No one was talking, but they happily gathered outside the office on the apartment complex lawn just to be near people and, maybe more importantly, near the light. We didn't have a lot of resources for big fires, but we did have wood for smoking some of the game that Cat and a few other people harvested. That first night, we worked with candles and built a fire pit right on the lawn. Our fire wasn't huge, but it was warm and bright. People were wrapped in blankets, and many got as close to the dancing orange flames as they could stand.

"Maybe you tell 'em what's going on," LB suggested.

By that point, my confident word of knowledge was starting to get shaky. Not that it was wrong, but my confidence in what I had understood was under attack in my own mind. I didn't hear voices, but doubts seemed to rain down on me.

"That's a good idea," Cat said.

"We've all got questions," Allie added. "Maybe you can answer them."

There are times in life when a person feels so inadequate for the task at hand that they fall into despair. I was quickly headed in that direction, but then one of Lorenzo's favorite verses popped into my head — *He gives wisdom to the wise, and knowledge to those who have understanding* — and I was suddenly flooded with a sense of calm. I nodded to my friends and LB got everyone to quiet down.

"I want to remind everyone that I'm not a guru. I don't have any special abilities or insider information on what's going on. The Bible says in Daniel 2:21 that if we seek knowledge, God will give us understanding. And I think I know what's going on."

"Why is everything a religious event to you, dude?" Eddy Felding said.

"Quiet, Eddy," Flex told him.

"Yeah," Lucern said in a shaky voice. "If he knows something, I want to hear it."

"He knows," Preston said.

Patty, a stalwart woman, both physically and spiritually, added, "Trust us, we've seen what's in the dark. There's no doubt about what it is."

"She's right," I said. "The Bible doesn't explain it in Revelation, where it talks about the fourth Trumpet judgment, but scripture does tell us that our enemy, the enemy of our souls, loves the darkness. I believe what is happening is that in this supernatural darkness, the demons have greater freedom."

"Can they hurt us?" a man named Vince asked. To my knowledge, he wasn't a believer.

I looked at Eddy and said, "You aren't going to like this answer, but I speak from personal experience."

"Whatever," Eddy mumbled, but he didn't leave the group or the light of our campfire.

"Vince, the truth is, if you haven't believed in Jesus and received the free gift of salvation he offers us, then yes, the demons can hurt us."

"What if we're believers?" Preston asked.

"Believers can be tempted, tormented, even oppressed, but they don't have to be," I said. "We have power in the name of Jesus to rebuke the enemy. How many of you saw something... awful tonight?"

Over half the community, including Allie, raised their hands.

"Did any of you hear them?" I asked.

Several kept their hands up. I felt for them. Every person in our little community was frightened. And I didn't think my explanation was much comfort.

"In my case, a demon came to me before the rapture," I started to explain.

"The what?" Someone asked.

"The disappearances," LB said.

"Yes," I continued. "I was helping a friend of mine who had been hurt in a car accident. At night, this being would come into my room.

I'll admit, at first, I thought I was hallucinating or dreaming. I felt like a child having a nightmare, but it was real. He showed me things, horrible thoughts tied to the events in my past, like how my parents died. He reminded me of all the things in my life I had messed up. Every mistake, every traumatic event was like a weapon the demon used against me. He also showed me hell or, at least, some version of it."

When I paused, the only sound was the crackling of the fire as it consumed the wood. Every eye was on me. When I looked out past the group members into the thick darkness, I felt like there were eyes watching me there, too.

"He taunted me and swore that he was taking me there. I was helpless. After a while, he sort of took control of me. To the point that I ended up in my friend's room with a knife."

People didn't speak, but there was shock on their faces. They looked from me to one another, then back.

"I know, it was insane. I can't remember how I got the knife. There was some time that night that was just blank. I have no memory of it. In fact, I just remember coming to, almost like I had been asleep and someone was shaking me. But it was my friend, calling on the name of Jesus Christ, binding the demon and casting him out of me. That was literally minutes before the rapture. And when my friend disappeared, I knew instantly what had happened."

"What?" Eddy asked. "You know what happened that the government doesn't know?"

"I know the truth," I said as kindly as I could manage. "The people who disappeared were not taken away by the aliens. They weren't removed for special treatment or education because they were bigots or racists."

"Says you," Eddy snapped.

"Says the Bible," I replied. "*For the Lord himself will descend from heaven with a cry of command, with the voice of an archangel, and with the sound of the trumpet of God. And the dead in Christ will rise first. Then we, who are alive, who are left, will be caught together with them in the clouds to meet the Lord in the air.* My mentor quoted that verse often and urged me to believe in Jesus. I thought I had time," I said with chagrin and a woeful chuckle. "Until it was painfully obvious that I didn't.

"I immediately called out to God and he had mercy on me. I dove into Lorenzo's teaching and even pored over his Bible. What had seemed so strange and out of touch before was suddenly like the very air I was breathing. It became vital and refreshing. God's word is alive and it will change you for the better, I guarantee it. It is truth and it teaches us what is and what is to come. That demon has not tormented me since then."

"You're demon-proof?" a woman asked.

"No," I said. "I have doubts and temptations still every day. And tonight, I had an awful vision, but I also had a word from God that helped me to understand what was happening."

"You hear God?" Eddy said. "What a surprise."

"Why are you so negative, dude?" Flex asked.

"I'm not negative, but I'm not a sucker either. I ain't buying all this religious mumbo jumbo. Y'all better not either. He'll have you all drinking poison or something just as crazy before long."

"All I'm trying to do is help people," I said.

"God's real, young man," Patty told Eddy. "My story is much the same. I was married to a good man for twenty-eight years. We went to church and attended conferences. All that time, I thought God was up in heaven watching me and taking note of every offense I made. And let me tell you, I made a lot of them. I was a gossip and filled with jealousy. Instead of trusting in God, I was relentlessly working to be a good person. The night that the rapture came, my husband and children disappeared. The members of my church, most of them, were rescued. I was left behind a broken and bitter woman. But after a while, I picked up my husband's Bible. I had my own, but to be honest, I didn't even know where it was because I never read it. But my husband read his every single morning and night. I read a lot of books about the Bible and about how to live or how to be happy, but I was confused about who God was and what he wanted from me."

"What did he want?" Hannah asked.

Patty smiled, "Just my heart," she said as tears ran down her cheeks. "He didn't want me to do anything. He didn't want my money, or church attendance, or my time volunteering in the nursery. He just wanted me. Talk about feeling unworthy. I was a wreck for a while as the truth finally broke through. I'll admit, I struggled with it. But Jesus said that all who believe in him will have everlasting life and I realized that I believed in the idea of God, but not in the person of God. I thought I had to believe and then prove my belief by living sinlessly, which no one can do. When I realized that God did it all through Jesus' death and resurrection, it changed everything. I didn't need to add anything or do anything. Knowing God isn't based on merit, it's based on his grace."

The stories went on and on that night. It was as if I had tipped over the first domino and one testimony led to the next. For six straight hours, we huddled in the darkness, stoking the campfire and sharing our stories. Some were short, others were long, but they all were similar. By the end of that first period of supernatural darkness, several of the younger members of our community prayed in faith to receive God's gift of salvation. When the lights inside the apartments came on and the stars appeared overhead, we all breathed a sigh of relief. The night was still dark, but not as thick and frightening as before.

"Remember, we have to conserve electricity," LB said. "Refrigerators and lamps only. We don't want to run down the power banks completely."

"Tomorrow, we can consolidate what we've got," Allie added. "So that the shorter days don't leave us without enough electricity."

There were still some people who didn't believe our testimony. Eddy Felding was adamantly against us. As soon as the power came on, he rushed to check the internet and was rewarded with news stories from the Regional Administration government.

"Look!" he shouted. "I knew it. You guys were wrong."

He was laughing almost hysterically as he he held up a laptop with a news site on the screen. The headline in bold black letters read **Apkallu Report Blocking Sunlight To Reverse Global Warming.**

"They did it," he said, pointing up but referring to the beings who claimed to be the progenitors of the human race. "They're fixing our mistakes again."

I glanced at LB and the big black man shook his head sadly. We didn't argue with him or try to explain away the news. We knew who the Apkallu really were and what they ultimately wanted.

"Time to get some rest," I said. "We need to be up and moving at first light."

"Roger that," LB said.

"I'll see to the electrical work," Allie volunteered.

"We'll need to start gathering wood," Cat said. "If this is going to happen again."

"I think it will," I told her.

The next day was dramatically different. Gone was the sultry heat of the South Florida summer. Instead, we were forced to bundle up in the cold. It was just above freezing when the sun rose, with frost glistening on what little grass had sprung up since the fiery hailstorm that we understood to be the first trumpet judgment.

"This is different," Cat said. "I had gotten used to being hot all the time."

She was from the north Idaho mountains and was used to long, cold winters. LB was not.

"Damn, I thought we didn't have to worry about the cold no more," he said. "I ain't even got a coat."

"We'll have to track some down," I said.

"There probably won't be many this far south," Cat said. "We'll have to adapt with animal skins."

"You know how to do that?" Allie asked.

"Sure," Cat said. "There's enough matter in every animal to tan its skin. God made it that way on purpose."

"We'll leave that up to you," I said. "In the meantime, we need fuel for fires."

"Ain't a lot of trees in Miami," LB pointed out.

"Right, but there's driftwood on the beach and a lot of the wrecked ships have some wood on them. We'll scavenge for what we can get. I'll take a few people with me."

"I need someone back on the roof," Allie said. "I'm not making that climb with this leg."

"I'm your man," LB said. "Your wish is my command."

We set out to get things done in the short eight hours of daylight available to us. I took Patty, Flex, Hannah, and Lucern with me. Flex and Lucern had put their faith in Jesus overnight and they had the excitement that came with their new belief. I remembered how relieved I had felt and how anxious I was to share the truth after my own conversion. We gathered wood along the beach, of which there seemed to be no shortage. I believe it was another blessing from God. We weren't immune to the judgment that had come upon the world, but God was faithful to provide what we needed despite his wrath that was poured out on unbelievers.

That afternoon, the darkness came again, but we were prepared. The fire was lit, and it was bigger and brighter than the night before. In the days that followed, the nightly gathering became a sort of celebration. We were ready each night with food and activities. No one wanted to leave the fire to collect things or do something else. We huddled near the light and warmth, swapping stories and huddling under blankets. The lack of daylight had a profound effect on the Earth's climate, kicking off a new ice age. Miami was radically altered. Much of the wildlife disappeared. Standing water froze everywhere. The Art Deco buildings that had survived the great earthquake and tsunami had once been festooned with neon. But after the fourth trumpet judgment, they were gilded with ice that glittered and dripped in the shortened days, only to refreeze in the long, cold nights.

Ten days passed and we were adapting. Game was not so plentiful and, even though the bloody waters around the coast had abated, there was very little aquatic life. Not that anyone was in a hurry to harvest it after seeing and smelling the bloated, rotting fish that had collected near the shores after the second trumpet judgment. That lack of warm clothing and food scarcity set us up for the biggest temptation of our lives. It caught us completely off guard.

9

They came on the eleventh day, not just three white EVs but nearly two dozen. Most were manned by soldiers. I had just gotten back to the apartment complex with a load of wood for that evening, which I pulled in a heavy-duty wagon that was made for landscapers. Patty often went with me, along with Hannah and Lucern. The beaches were hard-packed sand, most of it pink from the blood that had lapped up onto the shoreline for weeks after the second trumpet judgment. The tide surged through the wrecks of old ships, mostly sporting vessels of all sizes that had once filled the marinas along the Miami coast. There were some larger vessels too. We mainly worked an area between a cluster of large, ugly fishing vessels and a capsized cruise ship. White wood that was soaked in saltwater and bleached by the sun washed up onto the beach every single day. If it wasn't collected, it washed back out on the next high tide. We collected a wagon full, took it back to the apartment and let it dry, which it did quickly thanks to the salt. It also burned quickly, but a full wagon load kept our fire going through eight hours of darkness.

Eleven days were more than enough for our group to get our

resources in order and create a routine. At dawn, a member of the security team went up onto the roof. There were bound to be bands of roving criminals who would happily raid our little community. We had power, access to the wider world, clean water and some food. We weren't looking for a fight, but we didn't want to get caught off guard either. I had just gotten back to the office and settled into my desk, where I prepared a Bible reading for each night around the campfire. Not everyone liked it. We still had non-believers in our group. But there were eight hours to fill; my little devotions only took about half an hour.

We used walkie talkies someone had discovered, to keep track of people on resource runs and the security team. One was in the office and turned on. I was pretty good at ignoring the chatter on the small device by that point. But when Preston called out, "Incoming NARA caravan, I repeat, we have a caravan of NARA vehicles heading toward the apartments," I jumped to my feet. There was a rifle by the door and a pistol in the drawer of my desk, but I left them both behind. The plan was to play nice until we had to do otherwise with the local government agents. We had already read stories and seen videos posted about NARA. There were active settlements all along the western edge of what had been the United States. The rest of the country had fallen under a blanket of freezing snow after the Chinese attacked and the use of atomic weapons had created a nuclear winter.

NARA controlled everything down to South America, which was a separate region with its own government. Still, Mexico and the countries of Central America had surged in population during and after the war. Most of the government administrators were from those regions and had little empathy for Americans.

I stepped out and waited near the parking lot. We had successfully moved most of the cars from that lot into the street. It wasn't exactly a wall around our complex, although it left the parking area free for work and the small group of working vehicles we kept. Two of the white government SUVs pulled into our parking lot. The other vehicles were all pickup trucks, which waited in the street. Men in Kevlar armor and dark green uniforms got out. They all had military-issue rifles slung over their shoulders. It was a frightening display, to say the least.

Community members came out and gathered on the lawn. Cat had gone hunting and LB was on a resource run, but Allie, Patty and Flex joined me near the parking lot. A moment later, Floyd - of the three-piece business suit - got out and held the door open. A woman who looked to be in her mid-twenties with long, black hair and a heavy winter coat stood up beside him. She had a crimson NARA band around one sleeve of the coat.

"This is the group I was telling you about," Floyd said. "Their leader's name is Hank."

"Not sure I'd call me the leader of anything," I said as the woman approached us. "We're just living here and working together."

The woman was beautiful and, had I not known better, I would have thought she was airbrushed. She had no blemishes and every last strand of her hair was in place. I could see no makeup, and yet her features were perfectly accented on her light brown skin. When she spoke, her teeth were very white and perfectly straight. Standing in front of her, I felt old and my clothes felt very used. I was wearing long pants and two shirts, which were enough to keep me warm in the daylight hours, but felt frumpy at that moment.

"I am Administrator Nevina," she said in a melodic voice with a slight accent that sounded charming. "It is a pleasure to meet you all."

"They've done quite well," Floyd said, pointing up at the rooftops. "Solar power for their apartments, computers, vehicles, they even have hunting rifles to harvest game."

I wanted to ask if that was a problem, but something in my spirit kept me in check. The animosity I felt toward authority that I knew was backed by a demonic power wouldn't help us in the long run, no matter how good it might feel in the moment. We didn't need enemies. Our group was strong and resourceful, but we were not an army, nor did I want to see any of the people in our group killed in a senseless fight.

"Is there a place we could talk?" The woman asked. "I'm happy to address everyone soon, but I'd like to talk to you first, Hank."

She said my name with such familiarity that I was nearly speechless.

"You can use the office," Patty suggested.

"Yes," I managed, "this way."

Allie gave me an odd look, but didn't protest. Floyd followed us back toward the office, which wasn't far from the parking lot. I opened the door and let our guest in, then pointed to Allie and waved for her to come in with me. Flex looked a little disappointed, but he didn't complain. Inside the small office were two desks. One was where we kept the Starlink direct line. That desk was empty save for a single laptop computer, which was open. The other desk was where I kept my books and notes. I didn't have much left after all the travel and disasters we had been through. But there had been plenty of Bibles in the nearby homes we had searched for supplies and more than a few commentaries as well. I had almost a dozen books by that point, but kept them all stashed in the drawers of the second desk. There were a couple of cheap sitting chairs in the office as well. I waved to them and offered the North American Administrator a seat.

"Would you like to sit down?" I asked.

"No," she said. "This is a fine set-up. You have Starlink computers?"

"We have a Starlink sat receiver," I explained. "It has wireless capability, but we don't use that feature. It burns up too much power."

"Yes, solar energy has become a liability," she said. "Once the Apkallu move their ship, we shall enjoy full days again. I've been assured that it won't take long to reverse the decades of careless stewardship we have been responsible for."

I wanted to ask if cooling the planet down a couple of degrees Celcius was worth ushering in a new ice age, and killing all the plants and animals who couldn't survive the sudden change of temperature? We had seen several animals that couldn't adapt. There were no more alligators, which suited some of us just fine, but there were also no more loggerhead turtles or Key Deer either. In fact, I had a whole host of questions, but none quite as potent as how the Apkallu block out a third of the sun and a third of the stars all around the world, even in countries in different hemispheres and time zones?

Still, my instincts told me to talk as little as possible. So, I nodded and the administrator kept talking.

"I don't want to put you on the spot, Hank," she said, once more saying my name with a sort of friendliness that made me feel like there was something between us. It was almost as if she said my name with a sort of flirty-ness that made my skin tingle. I wouldn't have said that I was attracted to the woman, it was more like getting attention from a celebrity. It made me feel special even though I couldn't quite say why. "But, I've noticed you and the people here haven't registered with the NARA database. Is there a reason why you're hesitant?"

"I didn't know there was a deadline," I said.

"It's interesting that you use that word," she said. "No ultimatums were given because we hoped that you would join us willingly."

"What do you mean, join you?" Allie asked.

Nevida answered without taking her eyes off of me. "I mean, throw your lot in with the government. It's not lost on us that you Americans like your independence. But the world has become a very dangerous place. We need to pull together and help one another all that we can. There are resources being provided to everyone who registers with NARA. We want your people to bempart of that."

"I'll pass that information along," I said. "But I'm just one person. I can't guarantee what the others will do."

"I see," Nevida said. "What would it take to get all your people to register? Is there something I could offer you that would help us see eye to eye?"

I had never been bribed before. It felt sleazy. Despite all her beauty and charm, the offer to buy me off rolled off her tongue as easily as all her compliments had. She was clearly no stranger to political glad-handing.

"We have all we need," I said. It wasn't strictly true. We didn't have enough warm clothing. People had begun making clumsy garments from old blankets and towels scavenged from the apartments and nearby homes, but they weren't as warm as it seemed we would need. And then there was the lack of food. We had already consumed all the fresh meat and were back onto dry goods, although our supplies were dwindling.

"No one does," Nevida said. "I'll be frank with you, there are dangerous elements in this area. Criminals who would take what you have and kill you just for sport. The government is working to stamp out these lawless groups, but it takes time. And only with the help of everyone working together can we really make a difference. Won't you join us, Hank? Please, the North American Regional government is asking for your help."

Despite all I knew, there was something strangely enticing about her offer. Maybe it was because she was playing to my ego. Or maybe, the same unclean spirits that tempt us every single day were urging me to throw my cooperation behind the beautiful administrator. But despite the temptation, I found a way to resist.

"I'm happy to make your offer to the people here," I told her. "But I can't promise anything."

She frowned, and for the first time her mask slipped. I say mask because the skin around her eyes drooped a little and I saw what looked like scales. They were tiny little yellow and red dots. I might have chalked what I saw in that moment up to my imagination, but then a grayish, leathery eyelid blinked. Only it didn't come down from the top of her eye, instead it slid across from the outside in. When it pulled back she once more seemed to be the beautiful woman who had greeted me outside, but my mouth had gone dry and I felt my insides turn to water with fear.

Lorenzo Maltza had talked about creatures like Nevida. He had never seen one, but he had hundreds of testimonies of people who had. Some called them shapeshifters, others said they were reptilians in human disguise. There had even been a television mini-series about the concept of reptilian aliens who could put on a human costume and fool the entire world. My legs felt shaky and weak, but if Nevida noticed the lapse she ignored it and pretended nothing had happened. I tried to do the same. Thankfully, when I turned and saw Allie's face her skin was pale. I knew right then that I wasn't insane or simply seeing things. Allie had a good poker face, she didn't frown or act frightened. But I could tell that my friend was just as terrified as I was.

"I think it's best if I make my appeal directly," Nevida said. "Will that be a problem, Hank?"

"No, ma'am," I managed to say.

"Very good," she responded.

I stepped aside and she went to the door where Floyd pulled it open. Suddenly, I remembered shaking his hand. That had been before the fourth trumpet judgment had taken away a third of the day and caused the world to get cold. It had been hot then - sweltering hot - and yet his hand had been cold. Snakes were cold-blooded creatures, I remembered as the pair of them left the apartment building office.

Outside, everyone who wasn't off working on something had gathered in the grassy area of the property. The cold weather and short days had stunted what little growth the grass had achieved. It crunched under Nevida's designer shoes. Allie and I followed them out of the office, but waited beside it.

"Hello everyone," Nevida said in a loud voice that carried over the small crowd. I guessed there were maybe twenty-five people present, and another ten off the property. "My name is Innara Nevida and I'm the duly appointed administrator of the North American

Region. We are part of the new global government, a strong, reliable administration working hand in hand with the Apkallu to usher in a golden age on planet Earth."

There was some grumbling, but Nevida either didn't notice it or pretended not to.

"I know that things are difficult now. We've endured a lot in a very short time, but those hardships are behind us. Together, we are building a brighter tomorrow. Which is why I'm inviting you to come and register with us. The collective good will be able to provide you all with the resources you lack. Warm clothing," she said as she rubbed her hand down the sleeve of her coat. "Each of you will get a good winter coat, socks and boots, and whatever else you might need. Are you hungry?"

That got a more positive response. Many of the people nodded at the mention of hunger.

"We have food. Enough for everyone. If you prefer, you can even move to our NARA approved campus with power, internet, clean water, hot showers, regular meals, and maybe most important, protection from marauders. I hate to admit it, but in these desperate times some have given in to their baser instincts. Some have turned to violence and crime to get what they need and ensure they have more than others. Now is not the time for selfish ambition or greed. What the world needs now, what we here in what was once southern Florida need, is brotherhood, liberty, compassion and community. That is what I'm offering you, my friends. It is the chance to join something good. It is the chance to make a difference in the world. Come and be with like-minded people who enjoy the benefits of social communal living. Will you join me?"

She waited, and to be honest, I don't think anyone realized she was asking for people to respond. I certainly thought the question was rhetorical. But then she raised a hand toward the group. And, while I felt as though I had failed him, I was not surprised to see Eddy Felding step forward.

"I'm in," he said. "Where do I sign up?"

"We will take you," Nevida said.

"I'll go too," another man said.

"Yeah, I'm in," a woman with short hair and a scar on her forehead added.

I felt for them. It was like watching people jump off the edge of a cliff, but I had to remain silent. If the NARA people discovered that we were a religious group, they wouldn't be asking us to join them. They would probably just shoot us where we stood. So, I prayed silently for deliverance. It was all I could do. Allie moved up and stood just to my right but slightly behind me. Patty and Flex were to my left. The younger man started to say something when Eddy volunteered, but I reached out and put my hand on his forearm. He looked at me, his eyes open wide with shock and I gave him a little shake of the head.

"Just three?" Nevida asked.

I was relieved none of the believers had agreed to go. But we were still in danger and I had no way to protect the group. All we could do was wait and pray that the NARA people would leave us alone.

"I told you," Floyd said.

"Fine, take what we need," Nevida said.

The others all looked to me and I shook my head. Floyd waved toward the soldiers in the street. They rotated their rifles off their shoulders and then came marching toward us. I was convinced at first that they were going to murder us. Most of the people were praying silently. Their eyes were watching the soldiers, but their lips were moving in quiet prayers for help. I was praying, too, and I took Allie and Patty by the hand. They were both trembling, but so was I.

"Take the solar equipment," Floyd said. "The computers, the weapons and their food."

"You can't do that," Preston said.

"Actually, we can," Floyd snapped at him. "We are authorized to confiscate any resource that could potentially help the collective."

"If you take our food, we'll starve," said Miss Keller. She was seventy-seven years old, a former teacher and gymnast. Despite her age, she could outwork most of us and had a gentle, quiet spirit. I was surprised she spoke up.

"If you want to eat, then join us," Floyd said. "You can register at the Hard Rock Stadium."

Eddy and his companions, who agreed to join NARA, piled into one of our trucks. They didn't take from anyone, except to gather their own meager belongings. Once the soldiers had finished stealing from us, they followed the convoy of white vehicles away from the apartment. By that time, people were crying. I couldn't blame them. Everything we had, everything we worked for, was suddenly gone. There was nothing we could do to stop it.

"Get everyone together," I told Allie and Flex. "We need to make a plan."

"What about me?" Patty asked.

"I want you and Preston on the roof," I said. "If they come back, we need warning."

There was a look in her eyes. She had questions and who could blame her? But she didn't argue and she didn't insist on being part of the meeting. She was needed and that was enough. I could have hugged her for trusting me in that moment. Although the truth was, I had no idea what we were going to do or how we would survive the next few days. I knew that joining the enemy wasn't what I wanted to do and it certainly wasn't the safe thing to do, but was it what we should have done? I had no answers. While Flex and Allie gathered the community together in one of the larger three-bedroom units, I went into the office.

To my utter surprise, the drawers of my desk were still closed. No one had found my little library or the box filled with the Bibles we had collected since arriving in Miami. The guns were gone. The food we kept in the office was gone, but God had blinded the soldiers to the items that would have cost us our lives. I knew then that somehow, someway, we would make it through. It was time to keep the faith. Salvation wasn't a ticket to an easy life, no matter what some people say. Jesus himself told us we would have tribulation in this world, but he also said that he had overcome the world. Which was why I believed with all my heart we were going to make it. How long and for what purpose, I could not say. In fact, there were many times when I contemplated dying. If my eternal destiny was secure, why not give in and let the enemy kill me? At least I wouldn't suffer any more once I was dead. But deep down inside, I knew that wasn't right. God had saved me, provided for me and showed me his power in my life many times. He had me in Miami for a reason and I wasn't about to give up on that.

10

There was frustration, as you might expect, at having essentially been robbed of everything. But we were all old hands at dealing with disappointment by that stage.

"We'll need to see if there's anything left," Allie said. "They took our solar equipment—"

"And the computers," Flex interjected, his voice brimming with anger.

Allie nodded and continued, "...most of our weapons and food, but there is probably some of it left, and LB will be back with more before dark."

"Cat is hunting," I added. "If there's game out there, she'll find it."

"But the government is right too," Shawn North said. He was fifty-five years old with a bad knee and battered glasses that had been taped and superglued back together several times. "We don't have what we need here. It's getting colder every day and we can't defend ourselves."

"Never could," I told him. "Not really. Don't forget what we learned at the caves, God is our defender. Having guns is nice, but they aren't the answer."

"What is the drawback to joining the government?" Delores Smith asked. She was sixty-eight years old and clearly frightened. Some of the people around her put their arms around her. It was inspiring to see how the group cared for one another.

"Maybe nothing at this moment," I said. "But we know what's coming."

"The mark of the beast?" Allie asked.

I nodded.

"How soon?" Shawn wanted to know.

"I can't say for sure. And I can't tell you what it entails. What I know for certain is that the mark will be required for people to buy and sell."

"Is that bad?" Flex asked.

"The Bible also says that anyone who takes the mark has no place in God's kingdom," I said. "My fear is that if we are in NARA's database, they will hunt us down and kill us when we refuse their mark."

"Aren't they going to do that anyway?" Allie asked. "I'm not saying I want to sign up, but they did just rob us blind and leave us to die."

"She has a point," Flex said.

"We could at least send some people to check it out," Shawn said. "Like the spies who went into the promised land and brought Moses a report."

I wasn't Moses and we weren't the Israelites, not even close. We were a ragtag group of believers just trying to survive and, to be honest, I didn't know if that was even a good idea or not. At least dead would be in the presence of God, where there is no more pain. Believe me, I was ready by that point to see Jesus. But I also felt a compulsion to live as long as I could. Not because I feared death, but because I recognized that in every scrape with death it had been God who kept us alive. If he did that, then he must have a reason for us still being around. I didn't want to miss his purpose the way I had missed out on having a relationship with him all my life.

"It might not hurt," I said. "You volunteering?"

Shawn looked perplexed, but he was saved from having to answer by Flex.

"I could do it," the young man said. "You guys took us in, helped us when no one else did."

"Doesn't mean you owe us anything," I told him.

"Yeah, I get it. But it seems like it's right up my alley, if you catch my drift."

I did. Flex wasn't the only person in our group with a shady past. I certainly had done things I wasn't proud of.

"Alright, but let's do our inventory first," I said. "And let everyone get back before we decide for certain. If no one has a good objection, then we'll drive you north in the morning, Flex."

"I'll go with him," Lucern said. "We'll get more information with a girl spy anyway."

"If you're sure you want to take that chance," I said. "You both know if they discover that you're believers in Jesus, they'll kill you. The government is still beheading people who refuse to join the world religion."

"I think I can still pass for a thug," Flex said with a grin. "I doubt they'll be thinking about Jesus when I'm around."

With that, the meeting broke up. An hour later, we had a tiny larder of food. It was mostly canned vegetables, but there was a jar of marinara sauce and a small plastic bag of brown rice. When LB got back, he seemed frustrated. All his group of scavengers had managed to find were some extra blankets.

"What the hell happened here?" The former Marine asked.

"Long story," I said. "Any luck?"

"Nah, this whole section of the city's been picked clean," LB said. "Every home and business we came to had been broken into and ransacked. There's no food, no weapons. We found some old blankets, but..."

"It helps," I said. "NARA showed up today."

"That Floyd guy?"

"And his boss, North American Regional Administrator Innara Nevida."

"Really?"

I nodded. "They wanted us to throw in with them. Promised us clothing, winter coats, food, medicine, the whole nine yards."

"And you told 'em where they could shove their proposal."

"Actually, I didn't. I told them I would talk to the group about it, but Nevida wasn't the patient type. A few people threw in with their lot."

"Let me guess," LB said. "Eddy Felding."

I nodded. "Frank Milton and Tara Ketcham, too."

"Traitors," LB said. "Then they took all the gear we had?"

"Yeah, confiscated it. They had armed guards, lots of them."

"I imagine they did," LB said. "You did the right thing, not slugging it out. They got military vehicles rolling through town. That I did see."

"They've brought stuff up from down south, I guess. There's not much left up here to scavenge."

"Wish there was. What have we got left, a few pistols?"

"And Cat's hunting rifle."

The dark period wasn't like the end of the day. The sun didn't go down and there was no twilight. One minute it was bright afternoon, the next it was pitch black. Fortunately, we had a few wrist watches, the old school kind that had to be wound up. So we knew that between three and four o'clock each day, the blackout was coming.

Cat returned to camp just before everything went dark. She hadn't killed anything, but she did have two thick alligator tails.

"They were frozen," she said. "The meat should still be good."

"That's great," I said, before explaining what had happened with the NARA government people.

Several of the people in our group set about butchering the alligator tails. The hardest part was cutting the skin free. Once they did that, they cut two long, thick sections of boneless meat away from the bones in the tail. It was good meat, but tough and gamey. The cooks cut the tail meat into small chunks and, after pulverizing the brown rice into flour, dredged the alligator nuggets and fried them in the fat from one of the wild boars Cat had killed a few days earlier. I wouldn't say the meal was good, but it made the canned vegetables taste a whole lot better. Plus, there was enough to use in a stew that they started that night and let it cook most of the next day.

No one could argue that getting some intel on the NARA group was a bad idea, although LB wanted to go instead of Flex. Ultimately, it was decided to let the younger man have his way. Most of the dark period was spent together cooking or sewing new garments from the blankets that had been brought back to the Apartment building. But more than a few of us came under demonic attack that night. It was worse than before, as if the enemy knew we had been weakened. People were praying and singing worship songs, but still, I saw dark figures moving around us beyond the light of the fire.

If you read my first book, then you know I struggled at one point with visitations from what seemed to be aliens. I would have sworn that they were just that - short, thin creatures with big oval-shaped heads and large, black eyes. They gave me a very menacing impression, both in my past and as we huddled next to our fire that night. Nor did they disappear when the stars came out. As Cat and I went to bed, the memories of them flashed in my mind. And in the darkness, I felt as though I was being watched. Sleep was elusive and I thought I heard someone - or something - moving around in the little apartment.

The next morning, I was stressed out and tired.

"You look like I feel," LB said.

"Couldn't sleep?" I asked him.

"Nah, I hadn't had a night like that in a long time, boy, that's for sure. Feels like evil is rising up all around this place."

"Maybe you're just responding to being robbed," Allie said. "It's traumatic to have someone come in and take your things."

"Could be," the big, black man said. "But I can't shake this feeling."

"I feel it too," I told him.

"It's hard to tell what I'm feeling when it's this cold outside," Cat said.

"Pretty darn cold inside, too," LB said. "Better check on folks and make sure we ain't losing anyone from the cold."

It felt colder that morning than in the past, but I had a feeling it wasn't just the cold we were struggling with. I don't like to jump to conclusions or blame everything on the devil. Innara Nevida wasn't the devil, but I couldn't help but sense a correlation to her arrival and the rising tide of evil around us.

LB and I drove Flex and Lucern north. Hannah, who had been out with LB when Flex volunteered to spy on the NARA commune, wasn't happy about being left behind. Yet she took charge of collecting firewood after Flex promised to return to her. I hoped he could keep his promise.

"Y'all get to the stadium, don't let it get in your mind that you shouldn't be there," LB said. "Just be grateful that they let you in and you'll be fine."

"That's right," I agreed. "Take what they give you."

"And if they ask where we came from?" Flex asked.

"Don't lie," I said. "Tell them you were with us, but decided you couldn't make it after NARA took all our food."

"What do we tell them if they ask about the group?" Lucern wanted to know.

"Tell them people were arguing," LB said. "There were lots of different opinions. That's part of the reason you felt you had to go north."

"When you're dealing with people like those from the NARA camp, it's not hard to convince them that they're in a superior position," I said. "If you tell them we're in disarray, they'll believe it because that's what they're already thinking."

We stopped eight blocks away on a street lined with abandoned cars.

"This is it," I said. "You know where you are?"

I had studied a map, but Flex and Lucern had grown up in the Miami metroplex. They both nodded.

"We'll meet you right back here tomorrow night, four hours after the stars rise," LB said. "Watch your six."

"They might not let us leave," Lucern said.

"I don't expect they will," LB told her. "You'll have to be quiet about that. My guess is, ain't nobody wanting to leave in the middle of the night."

"If you can't make it," I told them. "We'll keep coming back every night until you do."

The two young people nodded. From the bed of the truck, they picked up their backpacks. It had all their personal belongings save for the Bibles we had given them. We hugged them both. They were part of our community, and while they hadn't been around all that long, LB and I still felt protective of them.

"Don't fight," he said just before the pair set out. "Blend in as much as you can. Now ain't the time to strike a blow. Get back to us and bring the information we need, that's the best thing you can do."

"And trust that God is with you," I said. "He'll guide you if you let him."

"You really hear God?" Flex asked.

"Yes," I said. "It's not like hearing with your ears. You have to learn to listen with your heart and trust that when you ask, he will answer."

They both nodded, then set off LB and I watched them go, silently praying they would be safe, but both of us knowing there was no real safety in the world any longer. Maybe, there had never been any all along.

11

"Think we'll ever see them again?" LB asked.

"I hope so," I said.

The next two days were difficult. Cat was right about the weather. It was getting colder by the day. And our meager clothing was no match for the almost constant wind blowing off the ocean. We knew we needed to move further inland and find better shelter. The apartments had been fine at first, but they were built for hot weather, not cold. There was no heat, and we didn't even have electricity after the NARA group stole our solar panels. Not that they would have done us much good those two days. Even before we got back to the apartments, thick clouds blew in. That night, snow fell. I didn't know if it had ever snowed in Miami before, but it fell hard on us that evening and into the next day, nearly a foot of snow covered everything.

The communities in North Miami were busy. As LB and I drove, we saw people in the streets. Some were scavenging goods, others were driving tow or lift trucks to move cars that were left in the middle of the road or overturned during the previous judgments.

Plenty of the abandoned cars were damaged from the hail, which had shattered windows and beaten down some cabs. Others had caught on fire and burned. There wasn't as much damage to the roads as in other places from the great earthquake, and it seemed like life was coming back to the northern part of the city.

At the apartments, we were forced indoors by the snow. The apartment didn't have a lot of insulation, but being crammed into a small space with just a few candles to ward off the darkness helped to keep us warm. We ended up sleeping all together in one of the larger apartments. It wasn't ideal, even though it was warmer than going it alone.

The second day, there was no food left. Cat had been unsuccessful at finding food. She didn't have snowshoes, and tramping through the thick, white powder was exhausting. It would have given her an idea of animal movements via tracks, but there didn't seem to be any. The lakes and rivers had frozen over, and along the coast, ice extended from the beach several hundred feet. The incoming tide washed over it, and when it receded, the ice was a little thicker.

"How cold does it have to get to reverse global warming?" Shawn asked.

"Ain't no such thing," Preston argued.

"I used to think so," Patty confessed. "I spent years of my life volunteering for every community clean-up and climate rally I heard of."

"You still think the world is too warm?" Delores asked.

"I think it was a distraction," she said. "An illusion that made me feel righteous, but that also made me hate people who disagreed with me. At the rallies, we would all cheer for the different climate initiatives and laws being proposed, but we also got pretty worked up when the speakers took the opposition leaders to task. I remember thinking that anyone who disagreed with my point of view was evil."

"Wow," Preston said.

"The enemy does that," I pointed out. "It wasn't just climate change, it was political, it was racial and it was cultural."

"I know that's right," LB said. "It's easy to demonize the other side, always has been."

"Now the other side are actual demons," Cat said.

"Or worse," Preston said. "I don't know how much more we can take."

He wasn't the only one who felt that way. That second day, LB and I managed to create some makeshift tire chains for the truck. I almost felt guilty when we had to leave to go get Flex and Lucern. The vehicles had heat and I won't deny that it felt good to be warm all over again.

"How long before the next one?" LB asked as we crept through the dark streets.

The snow was still falling, although much slower, and the streets were covered with it. There were no city services and Miami didn't have snow plows. Our truck did well enough, but we had to drive slow. Everything looked different at night. It didn't help that the shadows moved nearly everywhere we looked.

"One what?" I asked.

"Judgment," he said. "It's worse, right?"

"Yeah, it's going to get really, really bad."

"I don't get it," LB said. "How does Paul Eon keep everyone buying the hogwash he's peddling?"

"It helps to have a pet alien who can do supernatural miracles," I said. "And the media fawns all over him."

"But the world is literally going to hell," LB said. "I gotta admit, brother, I'm ready for heaven."

"Me too," I confessed. "But it isn't time for us yet."

"So, how long?"

"I don't know," I told him. "By my count, we've got about eleven months to the midway point. And we know the fifth trumpet judgment lasts five months."

"So, it can't be too long then?"

"I wouldn't think so," I said.

We reached the rendezvous an hour early despite the snow. The truck had plenty of fuel, so we kept the lights off, even those of the dashboard and the auxiliary running lights (which had to be disconnected via a fuse). If someone had come by, they probably would have noticed us but we weren't drawing extra attention in the vehicle.

The time for the meet-up came and went with no sign of Flex or Lucern.

"How long you want to wait?" LB asked half an hour later.

"Let's give them until sunrise," I said.

We didn't have to wait that long. An hour after the prearranged time, we saw a lone figure in the darkness. He was struggling through the deep snow. We waited, unsure if it was one of our people or just a stranger. Eventually, we could see that it was Flex. He was in a parka with a fur-lined hood, but when he reached the truck, his pants were sodden and his shoes soaked.

"Get him inside," LB said. "Crank the heat."

He sat hunched forward as the hot air filled the cab. I was sweating before he seemed to come out of the stupor he was in.

"Tell us what happened," LB urged him as the younger man began to relax.

"Lucern... she wouldn't... come," he said between the shivers that still racked his thin body.

"Was she afraid?" LB asked.

"Didn't want to leave," Flex said. "They got a tight thing going, man. The stadium's been converted to a solar farm. They got power, heat and clean water. People are living in the stadium, man. Like in the old souvenir shops and up in the executive sky boxes. They turned them into apartments, right? And down in the locker rooms, people can shower. They got hot water down there and other stuff."

He seemed not himself. I thought at first it was the cold, but the more he explained things, the more I realized he was traumatized.

"The government's there," he said. "I got a coat, some new clothes, but they put me right to work."

"Doing what?" I asked.

"I was on auto detail. They're collecting whatever vehicles they can find in good shape. The stadium parking lot is filled with them. But we take the bad ones too. They run them out toward the glades."

"Doesn't sound so bad," LB said.

"The work's not bad," Flex said. "But I... look, man, I didn't know what..."

He started crying. I had no idea what to do. Fortunately, LB was there. He put his arm around the younger man.

"It's okay," LB said. "You're safe. We got you."

I could tell that Flex was frustrated with himself, but he was also emotional. He leaned forward, his face inches from the dash and crossed his arms over his knees.

"Down in the locker rooms... you ever see them NFL locker rooms?"

"No," LB said.

"They're like a resort or something. Yeah, there's lockers for the players, but massage rooms and treatment rooms too. It's state-of-the-art, very high-end."

"And you went down there?" I asked.

"They said we could get hot showers down there," he said, tears rolling from his eyes. "I didn't know."

"Know what, Flex?" LB said.

"It ain't just showers," he said. "People are down there... I'm talking hundreds of people."

I didn't need him to tell me what they were doing. I remembered the temple at Chichen Itza, and how people were supposedly worshipping by having sex. It had been the largest hedonistic display I had ever seen and the people seemed unfazed by the fact that they were carrying out their illicit acts in the open for everyone to see.

"We get it," I said.

"I just got out of there, but Lucern... she got... selected. We didn't know what that meant, but she got taken up to the Owner's suite. And I... I heard what they do up there."

"Who? Nevida?" I asked. "Floyd?"

Flex shook his head. "I went up there tonight, after the darkness, you know. Most of the people there spend the whole time it's dark down in the locker rooms." I knew he was talking about the eight hours of supernatural darkness. It was so dark during that period of time that regular nighttime didn't seem so bad.

Flex continued his explanation. "There's something up there. I don't know what it was." He was breathing harder. "It was... it was real, you know. I mean, it was physical... but it was bad."

"Demonic?" LB asked.

"Is there something worse than a demon?" Flex said.

"Hang on," I interjected. "It was real, like you and me?"

Flex nodded.

"And it was doing what?" LB asked.

"It was impregnating people... I mean, that's what I heard. And I saw some of the skyboxes filled with pregnant women."

"Are you sure?" I asked.

Flex nodded. "Some of the guys I was working with told me. They were talking about it like it was some kind of big honor. Then, when I went looking for Lucern, I saw them."

"And they looked pregnant?" I asked.

"Oh, yeah. They were huge. Biggest bellies I ever saw," he explained. "They were being fed and pampered, but they looked miserable."

"Did you find Lucern?" LB asked.

Flex nodded.

"Was she..." I asked.

"I couldn't tell," Flex said. "We were only there two days. But she wouldn't leave. They were doing all kinds of treatments on her. Oils for her skin, massage, and they cut her hair. The food in the stadium was decent. They were using three or four of the concession stands to feed people. But up in the skyboxes, they had chefs and fresh fruit. Anything you could think of, they had up there. They had to be flying it in. There's no way they were getting food that choice, just scavenging."

"What did she tell you?" I asked.

"Just that she wasn't leaving. I couldn't say for certain, man, but she seemed to be under some kind of spell. Like I talked to her, but she wasn't herself. And there was this... I don't know... this thing on her hands. You ever see what they do to Indian women before they get married? The skin decoration stuff."

"Henna," LB said. "On their hands and feet."

"Yeah, that's it," Flex said. "She had that, but just on the back of her left hand. It went from her fingers up to her elbow. And I don't think it was temporary."

LB looked at me. "The mark?"

"Maybe," I said.

"Should we go in and get her out?" LB asked.

"You can't!" Flex said. His eyes were closed and he was shaking his head. "No, no, no, you can't."

"Why?" I asked. "Because of their soldiers?"

Flex was still shaking his head. "No, they don't... the soldiers don't stay at the stadium. They're set up at the Opa-locka Executive Airport. They're bringing in more soldiers and equipment all the time, is what I heard. But at the Stadium... There's a pair of... well... they're freaking giants, okay."

"Giants?" I asked.

"You have to believe me, Hank. I'm not kidding. These things, they don't even look human."

"I believe you," I said, thinking of the body that I had seen in the crate at Fairfield Airbase. That had been the event that changed everything for me ... that giant had been dead.

"They're freaking huge, man, and not just tall. I seen them picking up cars and moving them around like... like you would pick up a watermelon or something. It was nothing to those freaks. I didn't go anywhere near them, but if you tried to make Lucern leave…"

"We get it," LB said. "What do you think, Hank?"

I leaned back in the seat. The trucks had extended cabs with a bench seat behind the main two seats. I had given Flex my seat up front and had the back to myself, although it was still pretty tight quarters.

"I honestly don't know, but I'll tell you what it sounds like."

"We're listening," LB said.

"It sounds like Genesis six, when the sons of God came down and took wives from the sons of man."

"The Nephilim?"

"That's right," I replied. "Offspring of the Watchers. They were giants."

"But maybe not like the brutes Flex saw?"

The younger man sat half turned in his seat and didn't interrupt. LB sat facing forward, his eyes scanning the darkness outside their vehicle. Occasionally, he glanced up at the rear-view mirror and made eye contact with me. But I knew LB well enough to understand that he was on high alert. His demeanor might not seem like it, but he was fully engaged in our conversation.

"I don't think so," I said. "Lorenzo talked a lot about the alien breeding program."

"The what?" Flex finally spoke up. "Who's Lorenzo?"

"Lorenzo Malta was my mentor. He hired me right out of the Air Force. He was an expert on the paranormal, specifically the UFO phenomenon, but unlike most ufologists, Lorenzo didn't think the visitors were from other planets. He understood the reality of the spiritual realm and that we have an enemy who often makes incursions into our four-dimensional reality. He believed the aliens were demons masquerading as aliens, or, in some cases, genetic experiments of demons and fallen angels."

"We weren't the first ones to discover the human genome," LB said in a low, serious voice. "And we were late to the party when it came to DNA manipulation."

"For decades, people have experienced things they can't explain, like sleep paralysis, loss of time and physical symptoms that have no cause," I explained. "There are hundreds of thousands of people who claim to have been visited by aliens, and many of them were taken for short periods of time. There's been highly legitimate studies on these people by important academics through the years. They collected stories, compiled case studies and even used hypnotherapy to try and get to the truth."

"Which is?" Flex asked.

"That almost all the people who reported being taken had eerily similar stories of what happened to them. It involved the removal of semen from the males and implantation of fertilized eggs in the women. There are even documents from many of the females, medical records, photos from ultrasounds and pictures of their bodies that show them to be clearly pregnant. And all of them report that after another visitation, the fetus disappears. Some have even been taken and shown their offspring months and years after the pregnancy."

"You're saying aliens are getting women pregnant?" Flex asked incredulously.

"After what you saw tonight, do you doubt it?" LB asked, all business.

Flex started to respond, then stopped. A look of grief and shame came over him.

"We don't really know what these nefarious entities were up to, but Lorenzo theorized that maybe they were trying to replicate the Nephilim. You see, in the antedeluvian world—"

"The what?" Flex interrupted.

"Before the worldwide flood," LB said. "Noah's ark, you know?"

Flex nodded and I continued.

"Before that, there was an incursion by angelic beings called Watchers. They came to earth, took wives and had offspring. No one really knows much about them other than they were giants. The Bible calls them Mighty Men or Mighty Hunters, but the Hebrew word also means giants. And these hybrids, at least some of them, became kings over humanity. They taught the people dark magic and how to wage war. It's a long story but the gist is that many of the ancient myths were based on these hybrid beings of great power and strength."

"The question is, why are they trying to create them now?" LB said.

"I suspect it's because Satan knows what's coming," I replied. "Lorenzo believed they were building an army to oppose God."

"That's insane," Flex said.

"Agreed, but it seems to be what's taking place," I continued. "We should head back home."

"Time to move on?" LB asked.

"Seems like it," I said.

"In this weather?" Flex said. "Yo, man, it's seriously cold and wet out there."

"What about the other people from our group?" I asked. "Did you see any of them?"

"Saw Eddy," Flex recounted. "He was working cars too, but he told me he had something the lady in charge wanted. I didn't see him again after that."

"What could he possibly have?" I asked.

"Information," LB said. "The truth about us would be my guess."

"What's that mean?" Flex asked.

"You and Eddy were close, right?"

"Like brothers," Flex said.

"And so when you showed up, he probably felt he had nothing left to keep him from blowing the whistle about us being Christians."

"He wouldn't do that," Flex said, shaking his head. "No way."

"Why not?" I asked. "He had no love for us."

"We helped him. You did that, just like you did for all of us."

"But he hated the message we believed in," I continued. "He hated God. Hated me because he equated me with God."

"They'll be coming for us," LB said. "Best not be where they expect to find us when they arrive."

He shifted the truck into drive and set off slowly through the darkness.

12

We hunted that day, despite the snow, but not for game. Allie, LB, Cat, and I set off in search of vehicles. There were plenty to choose from on the streets, but they were all damaged by the hail of the first Trumpet Judgment. We needed cars that were indoors. We discovered a restoration shop just a few miles from the apartment complex. It still had over a dozen cars inside, in various stages of restoration and customization.

Under different weather conditions, we could have loaded everyone into the back of the trucks from Solar Solutions, but it was too cold for that. And even in bulky coats and hats made from blankets, it was difficult being outside for very long.

"Look at this place," Cat said once we got inside.

"It took some damage," LB pointed out. "Getting the doors open won't be easy."

He was referring to the metal overhead doors that were large enough to drive vehicles through. Most were clearly damaged from the great earthquake, but there were a lot of tools in the shop that could be used.

"I'll see to that," I said. "You guys find us some vehicles that run."

None of the vehicles were ready to roll. It had been years since anyone had worked in the restoration shop. Half the vehicles were in the middle of deep repairs, but there were four that seemed ready. All they needed were fresh batteries to get them going. We had one, and it was in the truck.

"You know," Allie warned us as LB unhooked the battery from the terminal outside. "If these vehicles won't start, and we run down our battery cranking on them…"

"Then we'll probably all freeze," Cat said. "This shop is like a meat locker."

"It'll work," I said, although I didn't feel as confident as I sounded. But it was hard to think the pristine vehicles weren't in good shape. There were two that seemed especially useful. One was a tall Mercedes G-Wagon with a cargo rack on top. The other was a four-door Jeep Wrangler with massive knobby tires and a snorkel that stuck up on the passenger side of the engine compartment, big spotlights above the cab, and a five-gallon metal gas can on a custom rack on the back.

There were also two sports cars that were next to useless in the deep snow. But next to them was a sprinter van with seats for twelve. It took us an hour to jump-start the three vehicles. Allie was careful. She checked every vehicle over to make sure they were in good working order, including the fluids. The van was the most difficult to start. Our truck battery was running down, but it got the job done, and the four of us took a different vehicle back to the apartment building.

There wasn't much to load, but what we had we got packed in the vehicles before the darkness fell. Then, we once again huddled in a single apartment. The cold was almost more than we could stand. No one slept much that night. We were hungry, uncomfortable and a little bit frightened. When the sun rose, we set out, moving deeper into the city.

The snow on the roads wasn't melting, but it was packing down.

Most of our people rode in the sprinter van with LB at the wheel. They drove in the tracks from the G-Wagon, the Jeep, and the Solar Solutions truck, which still had chains on the tires. I drove the Jeep, whose big knobby wheels and four-wheel-drive had no problem plowing through the snowy streets. As I went, I prayed for guidance. It was one thing to be in charge, but another to feel the weight of responsibility that came from knowing the lives of so many people were in your hands.

The Shiloh building was a fourteen-story condominium tower near The Falls shopping complex. There was something about it that drew me in. It wasn't the best-looking building, nor was it without damage from the great earthquake. But it was intact, and as I circled it, I discovered the underground parking garage. There was nothing blocking the entrance, so down we went. Inside, there were still a few cars, mostly older Cadillacs and Mercedes sedans. The elevator was obviously out of service, and the doors that led to the stairwells were thick metal security doors. They had marks where someone had tried to pry them open, but it didn't appear that they had been successful.

The underground garage was only slightly warmer than outside, but it was out of the wind and out of sight. I knew the garage wouldn't work as a shelter, but I felt compelled to try and get inside. It wasn't like I heard a voice telling me what to do. It was more like I was unexplainably curious and didn't want to leave without trying to get inside.

"Tell me what you're thinking," LB urged.

"Can't say for certain," I told him as we left our vehicles to inspect the doors that led into the building. "I just want to check this out."

"Doesn't look too promising," he said.

Most of the others had stayed in the warm vehicles, enjoying the heat despite the freezing temperatures outside. But Preston and Flex joined us as we approached the doors.

"Can't get those open," Flex said. "Look, electronic locks. You'd need power to open them."

"Could we jump them from the vehicle batteries?" Preston asked.

"Too risky," LB said. "If we lose a battery, we won't have enough space for everyone."

"Just... give me a minute," I said as I stared at the door.

There have been times since I put my faith in Jesus that he has moved in miraculous ways. I felt a little silly praying for a miracle at that moment. It seemed beneath God to help us open a door when the world was in the throes of the tribulation period. Yet again, I felt almost irresistibly drawn to pray.

Lord Jesus, I know you can show me how to open these doors. I'm sorry I have to ask, but I believe your word teaches that you want me to ask. So, please help me open these doors.

There are times in your life when the Holy Spirit brings a verse of scripture to mind. And sometimes it seems like the passage doesn't fit, or it's completely out of context. But at that moment, I thought of Matthew 7:7. It's from the famous Sermon on the Mount, and Jesus was speaking to the Jews in that passage regarding what God wanted from them. But I couldn't deny that it seemed appropriate. *"Ask, and it will be given to you; seek, and you will find; knock, and it will be opened to you."*

Feeling like a complete idiot, I stepped to the metal door. It was thick and heavy. A voice in the back of my head started mocking me. And for a moment I started to turn away, but then I thought to myself that if a person is going to ask God for directions, then he has to do whatever God tells him, even if it makes him appear foolish.

I raised a land and pounded on the door with the fleshy part of my fist on the pinky side. It thumped and echoed in the parking garage.

"Dude, I don't think anyone's at home," Flex said with a chuckle.

"Hello!" I called out in a loud voice. Then, swallowing my pride completely, I said, "The God of Abraham sent us here."

The words echoed for a second, then the garage fell silent except for the gentle rumble of the vehicle engines. I was on the verge of turning back to my friends when the intercom buzzed, and a voice said, "Who are you?"

I'll be honest, I almost fell over. I had to put my hand on the door to stay upright. Behind me, I heard Flex take a surprised breath, and it was LB who chuckled lightly as if he had expected a miracle all along.

"My name is Hank Downes," I said as soon as I regained my bearings. "I have a group of believers with me. We need a place to lay low."

"Are the authorities chasing you?" The voice asked.

"Not yet," I said. "But they will once they realize we're believers."

"Who sent you here?"

"God," I replied.

"You are descendants of Jacob?" The voice asked, pronouncing Jacob like *Yakib*.

"No," I admitted. "But we serve his God."

"And what is His name?"

"*Yod he vav he*." I spoke the Tetragammaton with as much reverence as I could. Lorenzo had taught me that the Jews revere the name of God as given to Moses at the burning bush encounter - Yaway, or translated *I Am*.

The door lock opened with a loud bang that reverberated through the garage. When the door opened, a short man with a protruding belly was waiting. He wore glasses and had several layers of clothing on. He looked at me for a moment without speaking, then extended a hand.

"Shalom," he finally said. "Welcome to Shiloh."

Perhaps it was a risk taking everyone into the building. For all I knew, it could be filled with outlaws just waiting to rob us blind. But if that was the case, the joke was on them. All we had were some poorly made winter clothing and Bibles. Plus, I was following the Holy Spirit, who I was certain had led us to the Shiloh building.

"Shiloh, wasn't that battle in the Civil War?" Preston asked.

"In Western Tennessee, 1862, that's very good," the short man leading them into the building said. "Almost thirty-five hundred soldiers were killed in three days of fighting, and over eight thousand were wounded on each side. I'm Saul Lukin."

"Hank Downes," I said as we reached a staircase that led down. "Can I ask where we're going?"

"I can't promise anything," Saul said. "To be honest, I'm just the doorman. But the elders are down here. It used to be storage for the condos, but since the government began hunting down our people, we've used it as a safe haven."

"Your people?" Preston said. "You're Jewish?"

"Didn't you know that?" Saul asked.

"Actually, we're just figuring things out as we go," I said.

The stairs led down to an open room. It was warmer in the storage area, which, by my guess, was thirty feet underground, maybe more. The space was filled with the golden light of candles. The concrete floor was covered with several old throw rugs that overlapped at the edges. Off the main room were dozens of small storage units that had been converted into bedrooms. And at the far end of the space was a makeshift kitchen.

It was a busy place. We waited by the stairs. I had two dozen people with me, and it felt a bit intrusive. At the same time, it seemed encouraging to see the little underground group. A man with a wide-brimmed hat came and stood in front of me while Saul hurried off to find the elders.

"My name is Daniel," he said. "I know you."

"Me?" I asked.

"Hank Downes, yes. I remember. I still have some of the videos you pirated. I knew Lorenzo. We were friends before the rapture."

He said the last word almost in a whisper.

"Really?" I asked.

"Indeed," the man said. He removed his hat, and I saw the mark on his forehead. It was almost a spectral image, sort of like a trick of the light. I saw parts of it and then they disappeared as other parts showed. He put his hat back on. "I wish I had listened more and talked less."

"He was a great man," I said, feeling tears sting my eyes suddenly. "I would love to hear how you came to know him."

"I will be glad to tell you," Daniel said. "In fact, I've been praying for you. I didn't know Hashem would bring you. It is a treat."

Saul returned with three other men. Everyone in the building was retirement age, but some were clearly older. The three following Saul were elderly and moved slowly. Daniel stepped aside, but most of the other people in the subterranean room moved in and listened.

"Who are you?" One of the elders asked.

I spoke for the group. "Hank Downes is my name," I said. "And these are friends of mine. We're believers. We were living in an apartment building on the coast, but the government came and took everything from us."

"Sounds familiar," one of the elders said.

"Governments have been doing that to our people for thousands of years," another said.

"We knew we had to move on," I said. "It's getting brutally cold and, on top of that, I believe a former occupant at the apartments where we lived has told the authorities that we are practicing an illegal religion."

"How did you know we were here?" The first elder asked.

"Honestly, I didn't know. I prayed, and we were looking for a safe place to take refuge. I believe the Almighty led us here. He certainly showed me how to make contact."

"You are not Jews," said a woman standing behind the elders.

"No," I admitted. "But we worship a Jew."

"They are Christians," Daniel said. "And Hank has Godly insight into the times we are living in."

"Is that true?" One of the elders asked, leaning closer to look at me with his watery eyes.

"Well…" I said.

"Don't be modest," LB said.

"He's a gifted teacher," Cat said.

"And full of wisdom," Allie volunteered.

"He changed our lives," Flex put in.

"That was God," I said.

"He took us in when we were living on the streets," Hannah spoke up. "He fed us, gave us shelter, and shared everything they had with us."

"Only we don't have much anymore," Patty said.

"We aren't looking to make things hard for you," I said. "And I'm not sure what we can offer you in exchange for helping us."

"We could use some muscle," one of the elders said.

"Would you be willing to help us with a few projects?" The first elder said again.

"Of course," I said. "We would be glad to help."

"And share your insights into what is happening in the world?" Daniel asked.

Again, I nodded, but before I could speak, the woman behind the elders said, "We have no idea what is happening. How can we?"

The elders frowned and Daniel explained, "Since the NARA people came back to Miami, we have hidden down here. We have food, we have shelter, but no internet."

"To activate the Starlink would reveal our presence in this remarkable structure," the lead elder said. "But, with your help, we might have the opportunity to get news."

"Like I said, we'll do whatever we can to help."

"Show them the recreation space. It's large enough for their group," the first elder said. "My name is Nathan. We are pleased to have you all. We can gather blankets from the units that were abandoned. There are mattresses too. It won't be grand, but we can make it comfortable."

"That is very generous of you, Nathan. Thank you," I said.

"You are welcome. My name is Matthias," the second elder with the watery eyes said. "Welcome to Shiloh."

"And I am Asher," the third elder said. "We have lived here the longest."

"Twenty-five years," Matthias said.

"Twenty-seven," Nathan added. "The last eight without my Dora, God rest her soul. I am glad she did not live to see these days."

And just like that, we had a new home.

13

There were enough hours of daylight that we were able to go up and gather what we could from some of the abandoned condos. Two-thirds of the building had been abandoned when the rapture occurred, or shortly thereafter, when Paul Eon made his peace deal between Israel and the world. That event saw an influx of Jews from around the world that was greater than any other time in the history of the reborn nation.

Cat and I climbed up to the eighth story and retrieved a queen-sized mattress, blankets, and a trunk full of winter clothing. The residents of the condo must have been believers. I saw a Bible on the nightstand beside the bed where we took our mattress. The condo looked as if whoever had lived there just disappeared into thin air, unlike some of the others that were stripped bare when the occupants moved out. The coats in the trunk were women's, but it seemed clear that the former owner had lived in a much colder place before moving to Miami.

By the time darkness fell, the rectangular room we had been given was neatly arranged. There were no dividers between our mattresses on the floor, but people set their suitcases and backpacks between them. We had blankets and pillows, room to stretch out, and plenty of insulation between us and the snow-covered surface where the temperatures were well below freezing.

That night, as the supernatural darkness fell, we were given bowls of warm soup. The broth was savory and filled with vegetables. There was bread too, freshly baked flat breads that were soft and warm. It was the first real dinner we had eaten since the alligator tail stew that was not so wonderful. But none of us would complain about a warm meal, so we had eaten it with gratitude.

Once everyone had eaten, Daniel asked me to share my story, which, if you've read my other books, you will know it's a long story filled with danger and, in some ways, disappointments. But through it all are the threads of God's miraculous intervention on my behalf.

"I hope you do not think you'll convert us to your Jesus," the woman who had spoken earlier and pointed out that we weren't Jewish, said. Her name was Liz, short for Elizabeth, and she was a widow. "All my life, I have heard the stories about this Jewish Rabbi from Nazareth who takes away the sins of the world. Bah, I think he is make-believe."

"We won't push our beliefs on anyone," I said. "But if you have questions, we'll happily answer them."

"Tell us why you believe the events since the disappearances are judgments from God," Daniel said.

"They're prophesied in the Bible," I responded.

"Your New Testament is not God's holy scripture," Liz declared.

"Actually, many of the prophecies are from your revered prophets, most especially, Daniel."

The man in the hat nodded, "My namesake."

"I was always told to beware of Daniel's prophesies," Nathan said. "Many believe it was written after the fall of Jerusalem."

"If it was written that late, how was it included in the Septuagint?" I asked.

"You know of the Greek translations?" Asher asked.

"I can't say that I've studied it, personally, but my mentor did," I shared. "Daniel, as you all know, was part of the first invasion of Judah by Babylon. He was carried into servitude and rose to become a high-ranking official in the Babylonian and Medo-Persian empires."

"Your grasp of the history is refreshing," Saul said.

"Spoken like a historian," Liz remarked. "This isn't a university, Saul."

"I taught for many years, this is true," Saul said.

"Continue," Nathan urged me.

"Okay, well, you know that Daniel predicted the rise of four empires. He was in the middle of the Babylonian Empire and lived to see the Medo-Persian Empire, but he also predicted the Greek Empire, including how it would conquer the Near East by Alexander the Great and be split into four sections upon his death. He also predicted the Roman Empire."

"What does any of that have to do with us?" Liz asked.

"It gives the prophet legitimacy," I said. "He was right about all that. He even correctly predicted the fighting between the Seleucid and Ptolemy territories and how they would impact Israel."

"I like him," Saul said to Daniel.

"Yes, he's very astute," the man with the black hat said.

"How many of you know about Daniel's prophecy of seventy weeks?" I asked.

A few nodded, although most of the group seemed oblivious. Behind me, LB's deep chuckle was encouraging. He had heard me explain the prophecy many times and knew that it was a powerful revelation of God's foresight into human events.

"Daniel was given a vision and, in it the future was divided between seventy sets of seven. We call them weeks because of the number of days in a week. Daniel chapter nine tells us that from the order to rebuild Jerusalem that a countdown of sorts would begin. It would take seven sets of seven, or forty-nine years, to rebuild the city with walls, defenses, the temple, and so on. Then another sixty-two sets of seven, or four-hundred and thirty-four years until the promised Messiah would appear in Jerusalem."

"So, his prophecy wasn't true," Liz said. "This is really fascinating. Will we get cookies and Kool-Aid when the story is over? Maybe you could use puppets in your story."

"Elizabeth, your sarcasm is not polite," Nathan chided softly. "These are our guests."

"I take it you believe that this prophecy points to Jesus as Messiah?" Saul asked.

"Better minds than mine have compiled the research," I said. "Four hundred eighty-three years from the time that Artaxerxes gave Nehemiah permission to rebuild Jerusalem is, to the day by most accounts, the day that Jesus rode into Jerusalem on a donkey's colt, while the people spread their cloaks and palm branches on the ground, shouting Hosanna. But we can talk about that later, if you'd like to know more. The prophecy said that after all but one set of seven, the anointed one would be cut off. Would you allow me to read it to you?"

"Oh, please," Nathan said.

Cat moved closer to me with a candle, and I opened my bible. As I flipped through the pages looking for the book of Daniel, I felt something stirring in me. I couldn't say what it was. It felt like excitement building and building.

"Here it is," I said. "Daniel 9:26 & 27 *'And after the sixty-two weeks, an anointed one shall be cut off and shall have nothing. And the people of the prince who is to come shall destroy the city and the sanctuary. Its end shall come with a flood, and to the end there shall be war. Desolations are decreed. And he shall make a strong covenant with many for one week, and for half of the week he shall put an end to sacrifice and offering. And on the wing of abominations shall come one who makes desolate, until the decreed end is poured out on the desolator.'* If you like, I can explain further."

"You'll have to," Asher said. "We have been without a Rabbi for some time."

"This man is no Rabbi," Liz snapped.

"Elizabeth..." Nathan said softly.

"He is learned," Daniel said. "We must let him finish."

"Finish what? That prophecy is as vague as Nostradamus," Liz said. "All my life, I've heard stories about Hashem and our people's plight, how we long for a messiah that never comes. Yet we endure atrocity after atrocity at the hands of gentiles all over the world. Why should I believe any of it? Why should I want to be a Jew and face the hatred that's been building up for thousands of years? I do not! Take my word for it, call it prophecy if you like, but the people of the world will find a way to blame all of this on the Jews, too."

She stood up and stomped away into a dark corner of the large room. Frankly, I was a little surprised. Not so much by her reaction as by the fact that I didn't see the shadows beyond the candlelight moving. There was no sense of the demonic down in the basement of the Shiloh tower. I couldn't say what was different, but that place seemed separate from the happenings on the surface.

"I apologize," Daniel said, his eyes sad under the wide brim of his black hat. "These have not been an easy few years."

"We came here for sunshine and leisure," Nathan said. "It was all so nice at first, before Covid. After that, everything changed."

"The holy city was destroyed by the Romans in the year seventy of the common era," Saul said. "It is a tragic tale. Does that fit into your prophecy?"

I smiled. "Yes," I said. "I was taught that the final seven weeks, or set of seven years, would be ushered in by the signing or strengthening of a covenant between a powerful ruler and Israel."

I paused and let that resonate. The retirees in the Shiloh building were like most Jewish people and kept tabs on the nation of Israel, which wasn't hard as the tiny country was almost always in the news. And I didn't have to explain what treaty I was referring to.

When I continued, it was with a somber tone. "This last seven years are known to Christians as the Tribulation period, and to the Jews as the Time of Jacob's Trouble."

"What's that?" An elderly woman in the back of the group asked.

"Judgment," Nathan said. "The final judgment."

"Are you saying the end of the world is upon us?" Asher asked.

It felt like the temperature in the room had dropped twenty degrees. The retirees looked concerned, and I felt bad for them. But at the same time, the sense of excitement was building in me, and I still didn't know why.

"No," I told him. "But we are in the final few years of judgment. In just under four and a half years, the Messiah will return and establish his kingdom. But there is a stipulation."

"What?" Nathan asked.

"Jesus told the people who flocked to him at Jerusalem that they wouldn't see him any more until they said 'Blessed is He who comes in the name of the Lord.'"

"Ah, it is always this with you Christians, always Jesus," Nathan said.

Suddenly, I couldn't keep my mouth shut. It was almost like I vomited the words. They came from me, but I felt such a compulsion to say them that it was like someone else was speaking through me for just a moment.

"You will hear a voice from heaven and know that what has been told to you is true," I said.

The elders sat back as if they had been smacked in the face. At the same time, I sagged in my chair. The building sense of excitement was spent. I felt numb and very tired.

"I think perhaps we have heard enough," Nathan said, his face hardening as he crossed his arms over his chest.

"Wait a moment," Daniel said. "Hank, do you believe that you are the Messiah?"

"No," I said, not even looking up.

"Are you... Jesus?"

LB chuckled behind me again, and I shook my head.

"He's just a man," LB said. "No different than me or you."

"Except he knows things," Flex said.

"Things found in the Bible," Cat said. "It's not him. What's coming, the judgments, are found in the Bible."

I held up a weary hand. "I'm sorry," I said. "It's not my intention to frighten you. And I'm not trying to force you to accept what I believe. I can't say why I blurted that out."

"Many have said such things," Nathan said. "I have been an observant Jew all my life, young man, and never have I heard from heaven. What makes you think I will now?"

"I think we all will," I said. "Everyone all around the world."

14

The next day we worked. Some of us went up and down the stairs, collecting things from the various apartments and taking them down to the basement. Others helped with the cooking, cleaning, and mending that the retirees were already doing.

As for myself, LB and I took Saul and Daniel out of the building in the Jeep. We drove west, deeper into the city, stopping when we were three miles away from the Shiloh building. It was cold outside. The snow had stopped falling, but there were thick, menacing clouds hanging low overhead. And the wind picked up the powdery snow, blowing it through the streets and over the buildings of downtown Miami.

"This looks good," I said

"I'll get the dish set up on the roof," LB said.

We left the Jeep running for both heat and power. The Starlink satellite receiver was on a tripod. We ran the cables down through the passenger window. One went into the power converter in the dashboard, the other went to a laptop computer that the retirees were using for news.

"It's connecting," Saul said.

As we sat waiting for the internet signal to lock onto the satellite, Daniel leaned forward. He had traded his wide-brimmed hat for a thick beanie that he pulled down over his ears.

"I am sorry for last night," he said.

I shook my head. "It's all good," I told him. "I know what we believe is in some ways offensive to your people."

"Our eyes were blinded for a long time," Daniel said. "I, like you, Hank, had many wonderful conversations with Lorenzo. He often urged me to see the truth, but I felt it was all academic."

"How did the two of you connect?"

"I was a guide and translator for many of his trips overseas," Daniel said. "My parents were diplomats. I have connections in countries all over the world, or I did have."

"I wish I could have been on some of those trips," I admitted. "In all my life, I never met anyone who was as encouraging as Lorenzo. He even took me in near the end, let me live with him."

"His children were estranged," Daniel said. "After his wife died, they didn't go to see him, and I know he was lonely. My guess is, your presence in his life was as much a blessing to him as he was to you."

I could have argued that idea. The truth was, from the day Lorenzo met me, I was a mess. My foundations in life had crumbled and then the one relationship I was really committed to blew up. I had been in a dark place right up until the end. Not to mention, I was driving when we wrecked his Lincoln on the way back from California. After losing both my parents in a car accident, the thought of losing Lorenzo that way had shaken me up.

But before I could say anything in reply to Daniel's kind assessment, Saul spoke. "I've got a connection," he declared. "I'm downloading a story now."

The news since the disappearances had come out of the Near East, new Babylon, to be more precise. It was an incredible city built on the ruins of ancient Babylon, just north of the Persian Gulf. In fact, several deep canals had been dug, allowing cargo ships to move their goods right into the new city. It had been built by aliens and giants, which the world seemed to accept as if it was of no interest whatsoever.

"Looks like the Apkallu are planning to keep their ships blocking the sun a while longer," Saul reported. "The good news is it's working."

I looked at LB and the black man just raised his eyebrows in wonder.

"Oh, here's another story. NARA is shifting its base of operations to the Caribbean. They're rebuilding cities in Cuba, Haiti, and along both coasts of Central America."

He fell silent as he downloaded a third news article. When he spoke, his voice was softer, almost husky with emotion. "Suicides are up nearly five hundred percent in countries around the world," he said. "The regional administrators are blaming it on Seasonal Affective Disorder."

"I'll bet they are," I said quietly.

For an hour and a half, Saul downloaded news articles and video reports. LB and I watched for any signs of the government. Unlike North Miami, the southern portion of the metropolitan area was scarcely populated. There were almost no signs of human habitation or movement on the snow-covered streets. We went the entire outing without seeing anyone, but we weren't complaining about that.

When we got back to the Shiloh building, Saul took the computer down for the other retirees to see, while I took my closest friends up to the highest level of the building. Climbing stairs was not fun. The Shilo building was twelve stories high. At the top, we found the penthouses unoccupied. Unlike the thick metal door that led into the building from the parking garage, the doors into the condos were left unlocked. We went in one that faced west and stood for a while looking out the big windows.

"What happened to the Everglades?" Cat asked.

"Looks like it all burned up," Allie said. "It's a snowy wasteland now."

She wasn't wrong. Almost all the trees were gone, with just a few blackened trunks sticking up out of the snow. The tall grasses were gone, too. The dark earth had been warmer than the city streets. It melted the snow, leaving dark swathes of land visible between the areas of standing water, which had frozen and was brilliantly white with snow.

"Lots of animals must have died in the fires," Cat said. "No wonder there was so much wildlife in the parks."

"Driven out of their homes," LB said. "I can relate to that."

"What's next for us, Hank?" Allie said. "We can't stay huddled down in the basement forever."

"I would if I could," I told them. "There's nothing good ahead."

"What is ahead?" Cat asked. "What's the next judgment?"

I hesitated to answer.

"You know it ain't nothing good when he don't want to tell us," LB said.

"The fifth trumpet judgment," I said. "I honestly don't understand it completely."

I was shivering by that point. It was well below freezing in the big penthouse on the top floor of the building. We moved to a room with a northern view. The city lay sprawled out as far as we could see. Normally, visibility was probably dozens of miles, but with the low clouds and dim light, not to mention the blowing snow, we could only see three at most. Fortunately, there was no sign of movement from the NARA base at the Hard Rock Stadium, or the military operation at the airport just southwest of the government headquarters.

"You're stalling isn't going to protect us," Cat said.

"I know," I said.

"Doesn't it have to do with a demon being set free?" Allie asked.

"Not just any demon," I said. "Apollyon... it means Destruction. He's king over the locusts that come out of the abyss."

"Bugs, huh?" LB said. "That don't sound too bad."

"These aren't regular locusts," I said. "They don't attack crops or vegetation. They're sent to torment humanity for five months."

"Now, I see why he didn't answer," LB said.

"We better head back down," I suggested. "Before we all freeze to death."

But before we had even left the apartment, something startling happened. The dark clouds split apart, not like an opening in the clouds, but like a knife cutting a thick layer of meringue. The dark clouds slide aside and an incredible golden light appeared. It wasn't the sun but I felt the warmth of it. We instinctively moved to the windows and stood with the brilliant light pouring over us.

"What is this?" Cat asked.

"I don't know," I admitted.

I should have had a pretty good idea; it was in the text after all, sandwiched right between the trumpet judges in Revelation chapter nine. We found out later that the golden light from the sky somehow penetrated all the way down to the basement of the Shiloh building. Everyone from our group and the group of retirees came up to see what it was. How long we stood there soaking up the wonderful golden light, I can't say. But in that light was the most peace I had felt since I was a child, if even then. I can remember feeling safe and loved with my parents, before they were killed when I was a kid. Since then, life had been stressful and often frantic. I had joined the Air Force straight out of high school and quickly lost contact with my foster parents. There were so many times in life, from adolescence to adulthood, when I knew that if I was going to make it, the onus was completely on me. But standing in that unexpected glow from heaven, I felt warm and alive, but mostly there was - in that moment - a total lack of fear.

Unfortunately, that feeling didn't last. A shadow appeared, followed by the largest bird I have ever seen. It was, without a doubt, several hundred feet long from beak to its ragged tail feathers and its wingspan was twice as long. To say that the creature caught our attention is an understatement. We drank in its every detail. The bird was powerful with thick neck muscles and huge talons. It had a yellow beak and yellow skin over its feet. The talons were black, but seemed to be speckled with gore, as were the feathers on its legs and belly. They were covered with a thick buildup of something, not just blood, but certainly, there were dark crimson patches, and soaked feathers that stood out from the body. The lower half seemed ragged and old, but as it flew, the giant bird dipped down out of the gap in the clouds, which slammed shut above it. The bird turned in an enormous circle over the city, flying slowly. The feathers on the wings and on the bird's back, all the way up to the crown of its head, looked like they were made from pure gold.

It was the most drastic difference in one creature I had ever seen. When it banked toward us, I could see the beauty, but when it banked away, I felt a revulsion and fear. It wasn't like seeing an eagle in the wild, maybe soaring on the thermals above the mountains, or diving low to snatch a fish from a lake. Those birds are graceful, even powerful images of strength and skill in motion. The giant bird was a harbinger of doom; there was no doubt about that. It had come from the heavenly realm, the spiritual dimension that lay parallel to our own. I stood speechless beside my friends, staring up at the great creature, and before any of us could find our voices, it spoke.

15

"Woe!" The bird said in a voice that boomed like a thunderclap. The sound shook the window and made the building sway.

I knew that tall buildings could move. The Shiloh tower was built to withstand strong winds, even hurricanes force gales. It did so by bending and swaying slightly. But I had never felt one move under my feet before. I grabbed Cat and she clung to me.

"Woe!" The bird said again, its voice like the roar of Niagara Falls. The building shook, and we trembled in fear. Tears filled my eyes and my guts turned to water. I could feel my knees wobbling as they struggled to hold me up.

"Woe!" Cried the bird, saying the warning for a third time, "to those who dwell on the earth, at the blasts of the other trumpets that the three angels are about to blow."

The words came slowly and pounded us like physical blows. There was no doubt about what the creature said. In my memory, the words are like thunder crashing, the kind that makes you huddle in your bed as your skin crawls with fear, the kind that makes you feel small and helpless before a power that you can't comprehend. Yet the words burned in my mind. I had read them in scripture, but the voice of the bird had imprinted the message on my mind like a traumatic event.

When it gave its message, the bird flew south and suddenly we felt cold.

"What was that?" LB asked in a shaky voice.

"The warning," I said. "The three woes at the end of Revelation eight."

"We're in trouble, aren't we?" Cat said, tears suddenly streaming down her face.

Suddenly, I felt a wave of overwhelming compassion come over me. My knees stopped shaking and I put my arms around my wife.

"It's going to be okay," I told her. "We're not alone. God is with us."

"How can you be so sure of that?" Allie said.

She was clinging to LB and he was clinging to her. I put a hand on the big man's shoulder.

"We don't have any promises that we won't suffer or even survive the tribulation," I told them. "But we do have the assurance that when we die, we'll be with God. One way or another, we'll be okay. Remember how you felt in that golden light."

"That was pretty amazing," LB said.

"I've never felt that good in my life," Cat said, wiping away her tears.

"We need to go check on the others," I said.

We held hands as we descended the tower stairs. By the time we reached the basement, the people there were abuzz, some with excitement, others with fear.

"There he is!" Flex shouted when he saw me. "Hank, Hank, tell us what that was, man."

The members of our little group of believers hurried toward me. And about half of the retirees, including Daniel, Saul, and Nathan, did the same.

"A warning from heaven," I said.

"But was it an eagle?" Hannah asked.

"Or a vulture?" Flex added.

I held up my hands. "I don't know. In the Bible, I believe the word is translated both ways, but I can't be sure about that."

"How did you know?" Nathan asked. "How did you know we would hear from heaven?"

"Did you see it?" LB asked.

"We did," Nathan replied. "The light reached us, even down here. We had to go and see what it was for ourselves. It was a miracle. Jehovah has spoken."

"It was pretty convenient, if you ask me," Liz said.

"You don't believe ... even what you see with your own eyes?" Daniel asked her.

"You believe it was from heaven because that is the seed of an idea planted in your mind by this... this charlatan."

"Hey, now, let's not go throwing words like that around," LB said. "My friend is no charlatan."

"It's okay," I said. "Look, this wasn't about me. I had nothing to do with it."

"It was the aliens," Liz said, throwing up her hands in frustration. "We all know animals do not talk."

"That wasn't just an animal," Flex said.

"I've never seen anything that big before," Hannah added.

"You can believe whatever you want," Liz said. "But I say it was a hoax. How do we even know this man isn't part of the anti-semitic government? He could be spying on us and reporting everything back to his masters."

"As much as I would like to believe I am important enough to be spied upon," Nathan said, "I know it isn't true. Yesterday, this young man prophesied that we would hear from heaven. Today, his people did more for us than we have been able to do for ourselves in weeks. And I would like to hear more. Perhaps he is sent from Hashem to prepare us for his Anointed."

"You are weak-willed old fools," Liz said.

"Of that, there is no doubt," the watery-eyed Matthias said.

Soon, the darkness fell on Miami, and we huddled together in the basement of the Shiloh building. I pulled out my duffel bag of books and shared them with the elders. Saul laid the books out on a folding table along with two menorahs and a copy of the Talmud.

Allie and Cat joined Saul. Preston and Patty helped LB and me as the group asked questions. It wasn't just the retirees who had questions; there were plenty from my own group. The most pressing being: what are the three trumpet judgments?

"The first is a swarm of hellish locusts," I said. "They come up from the abyss and torment humanity with stings like scorpions."

"I think I would rather die than face this," Matthias said.

"Many people will feel that way," I told him. "But the Bible says that even though people long for death, they won't be able to die."

"How long does it last?" Flex asked.

"It's the only judgment that has a definite timeline," I said. "Five months."

"Wait," Nathan said. "You're saying no one will die for five months? That's impossible. People die every day."

"They won't for five months once the angel blows the fifth trumpet," I said.

The questions and answers went on and on. That night, eight of the retirees put their faith in Jesus as the Messiah. It wasn't because of me or even because of the giant eagle from heaven. For the first time, they read or heard the gospel accounts of Jesus. And, hungry for more answers, they searched their own scriptures for prophecies of the Messiah, only to learn that Jesus had fulfilled them all. Lorenzo used to say there are over three hundred prophecies of the messiah that Jesus fulfilled. I didn't know even half that many, but when the retirees let the scriptures speak for themselves, they had no trouble seeing that Jesus was the clear fulfillment of their own sacred writings.

To be honest, Daniel did more evangelizing than I did. Of course, he understood the customs of his people better. He was able to show them things like how the Passover celebration the Jewish people had celebrated pointed directly to Jesus, or how God's command for Abraham to sacrifice Issac wasn't so much a test of Abraham's faith as it was a picture of what God would do for all mankind by sending his son to die for our sins.

The only person who resisted the possibility that God was at work was Liz. Late that night, another miracle occurred. It wasn't a divine miracle, but the lights coming on and the heat working in the Shiloh building felt miraculous. It happened shortly after the period of supernatural darkness ended. One minute we were going to bed, the next the building lights came on.

We all decided it was still better to stay down in the basement and out of sight. The power coming on was most likely the work of the NARA group. The new article that Saul had found earlier that day said the government was working to restore municipal services all around the Caribbean basin. And while we were happy to utilize the heat, lights, and WIFI, we weren't looking to draw attention to our presence in the old building.

The next morning, it was Flex who woke me up. I'm normally an early riser, but after the day we had experienced, I had slept hard and was still asleep after the sun had come up.

"Hey, Hank. Sorry to wake you, man, but you gotta come see this."

"What?"

"In here," Flex said, heading for the door to the community room.

I left Cat sleeping, pulled on a sweatshirt and jeans, then joined Flex. Someone had carried down a huge flatscreen television. It had internet connectivity and was running live reports from northern Israel.

"Where did this come from?" I asked.

Flex, his eyes glued to the TV screen, just pointed up. The newscaster was standing beside the road. A towering mountain filled the screen behind her. Nearby was a road sign with a message in Hebrew and English. It said **Mt. Hermon 4 kilometers.**

"... this area was once a highly trafficked site for hundreds of years. The Grotto of Pan was believed by many to be the entrance to the underworld. Archeologists have found hundreds of bones in the waters that spring up under the mountain, believed to have been sacrificed to gods in ages past by a variety of people groups from the ancient to as recently as the Roman Empire."

The video footage switched from the woman, who continued narrating, to drone footage that hovered above what had once been a national monument. Most of that signage was gone, as was most of the trail into the area near the mountain. It had fallen inward as a massive sinkhole continued to drop. The sound of it was eerie, a mix of crumbling stone and an odd, screeching.

"What is that sound?" I asked.

"Hard to tell over the reporter," Flex said.

We weren't the only people watching. Several more people had gathered near us, and more were coming along every minute. Within half an hour, everyone was standing and watching the sinkhole.

"... that's right, Amir, we are preparing to take the camera down into the sinkhole now," the reporter declared. "There does appear to be some strange audio, so we'll be silent and let the camera's microphone pick it up."

"We're ready on our end, Alana, you can proceed," the anchor man from the news studio said.

"This is crazy," Cat said.

"Can't even see what's down there," LB added.

"Except we know," I told them. "That's right at the base of Mt. Hermon."

Daniel was standing nearby. "The Canaanites believed that the grotto was the entrance to the underworld."

"It's where Jesus declared he would build his church, and the *Gates of Hell*, which was what the area was loosely known as, would not prevail against it," I added.

"How do you know so much about it?" Flex asked.

"My mentor studied everything that had to do with the supernatural. You'd be surprised at the links between ancient religions, Greek and Roman mythology, and the unexplained phenomenon happening in the world today."

On the television screen, technical readings appeared. The picture was from a drone that was over a hundred feet in the air above the sinkhole. The opening filled most of the screen. In bright green letters, the length and width of the hole revealed that it was nearly seventy feet in diameter. The circumference was two hundred and fourteen feet. The information was displayed in Hebrew as well as English as the edges of the screen.

The pit was dark. The top edges were visible for perhaps ten feet down into the hole. It was hard to assess on a flat, two-dimensional video display, but the light didn't reach very far down. And the darkness within seemed thick. It reminded me of the supernatural darkness that had taken over a third of the day and a third of the night.

"Ain't nothing good down there," LB said.

"There are older and fouler things than Orcs in the deep places of the world," Daniel said.

"What's that? The Bible?" Flex asked.

"Tolkien," the Jewish believer said. "Lord of the Rings: '*The dwarves delved too greedily and too deep. You know what they awoke in the darkness of Khazad-dûm... shadow and flame.*' Have you read it?"

"It's not a book man, it's a movie," Flex said.

Daniel looked at the younger man with a wry grin, but Flex didn't notice. The drone had begun its descent into the darkness, and it soon held everyone's attention.

16

"We're in trouble, aren't we?" Cat asked. "God wouldn't have sent that warning if it wasn't bad."

"It's bad," I said, speaking more from my feelings as we watched the drone drop down into the sinkhole, then from my knowledge of what the Bible said.

I didn't know how anyone could see what was happening in Israel and not recognize the danger that the world was in. It was like watching a horror movie, but it was real. I think most people remember where they were when they heard about the sinkhole or saw the video of it. The news had replayed videos captured by security cameras at the site. A few of the cameras on the mountainside were still operable and broadcasting footage to an off-site cloud storage. What had once been flat ground at the base of the mountain, most of it cleared for tourists, but with a few clumps of bushes and a handful of short trees, suddenly began to crumble inward as if there was nothing underneath.

As the drone descended to ground level, the rocky soil at the sides of the giant sinkhole was visible. The raw earth seemed solid enough. But as it flew down into the pit, darkness enveloped the camera within seconds. Lights on the electronic drone came on, but they weren't strong enough to pierce through the veil of darkness. They showed only dust in the yellow beams.

And then the sounds were heard. Not the crumbling of stone, or the cascade of noise from a landslide, but strange, eerie wails.

"Holy…" Flex started to curse.

"It must be some sort of noise caused by the pressure that's creating the sinkhole," Liz proclaimed.

I couldn't necessarily blame her. The woman was desperate to hold onto the concept of reality she had built her life on. And we had all been taught that there was no magic in the world, no monsters, no God. Everything had a basis in science, at least that was what we were taught as children. No one bothered to mention that most of the things we were taught concerning the world and the universe are untested assertions put in place to back up naturalistic ideas in an effort to explain the mysteries of life. I was taught the Earth was four billion years old based on the age of the rocks on our planet. It wasn't until I looked a little deeper into those scientific explanations during my time with Lorenzo that I discovered that most rock aging methods are based on the flawed idea of uniformitarianism. Perhaps it made sense at one time to believe that the same natural laws and processes at work today had always been the same throughout time, but that theory simply didn't hold up. Even in a single person's lifetime, and in many cases even less time, the conditions of our world change. And as I learned in my own personal research of the history of science, many of the bedrock foundations used to explain our past are simply made-up theories used more to negate the need for a supernatural creator than to explain where our world really came from.

What we heard next was a roar; there was no other word for it. Something large and angry was bellowing in rage, or perhaps pain, maybe both. Chill bumps appeared all over my body, even though my mind couldn't accept that what my ears heard was real. On the dark screen, the technical readout showed the drone's depth.

"Alana, we are hearing some odd noises," the news anchor said. "Can you tell us what that is?"

"No one knows for sure, Amir. There are scientists here at the site to observe what's happening in real time. We've asked several, and they have no answers."

"What's the range on that drone?" the newscaster asked.

"One thousand feet, Amir. We've just crossed four hundred feet from ground level, as you can see. There is still no bottom in sight. We're going to add a new reading from the drone now. Strangely enough, Amir, the air in the sinkhole isn't getting hotter, it's getting colder."

The temperature reading appeared in green letters. It was really the only thing to watch. The sounds continued, moaning, crying, harsh grumbles, even barking, although it was unlike any animal I had ever heard.

"Your New Testament talks about this?" a woman named Ruth asked me.

"Yes," I said.

"What does it say this is?"

"The shaft to the bottomless pit, the abyss where the Watchers were held in gloomy chains of darkness."

"The Greeks believed," Saul spoke up, "that Tartarus was where the Titans were imprisoned. They believed it was as far beneath the underworld as the underworld was beneath the sky."

"It's just a sinkhole!" Liz insisted. "You're all talking like fools."

"Liz," I said softly. "You're going to see smoke come out of that hole soon."

"If so, it's just from natural gas, or probably magma that is rising to the surface," she said.

Undeterred, I continued, knowing that everyone in the basement was listening to me. "Out of that smoke will come a judgment on the world for its unbelief. It's going to be supernatural creatures that you won't be able to explain away. I know this is difficult for you—"

"Don't pretend you know me," she snarled.

"But God is trying to get your attention. This seven-year span of time, and these judgments are for God's chosen people. It's a call back to him."

"There is no God!" Liz said.

But as she made her atheistic declaration, smoke appeared on the video. It was dark, black smoke, and it suddenly billowed up around the drone. The lights on the device seemed almost snuffed out. Visibility was down to inches.

"This is a new development," the female reporter said in a loud voice. "We have what looks like smoke rising from the sinkhole."

"Smoke?" the new anchor in the studio said. "Can you confirm that for us, Alana?"

"We'll be checking with the scientists, Amir, but my drone operator just informed me that he's got to bring the device back up."

"How did you know that?" Ruth asked me.

She was a kindly looking woman, short and thin with a slightly curved back. Her face was lined with wrinkles, but her face was bright. I could see no sign of God's seal on her forehead.

"It's in the Bible," I said. "Revelation, chapter 9, says that an angelic being was given the key to the shaft to the bottomless pit. And from that pit came smoke. It's going to block out the sun. Out of the smoke are going to come terrible locusts that will sting people like scorpions and make them wish for death, but they won't be able to die."

"Tell us about these creatures," Nathan said.

"They'll have five months to torture people," I said. "Anyone who doesn't have the mark of God on their foreheads will be fair game."

"We don't have the mark," Cat said.

All the believers who had come with me to the Shiloh building could see the mark on the heads of the Jewish believers. There were ten of them, first Daniel, then those who had believed in Jesus as their Messiah the night before. They all had the same translucent symbol on their foreheads. But none of the non-believers could see the mark. None of the gentile believers, myself included, had the seal of God on our foreheads.

"No," I said grimly, knowing that meant we would be targets of the creatures that were coming.

"Why not?" Allie asked. "Why aren't we sealed?"

"I can't say for sure, but my theory is that we aren't sealed because we aren't secure in our relationship with God yet."

"But we believe," LB said.

"We do and we are in a relationship with God," I said.

"But we have to be good or we'll lose our salvation?" Hannah asked.

"No," I told her. "Our sins are forgiven. But there is one thing that would separate us from God."

"Just one?" Flex asked.

"One thing that is explicitly spelled out in the Bible. If we take the Mark of the Beast, whatever that ends up being, for any reason whatsoever, we'll be separated from God forever."

The room was quiet for a moment. It was scary to think about. And the world was a scary place. Then Cat said something profound.

"The mark isn't just a visible sign, is it?" she said. "It has to be more."

"Many people thought it was more," I said, "especially theologians who were alive at the time of the rapture. With all the trans-human talk, most believed that the mark would be something like that, some sort of a technological device that would fundamentally change a human being into something else."

"And if we take the mark, we go to hell?" Flex asked.

"Yes," I said gravely. "All those who bear the mark will be cast into the lake of fire prepared for Satan and his angels. We are called to endure and keep God's commands and our faith in Jesus."

By that point, the video on the television had shifted from the drone back to cameras on the ground. It showed smoke billowing up from the sinkhole. It was dark black smoke, laced with gray. It shot up into the sky and created a hazy overcast. Within minutes, as we watched in silence, the bright, sunny day turned dark. It wasn't as dark as night and certainly not the same as the supernatural darkness, but it was thick. The people near the sinkhole were forced to move back as the smoke billowed in a thick plume.

As the news reporter gave an update, a new sound could be heard. It was like rolling thunder, only it didn't shift and it didn't end. It only grew louder.

"Alana, can you tell us what is making that noise?" the news anchor asked.

The reporter turned to look over her shoulder. It was a natural reaction, although before she could answer, she was bowled over by a horde of small creatures. The cameraman's self-discipline held for a couple of seconds, then he – too - was knocked down. The camera fell away and was pointed at nothing but the tire of their news van. What continued to broadcast was the audio. Joined to the roar from the creatures that came flying from the smoke, were the screams of the reporter and her cameraman.

17

There was no good look at the creatures before the video changed back to the newsroom and the anxious-looking anchor named Amir.

"It appears that we've lost the connection with our reporter on the scene, but we will continue our coverage of the event. At News Four, we are here for you."

I turned from the television and walked away from the cluster of people there. With the twenty-four people who had come with me to the Shiloh building, there were fifty-five individuals in the building's basement. I didn't have to ask LB to follow me. He was every bit the leader that I was, perhaps even more. He was a commissioned officer after all, and had experience leading Marines, during his career.

"Food or security?" he asked me.

"How do you know what I'm thinking?" I asked him.

"'Cause I'm thinking the same thing, brother. I've read Revelation eight. I don't want any part of the creatures coming out of that pit."

"We can't avoid them," I said. "I don't think any amount of effort to keep them out will work."

"How quick do you reckon they'll get here?"

"No idea," I confessed. "But once they do, we're talking about five months of hunkering down and trying to stay off their radar."

"And what comes after them is worse," LB said. "No one said this was going to be easy."

"That's true," I replied. "We need food and we need to think about heading south again."

"We're about as south as we can get without leaving the country again," LB said. "We know the resorts on most of the islands in the Caribbean were wiped out. You remember how Cuba looked."

"I do. But if we bypass those islands and head south, we could reach South America. I don't know what kind of shelter there is out there, but it's closer to the equator, and we might not have our back to the wall like we do here."

"Alright, first priority is food. We figure that out, then move on to security and transportation. The only food around here is at that football stadium. You got ideas about that?"

"I think we need to get our hands on as much of it as we can," I said. "Finding a boat big enough for all these people won't be easy."

"You think they'll all go?"

"I don't know," I said. "Maybe they don't have to. Maybe it's just my paranoia kicking in, but I feel like staying here isn't right."

"God's got something else for you," LB said.

"For us," I corrected him. "I'm not forcing anyone to come with me, but I'm pretty sure we all need to make tracks while we can."

"You know Allie and I are with you. Just say the word and we're gone."

"Thanks," I told him, feeling a little better with his support.

That entire day, people watched the television while LB, Cat, Allie, and Flex gathered supplies. More fuel was needed for our vehicles. We found plenty of vehicles in the parking around the Falls shopping complex. They were in bad shape, but we managed to fill our tanks as well as the five-gallon can on the back of the Jeep.

Cat did an inventory of the food supply at the Shiloh building. It was all canned goods and dry foods, but they had enough beans, rice, flour, sugar and pasta to last a month feeding all fifty-five people, maybe enough for six weeks. But it wouldn't be enough to hunker down for the next five months.

Flex was key to our plans. He hadn't worked in the food prep when he spent a couple of days in the NARA facility at the Hard Rock Stadium, but he had seen where the pallets of food were stored.

"Ain't no question I can find it," he said. "But they got guards, yo. We ain't just strolling in and taking that food without a fight."

"We don't want a fight," I said.

"How do you propose we get enough food to make a difference?" LB asked. "A smash and grab ain't going to help us much."

"True," I said. "Let's pray about it."

We did and no lightning flash from heaven came in response. By the time the darkness came, everyone was on edge. They say the anticipation is worse than the thing you're dreading. I thought that myself until the power came back on and there were updates from news services around the world.

"Funny how an alien spaceship supposedly blocking the sunlight also makes electronic devices not work," Flex said.

"An astute observation," Daniel said, "How do you explain that, Liz?"

They had all been together during the darkness. Some worked on puzzles or read books. I led a Bible study, then did my best to answer questions. That evening we ate spaghetti with lemon cake for dessert. It was delicious despite having limited resources and no meat. But when the lights came back on, we were drawn to the television like moths to an open flame.

"Who cares," Liz said. "They're saving the planet."

She had a few friends who didn't disagree with her openly, but I had seen them glance longingly in our direction when I was answering questions about the judgments we had already been through. Surprisingly enough, the Jewish retirees were fascinated by the revelation of prophecy in the Bible. I tried to use as much of the

Old Testament as I could to reinforce the fact that the God of the New Testament is the same God of the Old. And more importantly, I wanted them to see that Jesus was God the Son, Savior of the World, their promised Messiah.

"Yeah, that's right," one of her friends said without much enthusiasm.

"You should probably give her a little grace," Cat said to Daniel.

"Liz would reject that too," Daniel said, drawing a baleful glance from Liz.

"How do you know?" Cat said. "She might surprise you."

"After being married for thirty-five years, there's not so much she could do that would surprise me."

"You were married to Liz?" LB asked incredulously.

"Still am," Daniel said with a mischievous grin. "Although she would be glad to be rid of me."

"You have become an embarrassment, old man," Liz said.

I think we were all shocked. It was only the breaking news that pulled our attention back before more could be said about Daniel's revelation.

"It appears that the sinkhole opened over a deep chasm," a reporter in a long trench coat said. He was holding a microphone and standing in front of a university sign in a language I didn't recognize. "Earlier today, I interviewed the renowned geologist Immad Turk of the Kalifa University."

The video switched to an interview with an older man with glasses. The reporter was showing him video from the sinkhole on an iPad as he asked questions.

"Can you tell us why there is smoke coming from the sinkhole?" the reporter asked.

"It is not an uncommon phenomenon," the geologist said with a heavy accent. "Most depressions, crevasses and sinkholes are a result of shifting subterranean geologic forces. There is often a great amount of heat involved and there are a myriad of minerals that would burn and smoke."

"I see," the reporter said. "There are eyewitness reports of strange insects coming out of the smoke."

"Again, that is not unusual," the reporter said. "There are many subterranean species that most of us are unfamiliar with. The good news is that none of these underground fauna can exist for long on the surface."

"You're saying they'll die off quickly?"

"That's correct."

Cat had a laptop computer open and began reading a report out loud. "That's not what this is saying. This is from a Syrian blog: 'They look like big grasshoppers from a distance, but upclose they are hideous insects with curving tails like a scorpion. What we saw were swarms of these objects coming out of the smoke and attacking people. I know that description may be triggering, but that's how it appeared. We have a dog and were near a sheep pen as the smoke drifted toward us. It was thick and hazy, blocking out the sun almost entirely. Then came the insects. They ignored the dog and the sheep, but seemed to swarm the people.'"

"That's in Syria?" I asked.

"Yeah," Cat said. "North of Mt. Hermon in Rashaya, Lebanon."

"Whoa! Look at that. The smoke is really spreading fast."

Back on the television, the picture had changed to a satellite feed. The smoke showed up from orbit as a dark smudge. It had moved north as far as the Black Sea and split south on either side of the Red Sea. It covered almost all of Saudi Arabia to the east and all of Egypt down into the Sudan on the west.

"Is it going to cover the entire planet?" Hannah asked.

"It doesn't have to," I said. "All I can say for sure is that the locusts will torment the entire world for five months and they come out of the smoke."

"Hank, look at this," Cat said. "Somebody got a video of one."

She turned the computer so that everyone could see it. On the video, there was a close-up of a locust that had landed on a woman. There was no sound. The video was a bit fuzzy from the zoom, but it showed the locust clearly enough. It had a thick, rectangular body front to back, not unlike a grasshopper, and two powerful legs for jumping. But that was where the normalcy ended. Around their bodies was an odd feature, a sort of overlapping set of scales. They seemed to hang on the creature, which was about as long as a grown man's index finger. The scales were colored red and yellow, brown and green. It was almost like there were designs on the scales. It reminded me of a horse in the Middle Ages that was covered with chainmail armor and on top of that were silks with the rider's motif sewn onto them.

They had no arms, but along their backs were long wings that fanned outward so that they looked like a dragonfly's wings. The long body angled upward from the powerful rear legs to the head, which was without a doubt the strangest feature of the creature. It didn't look like a bug, or even an animal, but a human. The one captured on video had an oval-shaped head, high cheekbones, a square chin and a broad nose. The skin was as white as my own. And the hair was long. It hung in ringlets on either side of the horrific face. Around the top of the head was what appeared to be a gold band with tiny spikes. It looked like a crown that an evil king might wear. The gold shone bright as if it were actual metal. It even reflected the features around it.

Across the broad chest of the insect was a dull iron plate. In fact, the locust looked like a fusion of metal and organics. It was, without a doubt, the strangest creature I had ever seen. The worst part was the tail. At the rear of the creature was a long, curving scorpion tail with a huge red stinger. There was venom glistening on the stinger that made a shiver run down my spine.

"That's the worst thing I've ever seen," Allie said.

"Can't be real," Hannah said. "It can't be."

"It's like a mythological beast," Saul pointed out. "There are many hybrids or chimeras in ancient writings, from the Greek Minotaur to the throne guardians of ancient Babylon."

I had to work my tongue around before I spoke because my

mouth was suddenly dry. "The book of Enoch says that the Nephilim sinned against the flesh of animals and birds. A lot of commentators take that to mean that they were creating hybrids. Some scholars believed that what the Bible called an unclean spirit was something that was mixed."

"I'd say that's an unclean thing," LB said. "Look at the teeth on it."

The mouth of the locust was open, and the teeth were visible. Four massive canine teeth stood tall above the other, smaller teeth, but they were all pointed.

"The Bible says they will have teeth like a lion," I said.

"Yes, that qualifies," Cat said.

We watched more videos coming from the Near East. The authorities were already censoring much of it, but so many people were uploading footage that there was still plenty to haunt our dreams. The videos were like scenes from horror movies. People were running, shouting, trying to find safety … but there was none. One video showed the locusts chasing a woman to her car. She made it safely inside, but the locusts weren't slowed for long. They broke through a door window and flooded inside. The video picked up her screams before the person filming had to flee the swarm.

Another video showed people running on a street from an elevated position. It was clearly pulled from a security camera as swarms of locusts flew past the camera. Another showed people falling on the ground and writhing as the locusts attacked. I could even make out the tails striking like vipers over and over again. The locusts showed no mercy. They went after every human in their path and stung them with unrelenting fury. Another video showed a man with a tennis racket. He batted one locust to the ground and then stomped on it. He was grinning victoriously and chattering in a language I didn't understand. But his smile vanished and his words turned to shrieks of pain as the locust not only survived being stepped on, but managed to sting through the bottom of the man's shoe and into the sole of his foot.

The professional news outlets tried to downplay the horror. They had experts saying the locusts were benign. Then the story shifted to warnings not to try and stop the locusts. I didn't think many people were trying to stop the swarming creatures. It was the locusts who were targeting people. But I had learned long ago not to trust the regular media. There were simply too many groups trying to manipulate the masses through the mainstream news outlets.

"What do we do, Hank?" Cat asked.

"We get ready," I said. "And warn as many people as we can."

18

Throughout the last two and a half years, since the rapture of the church, I had been posting videos. At first, I just uploaded Lorenzo's videos, as many as I could. Living in his home and working as his curator helped in that endeavor, but eventually I had to leave Spokane, Washington, as war broke out across the United States. And when I lost access to Lorenzo's videos, I used what I had learned to make videos of my own.

The first rule of making videos that called out the elites of the global government, along with their supposedly alien counterparts, and holding up the truth, was that you never revealed your identity. The world had, at least in North America, become very crude. We went from being a world power to being a third-world nation where people struggled to survive and things like IDs were rare. It was one of the reasons the NARA group at the Hard Rock Stadium was urging people to register. I hadn't shown my face in a video in a very long time. That didn't change as I made a series of short videos revealing what the Bible had to say about the locusts and the next five months on planet earth.

We made the short videos using a burner phone, which had no service, but which could still access the internet. And, in an attempt to kill two birds with one stone, LB, Cat and I took the Jeep north to take another look at the stadium. The snow allowed us to move slowly through the streets while also watching for any sort of roadblock or checkpoints. The plan was to get close enough to the stadium that I could patch into their internet to upload the videos and disseminate them across as many channels as I could. The government had a powerful AI system that scoured the internet for what it deemed misinformation. It had the power to censor anything it found to be inappropriate, which was really just newspeak for anything that was critical of the government or anything that promoted biblical truth.

"Can you believe it?" Cat said. "They're acting like nothing is happening."

"It ain't happened here yet," LB said.

"But it's only a matter of time," she insisted.

"We know that," I said, "but most people these days don't want to know the truth. They just want to hear what's going to make them feel better."

"Always been that way, I reckon," LB said.

He was driving. I was in the backseat. Between us, we had two pistols. It wasn't much protection, but it was better than nothing. We weren't looking for a fight. The farther north we went, the more surprising things became. There were snowplows working the streets. They were really just construction vehicles with makeshift snow plows welded to the front, but they were effective. The streets weren't exactly clear. Nothing was melting in the new ice age that had overtaken Miami, but it was packed down to a thin layer. On many of the main roads, there was a layer of sand.

"Pretty smart using sand," LB said. "They got plenty of that at the beach. And ain't no body spending time out there anymore."

"Look at this," Cat said, pointing to a grocery store. "What do you think they're using for money?"

"Digital currency," I said. "The whole world will be using it soon."

"They're just buying and selling and going to work and... is that a school?"

We looked, and sure enough, a local high school had been staffed and reopened. There were large banners with messages to parents and teens, such as: **School is back in session, Register for classes here,** and **Welcome back students!**

"I guess if people are going back to work, the kids gotta go back to school," LB said.

"I can't believe how many people there are here," I said. "The city seemed deserted when we arrived."

"The weather is pushing people south," LB said. "Only a matter of time before they have to abandon Florida altogether."

"You think it will get that bad?" Cat said.

"Yeah, I do," LB said. "Don't get me wrong. I ain't no weather man, but as long as it's dark twice as long as it's daylight, then I don't think it's gonna get any warmer."

We passed people working on utilities and repairing buildings, others were moving into apartments and houses. There were thousands of people in North Miami and the city was rebuilding despite the weather.

When we got close to the stadium, it seemed oddly deserted. Most of the vehicles that had filled the parking lot were in use. And although thousands of people were still living there, most were working at jobs that were off the stadium grounds.

We pulled up beside the rear of the building, where we had a view of several large trucks making deliveries. I was able to connect to the WIFI and upload my videos while we observed the process.

"Where are those trucks coming from?" Cat asked.

"Gotta be the airport," LB said. "They're shipping in goods from down south."

"When the first trumpet judgment fell and burned up a third of the forests, it left plenty of room to plant crops," I said. "I'll bet

Central America is busy growing food that's being shipped all around the world."

"It's still hard for me to wrap my mind around," Cat said. "We're in the middle of the most supernatural judgments ever put upon the world and yet people are just going about their lives like nothing is happening."

"That's the way Jesus said it would be," I told her. "As in the days of Noah, people were eating and drinking, marrying and given in marriage, right up until the flood swept them away. So it will be at the coming of the Son of Man - Hank's rough paraphrase."

"Pretty darn good," LB said.

"Still, hard to believe," Cat said.

The workers driving the trucks didn't get out of their cabs if they didn't have to. It was warm in their trucks, and freezing cold outside, where workers were unloading the goods. But I noticed that the few who were coerced out of their trucks were not soldiers.

"Looks like the drivers of those trucks aren't soldiers," I said.

"Should they be?" LB wondered.

"I'm just saying that if we had to take one, it might not be much of a fight," I said.

"How is it we're sitting here plotting a robbery if we're the good guys?" LB asked.

"We're contemplating, not plotting," I said. "Does that help?"

"Not really," LB said. "Don't get me wrong, I know there are dark days coming. But I'm not sure if this is the best way forward."

"We need a place to go," I said. "My guess is, once the locusts get here, we won't be able to do much of anything."

"Because we'll be in hiding?" Cat asked.

I knew she wanted me to say we had nothing to worry about, but despite my own fears, I didn't think that was true. The Bible says only those with the seal of God upon their foreheads would be spared and the only seals I had ever seen were on Jewish believers.

"That, or we'll be incapacitated," I said. "Maybe I'm wrong... I hope that I am, but..."

"We have to plan for the worst," LB said.

"Let's head south tomorrow," Cat said. "Maybe we'll find something that can get us through the next five months."

The following day, we left before dawn. We took the Jeep once again, this time taking Allie along. The four of us plowed through snow that was over a foot deep as we moved south. Eventually, we hit Highway 1, which took us out over the ocean and into the Florida Keys. The water was frozen along the coast as far south as Key Largo. Everywhere we looked were the icons you would expect in ocean communities: anchors, nets, pirate ships, fish, crabs, shrimp, and lobsters. It seemed starkly at odds with the snow and ice everywhere.

If the bridge was damaged, which we all expected it to be, the snow hid it. Maybe even the ice held it together; I had no idea. We went slow and careful, especially after we reached open water. The stretch between Islamorada and Marathon was sketchy. When we reached Big Pine Key, we saw widespread flooding. What we didn't find were places where fifty-plus people could take shelter and feel safe. We pressed on, past homes and small motels, but mostly just stretches of icy waters and snow-covered mangrove islands.

We were on the verge of giving up when we reached Key West. It was literally the end of the road, but also one of the biggest cities along the string of limestone islands. There was a lot of destruction on Key West. Sunken boats littered the shoreline. Entire marinas had been demolished by the tsunami that took out a third of the world's ships. If any people had survived, they had left the island, it seemed. Only a few buildings were intact. One happened to be a grocery store. It was not only still standing, but it hadn't been looted either. Another structure that survived the judgments from God was the Casa Marina main building.

"Would you look at that?" LB said.

"It's big enough," Cat said. "Let's check and see if there are people inside."

LB pulled the Jeep right to the front of the building. The main entrance faced the resort's green space. Hedges, palm trees, gazebos, and water features had been beautiful at one time. When we arrived, it was overgrown and covered in ice and snow.

"It's a shame to see dead palm trees," LB said. "They can't survive the cold."

"We can't either," Allie said, hurrying from the warm Jeep into the building.

It was cold inside, too, and dark as well. There was no sign of anyone staying in the building. A quick search proved that to be true as well. The resort was abandoned, but still habitable. The wide lobby had dark wood floors and black support pillars. There were green sofas and tan sitting chairs grouped in small clusters with throw rugs and wooden accent tables. Across the lobby from the wide check-in desk was a bar. There were still bottles of whiskey, tequila, and vodka on display shelves and a tall wine rack filled with dark bottles from around the world.

"We got shelter, but no heat," LB said. "I'd almost rather sleep in the Jeep than freeze in this swanky place."

"They're not connected to Miami's power grid, but what do you bet they've got generators on site," I said.

"They would have to for hurricane season," Cat said.

We gave the girls the pistols and had them search for the kitchen to see what was salvageable while LB and I went down a set of stairs to a maintenance level below ground. It didn't take long to find the generator. It was the size of a small car and connected to a huge tank of liquid propane.

"This looks promising," LB said.

"Tank's full," I said, shining my little flashlight at the transparent window on top of the tank.

"The only question is, how long will it last?"

The basement level was dark like a cave, and it took me a few minutes to find the main breaker box. We walked over to it.

"Should be able to conserve power," I said. "We don't need the entire resort to be up and running."

Let's see what we've got," LB said. "Don't need the Grand Ballroom or the Lobby."

He started flipping breakers to the off position.

"Don't need Fitness Room or the Spa," I added.

"Be nice, though, wouldn't it?" he said. "I would not say no to a massage and some time in the steam room. I feel the cold seeping into my bones."

"Looks like there are four resident areas. I say we reserve power for the Suite Wing, and keep the Flagler Building A and B, along with the West Wing, without electricity."

"Agreed. If we have to stay in this dump, might as well be the Penthouse Suite."

After turning off all the breakers but one, we turned our attention back to the generator. And like any good facility that caters to guests, there were instructions printed on the wall next to the controls. We had to use a hand pump to prime the generator, then we checked all parts of the device to make sure nothing was missing. There were two separate switches on either side of the device. They had to be turned to the on position. And then a safety lever had to be pulled down. Like everything near the ocean, oxidation was an issue. To keep the battery for the starter from getting corroded, it was kept in a plastic box with a lid and the terminals were further sealed in a removable plastic cap. We had to pull the tabs that unsealed the terminals, then attach the wires to them. But with all that done, the generator started with the push of a button.

It was loud and the exhaust vent was plugged with snow. I hurried outside, found the utilities on the side of the building and cleared the blockage. LB started the generator again and we met the girls back in the lobby.

"Lots of food," Cat said. "Good stuff too. Steaks, seafood, a bunch of stuff in big freezers that were vacuum sealed."

"You think it's still good?" I asked.

"Only one way to find out," Allie said.

We carried some of the frozen food along with a portable grill that was used for beach parties and kept in a storage area of the kitchen, up to the suites on the third floor. The girls had also found a set of lockers where the employees had kept their things, including the housekeeping staff. We had a pair of keycards we hoped would open the electronically locked doors, but once we got to the residential sections, we found the doors were all open. We had to pass through Flagler Building B, which was connected to the lobby on one end and the Suite Wing on the other. It was a three-story, rectangular building with guest rooms eighty-one through ninety-nine. At the end of that dark hallway, we entered the only part of the building with power. It was a relief to find the heat already running.

"How often do you think they had to run the heat in this place?" LB asked.

"Not very," Allie answered him.

"There were probably times when it got chilly at night, say in February," Cat added.

"I'm just glad they have heat," I said.

The heater hadn't been running long and it was still cold in the Suite Wing. We took the stairs up to the second floor after making sure no lights were on in the rooms on that level. There was nothing we could do about the lighting in the hallways. If they used too much power, we would be forced to remove the bulbs, but that would be decided later. We also made sure the heat wasn't running in the individual rooms, which were very upscale. The suites all had sitting rooms and bedrooms. On the second floor, the suites had two bedrooms and mini-kitchens. We checked all the rooms there, too. Most were clean, but a few had been left unkempt. It was impossible to know how quickly the resort was abandoned. Yet it seemed that some things were left undone.

We didn't have time to drive all the way back to Miami before the supernatural darkness set in. Unlike some of the other judgments, whatever God had done to the sun and stars to keep them from shining for a third of the day and a third of the night was continuing even as the other judgments continued. Electrical power was strangely affected by the supernatural darkness as well. For instance, the heat continued to work, but nothing that produced light would work other than fire.

In the waning moments of daylight, we gathered extra blankets for the beds in the two rooms that adjoined the living area of the suites on the top floor. There were excellent views of the ocean through the big windows. Gone were the waves lapping onto the beach. Instead, an ice shelf extended into the water, which was dark blue with white caps at the peaks of the undulating waves.

We set the room thermostat at seventy-two and set up some emergency candles Cat had found while searching for food. When the darkness hit, it was sudden, but we were warming up and had a cookstove set up on the balcony, thawing the steaks.

"Bad news," LB said as he came back into the suite from the frosty balcony. He stomped his feet to get the snow off his boots. "The meat is no good."

That was a disappointment, but not a surprise.

"It was worth a shot," Cat said.

"We'll have to go get something else," Allie said.

"Once more into the cold," I said.

We bundled up and went together. Perhaps that wasn't necessary, but as I feared, with the supernatural darkness came a sense of terror that was hard to shake. We were in a massive resort that was completely abandoned in the dead of winter. All I could think of was the Stephen King book *The Shining*. And, to be completely honest, it wasn't surprising when we saw ghosts in the resort.

The first one appeared as soon as we stepped out of our suite and into the dark hallway.

"What the—" LB exclaimed as a luminous woman appeared suddenly at the end of the hallway. She was only there for a moment and appeared to walk into one of the other suites without opening the door. She was ethereal, like a hologram from a sci-fi movie. She wore a bikini top and a wrap around her waist that hung to her ankles. She had long, blonde hair. At first glance, and like I said, she was only there for maybe a second or two, she seemed young and beautiful. But when she turned her head to look at us, we could see that her eyes were missing, and the far side of her face was a bloody mess. Worse still, there were worms, thick white worms, not tiny maggots, but worms like I remembered seeing in my visions of hell. They were consuming her flesh and writhing where her eyes should have been.

"No, no, no…" Cat said, grabbing onto me.

"Was that a ghost?" Allie asked.

"It was a demon," I said. "They masquerade as all sorts of things, from ghosts to aliens."

"You think?" LB said.

"I've seen them for a long time," I admitted. "Scripture isn't clear on that point, but we know there are evil spirits that torment people."

"What about ghosts?" Allie said. "Any mention of ghosts in the Bible?"

We were all students of the Bible. We each had our own copy and read the passages carefully, but I had been a believer the longest. Plus, I had been mentored by Lorenzo Maltza, who was a Christian expert on the paranormal. I had watched hundreds of hours of his lectures. That didn't make me an expert, but I was the guy everyone tended to ask about things like ghosts.

"No," I said. "When a person dies, their spirit goes either to Paradise or to Hades, depending on their relationship with God."

"And none get stuck here in our world?" LB asked.

They were standard beliefs about ghosts. Most people believed that the reason a ghost haunted a place was to resolve some unfinished business in their former life. But that wasn't a biblical concept.

"The only mention of a ghost in scripture that I'm aware of was the Prophet Samuel. King Saul went to a woman in the town of Endor who was considered a medium."

"Endor, like in Star Wars?" LB asked.

"In name only," I told him. "It was a town in Israel. Saul had decreed that all mediums and necromancers were to be removed from the land, but there were still some left, I guess. They go to this woman in Endor, Saul tells her to summon the prophet Samuel, and she does it."

"I didn't know stuff like that was real," Cat said as we headed for the stairwell.

"It's all become fantasy, I guess," I told her. "But archeologists have found ritual pits littered with bones and ancient writings that describe people making offerings to the dead, and communicating with them. Lorenzo believed that in most cases, they were dealing with deceptive spirits. In fact, the Bible records the medium at Endor screaming in fright when Samuel actually shows up. Saul asks her what she's seeing, and she said, 'I see a god coming up out of the ground.' Apparently, she wasn't used to seeing actual human spirits."

We were halfway down the stairs when a loud noise sounded above us.

"What was that?" Allie asked.

"Could have been something to do with the power," LB suggested.

"I'm not sure I like this place," Cat said.

"Just remember how things were when the darkness first came, and we were at the apartment facility," I told them. "We all saw things there, too."

"Feels different, I won't lie," LB said. "You sure it's safe here?"

"It's safe for us," I said. "We should pray."

And so we did. At the bottom of the stairwell, with our eyes wide open, huddled around our candles, we prayed that God would protect us and that his angelic warriors would surround the resort. We asked the Holy Spirit to move in that place, to fill it with his presence and drive out every evil and unclean spirit.

I wish I could say that God answered our prayers and the night went on without another scare. What I can say is that we all felt better and, while we continued to see frightening things, they were all outside our sections of the resort. Unfortunately, a beachfront resort is designed to give guests views of the ocean. And in the darkness, sometimes right outside those panoramic windows, shadows moved. We heard moans and screams from the darkness outside. If you can imagine how it might be in a haunted insane asylum, that is what we experienced that night.

We had to go all the way back to the lobby and through a side door into the staff work areas to reach the pantry. It was a large space with lots of commercial-sized food containers. The cans were almost all as large as an old-style coffee can, and the bags of dry goods all weighed more than ten pounds. We were in no mood to linger. It took just a few moments to grab a can of chili and a box of crackers, then we headed back upstairs. LB carried a flat of water in plastic bottles, which he almost dropped as he caught sight of the bar on the far side of the lobby.

"What is it?" I asked.

I couldn't see anything, but my big friend was clearly frightened.

"It can't be," he said in a whisper.

"What?" Allie asked.

She and Cat were still carrying pistols, but also the candles. I had the chili and crackers, LB had the water bottles, and we were all pretty frightened to see our big friend looking so shocked.

"Haven't seen him since I was a kid," LB said.

"Who?" I asked.

"That's my father," he said, nodding his head toward the bar.

I couldn't see anyone, and a glance at Allie and Cat revealed they couldn't either. But LB could; he was so moved there were tears welling up in his eyes. I didn't know if he was happy or scared.

"You see him? He's drinking whiskey, probably the cheapest they got."

"We don't see him," Allie said, putting her free hand on LB's shoulder.

"That's him, alright. Same slouchy hat, same frayed jacket he was wearing the night he killed a family driving drunk. He lived but only for a few weeks. Never woke up from the coma he was in, but there was plenty of people said he got off easy."

"That's terrible," Cat said. "I'm so sorry, LB."

"Still drinking. That man never could get enough."

"It's not him, LB," I said softly. "Not really."

"Let's go!" The big man said suddenly. "He ain't worth a minute of our time."

We returned to the suite in silence after that. The resort seemed deserted. There were no more sounds, no more moving shadows and no more ghosts that night. We used parts from the gas grill to hold up the can of chili and put candles beneath it. The food warmed right in the can and we ate it in small bowls with stale crackers.

"I got a feeling this place was abandoned right at the start of the war," Allie said. "All the food 'use by' dates are for over a year ago."

"I suppose it's a good thing everything was packed with preservatives," Cat said. "Otherwise, we'd be going hungry tonight."

"I appreciate this fine meal," LB said.

"You're losing it," Allie said. "This is just barely worth eating."

"Hey, compared to MREs and field rations, this is a feast. The only thing better would be some ice-cold beer instead of this water."

"I don't mind chili, but it's not my favorite," Cat said.

"Hot food and a warm bed for the night sounds pretty good to me," I said.

"Me too, partner," LB said. "Is this it then? This where we're headed?"

"I think so," I told him. "At dawn, we check the propane situation and shut down the generator. If we're not burning too much fuel, then we could bring everyone back here."

"We should check out that grocery store before we make a decision," Allie said. "There's a good bit of usable food in the resort, but not enough to feed everyone for long."

"Sounds like a plan," Cat said.

The next day, we set out for Miami. The generator had used so little fuel through the night that I couldn't discern how much was gone from the big tank. Before we left Key West, we happened upon a small business that distributed propane gas to the various homes and businesses on the little island.

The grocery store was everything we hoped it would be. Fully stocked and easy enough to get into. There was enough food inside to feed our group of fifty-five people for several months, more than enough time for us to find a vessel that would take us south.

The drive back was without incident. We followed the tracks we had made on the way down and got to the Shiloh building with half a day left. All we had left to do was convince the rest of our group that what we had discovered in Key West was better than what they had in Miami. Only before we could do that, the first of the supernatural locusts arrived.

19

"What if we don't want to go?" Liz demanded.

We were in the basement of the Shiloh building and had given our report about Casa Marina, along with our recommendation that we all move down to Key West. The women who were Liz's friends looked very uncomfortable.

"We aren't forcing anyone to do anything," I said. "But I have a feeling the NARA people will."

"They were patrolling this area just an hour before you got back," Flex said. "The snow plows still hadn't gotten this far south, and the soldiers saw our tracks in the street."

"It's only a matter of time before they come," I said. "I don't want to frighten anyone, but if they know you're here, they will come and take whatever they want."

"Says you," Liz demanded.

She was an outspoken unbeliever, yet she was also keenly aware of the rampant anti-semitism that had been so prevalent before Administrator Eon brokered the peace deal with Israel. She seemed like a big talker with us, but I didn't think she wanted anything to do with NARA, either.

"This is our home," Matthais said. "You are asking a lot of an old man."

"I just want to make sure you're safe," I said. "We need to find a ship capable of taking us south. The weather isn't getting any better, and eventually, you will run out of supplies."

"That happens, you'll be forced to join NARA," LB said. "They may pretend they're your friend, but in less than a year they're going to turn against the Jews in a very public way."

"A violent way," I said.

"Why should we believe that?" A silver-haired man named Oscar asked. "I respect you, and I respect your faith, but the government has shown no signs that it has anything but goodwill for our people."

"It's a farce," I told him. "You don't have to believe me, Oscar. I'm not trying to frighten anyone. But I've grown to care about each and every one of you."

"Even Liz?" Daniel joked.

"Yes, even Liz," I said, as the group chuckled.

"Whatever," the unhappy woman said. She turned away from me, but she didn't leave.

"I can't guarantee anything about anyone's safety. But I can guarantee that we will help one another and work toward keeping everyone safe."

"The sooner the better if you ask me," Flex said. "I want to get as far away from NARA as I can get."

I didn't have the heart to tell him that eventually we would have to sail south and settle somewhere more hospitable where NARA probably had an ever greater presence.

"All of your people are going?" Nathan asked.

I glanced around. All the believers from my group nodded in agreement.

"And I will go," Daniel said.

"Count me in," Saul added.

All the new believers that Daniel had helped realize Jesus was their Messiah spoke up and volunteered to go, except for Matthias and Asher.

"Let us discuss it," Nathan said.

I let them go talk it over and turned my attention to the next issue before us as Preston came hurrying down the steps.

"Anything?" I asked.

"Actually, I did find a couple of passenger vans in the Emerald Gardens," Preston said.

"Sounds like a nice place," Cat said.

"Why would a Chinese restaurant have vans?" Flex asked.

"It's a retirement village," Preston said. "The vans are in pretty good shape, but they won't start."

"They'll need to be checked out," Allie said. "I've got the time."

"Not without me," LB said. "If there are soldiers in the area, we need to be careful."

"Agreed," I said. "And you need to be back before dark, with or without those vans."

I bundled up and went upstairs to stand watch while Allie, LB and Preston were gone. There wasn't much more to do. Some people were packing, but Cat and I didn't have much to pull together. The retirees at Shiloh had given us access to the empty apartments. We had discovered coats and boots and had moved mattresses and blankets down to the basement. But other than what we would wear, we wouldn't need to take anything from the Shiloh building. The resort on Key West would have everything we needed.

"Thought I would find you here," Cat said as she came into the apartment where I was watching the city.

"Any decision from the others?" I asked.

"Nathan and half of the non-believers have decided to come along. Matthias and Asher want to stay, Liz won't say what she's doing, but her friends want to leave, so..."

"So, she'll probably come too. Her husband is with us."

"She really hates him," Cat said. "I can't imagine that."

"He accepted Christ as the Messiah. I know that a lot of Jewish people in the past were shunned for coming to the truth."

"It's sad," Cat said. "I can tell he still loves her."

"That's a tricky situ—"

I was cut off by a loud ~*Thud!*~ as something smashed into the window. Cat and I both took a step back. I thought that someone was shooting at us, although how they had spotted us in the darkened apartment wasn't clear. There was a tiny crater in the window and cracks spreading out from it.

"What was that?" Cat said.

"I don't know," I admitted just before another impact caused the window cracks to extend almost to the edges.

"Hank! Look!" Cat said, pointing.

On the window was a wicked-looking creature. Seen from the bottom, it resembled a grasshopper, only bigger, the body thicker, and from the rear curled a frightening-looking tail.

"It's the locusts," I said. "Get to the basement. We've got to seal up the doors."

To her credit, she didn't hesitate. We rushed out of the apartment just as another blow to the window shattered the glass.

"Oh, no!" Cat said as we sprinted to the stairs. "Can they get to us?"

"Probably," I said.

We had done what we could to prepare. We added extra rubber seals around the edges of the doors and had tacked up screens over all the vents in the basement. But if the locusts could break through windows, they would tear right through our screens. The metal vent covers might hold them off long enough for us to prepare for their arrival, but I didn't think anything would stop them forever.

"What about Allie and LB?" Cat shouted as we hurried down the stairs.

"We've got no way to warn them," I said.

"Someone has to," she said.

I didn't disagree, but I felt a rising sense of fear in my gut. I didn't want to leave and I certainly couldn't tell anyone else to go in my place.

"I'll go," Cat said.

"No," I told her, feeling ashamed that she would volunteer before me. "You get down to the basement and help the others. I'll find LB and Allie. Don't worry."

When we reached the level where the garage was situated, she stopped and turned to me.

"Come back, Hank," she said.

"The locusts aren't deadly," I said.

There was a look of uncertainty in her eyes. We had both seen one of the locusts and, having seen them, we were filled with terror. The Bible said that they weren't allowed to kill, only torment. But it felt like the little creature wanted to kill and, in that moment, our faith was on shaky ground.

"Just come back to me," she said. "I... I can't do this without you."

She pulled me close and we kissed. Danger has a way of heightening all our senses. That kiss wasn't the sweetest, or even the most passionate, we shared. But the details of it are burned into my brain. I don't think I'll ever forget it or the way she felt in my arms at that moment.

Then she sprinted off toward the narrow set of stairs leading to the basement and I was forced to swallow the lump in my throat and push open the door to the garage.

I hadn't really thought of what to expect. I just felt an almost crushing sense of terror at the thought of leaving the safety of the building. But my friends were out there and the woman I loved wanted me to get them. When I stepped into the underground garage, I was relieved to find nothing waiting for me. There weren't swarms of locusts. Other than our vehicles, the garage was empty. We kept the keys to the truck under the driver's seat. The Mercedes G-Wagon utilized a wireless fob instead of an ignition key. I was more comfortable in the pickup, but it didn't handle as well in the snow. I couldn't risk going out and getting stuck somewhere. The ignition fob for the wagon was kept on top of the vehicle. I stepped up on the side rail, spotted the small black device and unlocked the cab.

The interior was black and red leather that creaked as I slid behind the wheel. When I closed the door, it made a ~*Zoomp!*~ sound that I took to mean the cabin was well sealed. It was dark inside the garage. We kept the garage overhead lights turned off so as not to attract unwanted attention. Not much exterior light was coming in from the ramp that led up to the street. The Mercedes also had darkly tinted windows. After a few seconds, the interior began to light up, not with an overhead bulb, but with a neon glow under the dash and in pin stripe LEDs built into the door and dashboard. The instrument panel was all digital and looked like it belonged on a video game screen rather than a vehicle and it had a wide touch display. I pressed the green start button and the vehicle grumbled to life. I felt more than heard the engine. The cab had excellent soundproofing. I did a quick check to ensure that I was in four-wheel-drive, then slid the vehicle transmission into drive.

It was my first time driving this luxury vehicle. I was so impressed with the smooth, quiet ride that I nearly forgot about the locusts. But, as I drove up the ramp, I felt the terror constricting my chest again. Outside it was gloomy and gray. If there were more locusts, I couldn't see them. I pulled out onto the street and started looking for the Emerald Gardens. Had things been normal, I probably could have pulled up the address on the vehicle's computer display. But there was no internet available via cell signal anymore. The luxury SUV handled well even in the snow. I drove swiftly down streets, working my way south, which I figured was safer than driving north.

And then I saw one.

A locust zoomed by right in front of the G-Wagon. There was no doubt about it, the fifth trumpet judgment was upon us.

20

The swarms hadn't reached us, just the vanguard, like scouts pressing ahead of the main army. Only the locusts weren't an army; they were a plague. They had human faces, but they were driven by something other than intellect. Some would call it instinct; I think it was more of a divine set of orders. There were no reports of resources being consumed by the locusts. What they ate or drank was a complete mystery. Why they focused all their animus on humans could only be explained in spiritual terms. They were supernatural creatures from another dimension that had been set loose upon the earth with orders to torment humanity for five months.

And they were very good at it.

Fortunately, none attacked the Mercedes as I searched frantically for my friends. Along the way, I saw small groups, usually just two - but sometimes three - individuals in uniform, who were moving through the area on ATVs that had been modified to handle the deep snow. They traveled slowly through the streets and I saw more than one using handheld walkie-talkies. What they were looking for, and reporting on, I didn't know. But there was no way to hide the big, black SUV I was in. I wasn't too concerned about being seen, not when my friends were in danger.

The locusts weren't deadly, the Bible assured us of that. Still, I felt that it was important to warn LB and Allie. They were the closest thing to family Cat and I had. We had survived so many brushes with death together and, while the sight of the locusts terrified me, I knew I couldn't rest until I found my friends.

It took most of an hour of searching, but eventually I found the Emerald Gardens complex. It was a large property with adjoining bungalows around the perimeter. I pulled in and discovered the reason for the name. The interior of the retirement village had been a parklike series of green spaces with walking paths, pools, fountains and gazebos. In the back was a larger building, three stories tall. It looked like a hotel and I figured that it was for the residents who needed a higher degree of attention and care. To one side of the large building was a garage. The metal doors had been opened, and I could see an ambulance in one bay and a matching pair of passenger vans in the other. One van had its hood up, and there were jumper cables that led to the Jeep LB and Allie had left in.

What I couldn't see was any sign, other than footprints in the snow, of my friends. I got out and looked around for the locusts. I didn't see or hear them, which should have given me a sense of relief but, to be honest, I was too scared. As a kid growing up in Texas, I had seen my share of scorpions. They were terrifying to me, almost like they were made of bones with no flesh. And once I had been stung. It had been after school, waiting for my foster parents to pick me up. I sat on a brick retaining wall where most of the children waiting for pick up lingered. I hadn't seen the scorpion when I sat down. It most likely crawled up from the backside of the wall and onto the surface where I sat. When I saw my foster mother approaching in her car, I put my hands on the wall to either side of my body to launch myself off the short wall. I didn't put my hand right on the scorpion, but close enough for it to strike at the side of my palm. It felt like I had been hit by a hammer. The memory was vivid in my mind as I stepped out of the G-Wagon. First, a sudden, terrible pain that quickly transformed into what felt like electric currents of fire, which lasted for a full thirty minutes. I know because I couldn't stop crying all the way home, which was, for us at that time, a half-hour drive. When we did get home, my hand was numb on the side with the sting, including my pinky and ring finger. The numb feeling extended from my fingertips to my wrist and covered half my hand. You might think that when I say it was numb, that I mean it had no feeling and no pain. But you would be wrong. It was numb like when your leg falls asleep and you can't walk. Touching it brings none of the normal feelings; it's almost like your leg is dead, only it feels like it's full of tiny fire ants running up and down the leg. Putting weight on it makes the tingling sensation worse. The same was true for my hand. It was filled with the tingling numbness for two hours. Plus, it swelled and turned red. Fortunately, the pain didn't last, and by the next morning, the swelling had gone down. Still, the memory was strong and probably intensified my fear. Despite the freezing temperature, when I got out of the Mercedes, I was sweating.

"LB!" I shouted. "Allie! Preston!"

There was no response. I thought perhaps they had taken refuge inside the retirement village's main building, but there was no visible doorway into that structure from the garage. And no tracks leading to the front entrance. I had to squeeze between the support beams and the front of the ambulance to get inside the garage. The big vehicles filled most of the space. It was gloomy in the rear, but as I went toward the back, I heard raspy breathing. Hurrying forward, I found my friends. LB lay across Allie's legs. He had probably been trying to protect her from the locust, but I could see three large, red splotches on her neck and face, which were swollen. LB's black skin didn't show the red as prominently, but the swelling on the back of his neck and on both his hands was terrible. His right hand was so bad it looked like the skin might burst. A few feet away, Preston lay curled in a fetal position.

I hurried to my friends and rolled LB over. His eyes were open. They shifted toward me slowly, and he groaned. I was hit by a strong urine odor and glanced down at the front of his pants. They were wet. That really frightened me.

"Come on," I said. "Time to get you out of here."

"Hannnnth," LB said.

"Yeah, I got you, man."

LB was bigger than me. I couldn't easily lift him up, so I pulled him across the garage floor. At the big overhead doors, I stopped and looked around. There was still no sign of the locusts, but I felt certain they would return. I hit a button on the key fob that opened the back door of the G-Wagon. Then I folded down the rear seats. The cargo bay in the big SUV wasn't long enough for an adult to lie down in, but it was close. Getting LB into the back of the vehicle wasn't easy. I had to strain hard just to get him halfway in, then I went around to the passenger doors on the side and pulled him the rest of the way up. He lay there, panting almost as hard as I was. Just before I went off to get Allie, I grabbed a handful of snow and put it on his right hand.

"Try not to move that," I said. "We gotta get the swelling down before it causes permanent damage."

LB grunted and I hurried away. Allie was wearing a thick coat. I scooped her up. Her eyes opened and she groaned a little as I made my way between the vans.

"Hank," she said. "LB's hurt."

"I know."

"He was... trying to get it... off me."

"That doesn't surprise me one bit," I said.

"Don't let him... die," she said.

"He's not dying and neither are you."

I could speak with confidence because I believed what the Bible said about the locusts, that they were given the power to torment but not to kill. The only problem was I had no idea how bad the torment could be or how lasting the damage might be. Time would tell.

After setting her in the back of the G-Wagon, I went around and pulled her in beside LB. He grunted and I saw a fat tear leak out of his eye. Then I dashed back in for Preston.

I learned later that he had been stung first. He was wearing a makeshift coat fashioned from blankets that were quilted together with cotton batting between the layers. The front overlapped like a bathrobe and he kept it together with two straps of material that were tied around his waist and chest. The locust had landed on his shoulder, struck the side of his neck, then slipped down the back of his coat. He was screaming in pain and jumping up and down. LB and Allie had no idea what was happening. Preston threw himself into the wall backward, but that only made the locust sting him more. When we got him back to the Shiloh building, we found over a dozen different sting marks on his back.

When I reached him and bent over, he had one eye open. The other was swollen shut from where he had fallen, and his cheekbone had smacked into the oil-stained concrete floor.

"Hank," he croaked, his voice weak and gravely.

"I'm here," I told him. "Gotta get you home."

"Leave... me..." he said in a weak voice. "Let me... die."

"I can't," I told him.

"Please," he said. There was such desperation in his voice that I almost started crying over him. Instead, I prayed.

"Father, please help me get Preston out of here. Ease his pain as I move him. Give me strength."

It was the same prayer I had been praying silently since finding the trio. When I took hold of Preston's arms, he screamed in pain, then passed out. I didn't think his passing out was a good sign, but it did allow me to get him into the SUV without the poor man enduring the agony of being moved.

I was just pulling him into the back of the G-Wagon when I heard a deep, thrumming sound. I'll admit, at the time I thought it was a vehicle passing by with big subwoofers, even though I hadn't heard anything like that in years. Then I realized it wasn't a vehicle or the sound of a stereo with big speakers. I glanced over my shoulder and saw the locust flying straight at me. I dropped to the ground on my back into the deep snow and kicked the rear door of the Mercedes closed. My boot left a mark on the luxury vehicle's paint, but I was more worried about the crack in the glass caused by the locust crashing into it.

I wasn't sure how they did it. The Bible describes them as being arrayed like a war horse and with a breast plate of iron, but how they kept their faces from smacking against the glass when they ram into it was a mystery to me. I rolled to my side and scrambled to my feet. Unfortunately, the snow that softened my fall also slowed my run. I had to get around to the driver's side of the vehicle, and I just wasn't fast enough. As I turned at the front of the vehicle, I saw the locust and ducked. It raced over me and turned around. Meanwhile, I was scrambling to my side of the vehicle. The driver's door was already open. I jumped inside just as the locust struck. I wore several layers of clothing but no gloves. The locust landed on my hand, just like when I was a kid. The tail stabbed down on the back of my hand. It felt like I had been stabbed by a dull knife. I shouted in pain and shook my hand hard enough to fling the locust away. I had just enough time to slam the door closed before my hand cramped. Electric fire raced through my hand and stole my breath away. It was like putting your hand on a stovetop made of raw electricity.

But the pain was confined to my hand and forearm. It didn't race up my arm or spread through my body. I cradled my hand against my chest and hit the start button on the Mercedes. The engine reacted instantly, and I shifted into drive just as the locust landed on the windshield. I hit the rain wipers and knocked the creature away. Then I punched the accelerator and raced out of the retirement village.

I don't know if the locust followed me, but that fear was like a warning klaxon going off in my brain. My hand hurt so bad I caught myself holding my breath several times on the drive back. I would hold my breath, tensing my core muscles, trying anything to fight the pain. When that didn't help, I ended up panting to catch my breath while my diaphragm spasmed and I had chills. It felt like someone had cinched a tourniquet around my forearm, and with every beat of my heart, the electrical pain jolted through me. How it could feel like an electrical fire was beyond my comprehension. All I knew was pain so bad that I can't remember the drive back home. Had there been traffic on the streets of Miami that day, I'm sure I would have crashed. But somehow I ended up near the Shiloh building. By that point, my hand was swollen and stiff. Moving my fingers was excruciating, nor did I have any strength in that hand.

I had just turned the corner and was heading toward the garage entrance when a pair of ATVs raced toward me. Maybe they were already there and I just didn't see them, Maybe they had been following me. I didn't know for certain. I hit the brakes and slid a few feet in the snow before coming to a complete stop. The soldiers on the ATVs had machine guns pointed at me and more were coming toward the Mercedes on foot from either side.

"Get out!" the soldier in charge shouted. "Get out right now or we will open fire."

I raised my hands. The side windows were too tinted for the soldiers to see through, but the front wasn't. I could see the man in charge. He had silver bars on his collar that stuck up high on either side of his neck.

"Exit the vehicle!" the soldier shouted.

But before I responded, I heard the low thrumming again. Having a military-issue machine gun pointed at your face was frightening. But it didn't match the terror I felt at hearing the awful buzz of the locust's wings.

The demon creature struck fast. I heard a soldier scream. The man in charge kept his rifle pointed at me, yet he turned to see what was happening. Then another scream. The sound made my blood run cold and my insides felt like they had turned to water.

Then the shooting started. I didn't know if it was someone trying to kill the locust or just a reaction to being stung. There was a staccato series of pops behind me and then another scream. The man in charge stepped off his ATV and swapped his aim from me to something else. He fired a single shot. I heard a thump followed by a grunt as the bullet from the leader's rifle hit one of his own men. Then the man in charge was knocked off his feet. I leaned forward in my seat to see him on the ground. The locust was on his chest. It jumped, using its powerful legs like a grasshopper, and landed on the man's face, which was covered with a ski mask. The scorpion tail snapped down on the exposed skin just above the man's eye, right at the brow. He screamed and clamped a hand over that eye just as the locust took flight.

I had seen enough. I hit the accelerator again, steered between the ATVs and drove past the Shilo building. I didn't stop until I was in the parking lot of The Falls shopping complex. There I turned around and waited. The Mercedes had plenty of fuel and it was warm inside. I sat panting for a few minutes, holding my left wrist in my right hand.

"Hanth," LB said, his voice slurred from the swelling in his face. "You okay?"

"Yeah," I said in a shaky voice. "It just got me once, in the hand."

"Onth ith enouth," he said.

"Yes, it is."

We waited a bit, then drove back to the Shilo building. There was blood on the snowy street, but the ATVs were gone and so were the soldiers. I breathed a sigh of relief, then drove down into the garage. I was grateful the Mercedes handled so well. Even in the snowy conditions, I could easily steer it with one hand. Back in the garage, I had to force myself to open the SUV door. There was no sound in the garage but the metal ticking as the hot engine began to cool. My knees shook as I closed the door to the Mercedes and walked over to the metal door that led inside the building. There was still no sound of the ominous thrumming, so I knocked using the rhythm we had agreed upon. The door opened instantly,and Flex came out with a few other men.

"You okay?" Flex asked, looking at my hand.

"I'm fine," I told him. It wasn't true, but comparatively speaking, I was much better off than our friends in the back of the SUV. "Help them."

LB and Preston couldn't walk, but Allie managed to stand up with a little help. She leaned on me while the others carried the men inside. I felt better when the metal door to the garage closed behind me.

"Did they get to the basement?" I asked.

"The locusts?" Flex asked, then shook his head. "Nah, we haven't seen them."

We had survived the first of the locusts, but I couldn't imagine how we would make it the next five months.

"You did it!" Cat said as she hurried to help Allie.

"Barely," I said. "Got stopped by the NARA soldiers right outside."

"How'd you get past them?"

"Got lucky," I said. "The locusts hit them as they were detaining us."

Cat's eyes widened. "They know we're here."

"Yeah, we have to bank on that fact."

"What do we do?"

"We leave, just as soon as possible," I said. "There's just enough time left to get the vans."

"You can't be serious," Cat said. "You're going back out there?"

At that moment, I didn't know why I felt the compulsion to go back. I even considered the fact that the scorpion venom was affecting my brain. But I didn't think we could keep hiding in the basement of the Shiloh building. Soon, the swarms of locusts would sweep through Miami and it would be too late to do anything. So, I nodded, and after getting Allie settled, I headed back upstairs to go after the vans we needed to make our escape.

21

Flex, Patty and Saul returned to the Emerald Gardens with me. I drove, despite my throbbing hand, since I knew the way. Even in the snow, it took less than ten minutes to get back to the vans. Both started relatively easily. Whatever Allie had done to prep them worked well. It wasn't until after Saul and Flex had driven the vans out of the garage that I saw a nice looking tool box. It was glossy with an airbrushed American Flag on the metal exterior and the initials VGG on the top. Daniel loaded it and a battery charger on a rolling stand into the back of the Jeep. We managed to get everything back to the Shiloh building without incident.

Back in the basement, people were either fussing over LB, Allie and Preston, or watching news reports from around the world. Europe, North Africa, and Southeast Asia were under a swarm alert. Videos from major cities showed crowds of people being overwhelmed by swarms of locusts. The carnage was awful and the new ice age wasn't helping matters. People were being pushed down into a band around the center of the Earth. From the equator north to the tropic of Cancer and south to the tropic of Capricorn, the climate was still hospitable. Outside that zone, life was becoming increasingly more difficult. The one exception was the Near East and specifically New Babylon. Somehow, even though that area was on the same latitude as most of the United States, it was experiencing a wonderful, balmy climate, while North America, most of Russia, and China were being enveloped in ice.

"Heading south is the right thing," Flex said as he stood watching the news feed on the big television across the room. "Seems to me that we can't fight the cold and the locusts at the same time."

"True," I told him as I adjusted the icepack on my hand. It had gone from terrible pain to the numbness I remembered from my childhood. The flesh had swollen up too, nearly twice the normal size. My fingers looked like sausages and the skin on the back of my hand around the sting was so red it looked sunburned.

"If the locusts are drawn to people, it seems to me that we should go where there aren't many people. That way, maybe we won't be such a tempting target, you know?"

"That's sound logic," I said.

Later that evening, we caught a news program talking about the locust stings in an interview with a biologist who claimed to have captured and studied the demonic creatures.

"So, what you're saying is they aren't poisonous?" the reporter asked.

"No," said the biologist, a woman with deep wrinkles in her neck, but none on her forehead or around her eyes.

"That woman is using Botox," Liz declared.

Her name was Doctor Stine and she was from Turkey. She explained herself a bit more to the reporter in a thick accent. "The venom is much like a scorpion; it is a nerve agent. It does not enter the bloodstream, therefore it cannot impact the heart, lungs, or brain."

"When you say nerve agent, what exactly does that mean?"

"It inflames the nerve endings in the area it stings. These areas will experience pain, tingling, swelling, etcetera. But you won't die from it, even if you wish you might."

"She got that part right at least," Daniel said.

Another story caught everyone in our little enclave's attention. Reports were coming in from all the major hospitals around the world that, for the first time in history, there had been no deaths reported in more than twenty-four hours. The reporters had reached out to a growing number of metropolitan areas across the globe and, while the sick remained sick and many of the hospitals were glutted with people suffering from locust stings, there had been no deaths.

"Just as you predicted, Hank!" Saul said.

"Not me," I said. "The Bible said that we wouldn't be able to die during this judgment."

That night, everyone but Liz and Oscar put their faith in Jesus as the Messiah. Thirty-two of the retirees had seals on their foreheads. Everyone could see them except for Liz and Oscar. I was just as surprised to learn that everyone was willing to go to Key West. That night was spent packing up and, at first light, we loaded the vehicles. My group would continue to travel in the four vehicles we had salvaged and the retirees would take the two new vans. Personal belongings were packed and loaded into the back of the Solar Solutions pickup truck. And, to everyone's relief, LB and Preston were back on their feet. The pain and numbness had lasted six hours. After that, they were left to deal with the swelling, just not the overwhelming pain. LB's hand was the worst of his injuries. He had hit the locust several times trying to kill it. In that endeavor, he was inflicted with eight stings in the palm of his hand. The following morning, it was still twice the normal size and much hotter than the rest of his body. The swelling made the tissue so tight he could hardly move his fingers and making a fist was out of the question. But his spirits were up.

Likewise, Allie was okay. Her neck and face were still swollen, but no longer hurting. We were in the process of loading everyone up when a voice boomed from a loudspeaker outside the building.

"Tenants of the Shiloh building, this is Assistant Administrator Floyd Nigel. You are harboring a group of illegal religious zealots. We insist that you send them out immediately."

"Is he talking about your group or ours?" Daniel asked me.

"This isn't good," I said.

"What should we do?" Flex asked.

"What can we do?" Cat said. "We don't have the resources to fight them off."

She was right, but I didn't think surrendering ourselves was the answer either. I pointed at Flex.

"Head upstairs. Don't let them see you, but get me a count. I need to know how many we're dealing with."

"Maybe we should just surrender?" Oscar said. "How bad can it be?"

"That's what the Jews in Poland said," Daniels snapped. "Don't be naive."

"I am not," Oscar said. "I'm only trying to point out the obvious."

"He's right," Liz said. "We could be killed if they attack the building."

"They know we're Christians," Cat said. "Once they have us, we'll either have to renounce our faith or they'll execute us."

"I would rather die than betray God's Anointed One," Daniel proclaimed.

"We've all known this time was coming," Saul said. "At least we have found the truth before it was too late."

"I think of all the years I wasted," Matthias said. "How could I be so blind. I open the scriptures now and I see Jesus on every page."

"Giving up isn't an option," Nathan said. "What other choices do we have?"

Before I could answer, the booming voice from outside spoke

again. "Send out Hank Downes and the people with him, or we will come in after him."

"We can't stop them," Cat said. "All we have is two pistols, one hunting rifle and a shotgun."

"Better to go down fighting," Patty said.

"Let's move the elderly back," I said. "At least into the corridor behind the steel door. Patty, let's move the vans to the entrance ramp. We'll back them up to the entrance side by side and leave them there."

"That won't stop the soldiers from getting inside," Cat said.

"We don't need to stop them if we can slow them down. Cat, you take the rifle and move to the metal door. Daniel, you and Saul take the shotgun to the front entrance."

"It's barricaded," Daniel said.

"Good," I told him. "When they start to break through, blast away."

"This is it, then," Saul said, his eyes glistening with tears. "I wish we had more time."

"We'll have all the time we want in eternity," I said, putting a hand on the retired historian's shoulder. "If this is where we end our story, let's go out with a bang."

Patty and I hurried to the vans. We moved them into position, then slowly backed them up the ramp side by side. When we reached the opening, we put the vans in park before crawling back out. By the time we finished, Flex was back.

"There's only eight soldiers," he said. "They're in full riot gear, but I don't think that's for us."

"Protection from the locusts," Cat said.

"That's what they think," Preston said.

He was on his feet but moved slowly. His body was stiff and sore from the reaction to the locust stings.

"Those things find a way through your clothing and then it's worse," Preston continued.

"It's too bad we can't call the locusts back here," Cat said.

"I'm not sure that would help," Eric said. "They brought along one of the giants."

As if Assistant Administrator Floyd could hear our conversation, he continued his warning from outside.

"If you will not send out the religious heretics, we will be forced to knock down the entire building. You have sixty seconds to comply."

"Now we're the ones that are trapped," Hannah said.

She was right and I didn't know what to do. Little did I know, I wasn't the only person trying to figure things out.

"Load everyone into the vans," Asher said. "Get ready to flee."

"We can't just run," I said. "The giant will stop us, and if it doesn't, the soldiers will shoot our vehicles to pieces."

"Didn't you say that people will long for death but not be able to die?" Matthias said. "If that is the case, then you have nothing to fear, young man. Leave the giant to us."

"Our people have been slaying giants for thousands of years," Asher proclaimed.

We moved the vans and I got my first glimpse of the giant. He was eighteen feet tall, with dark red hair and a horrifying face. His lower jaw was wider than his brow and. in the open mouth, I saw two rows of teeth.

Saul took charge of one van and Daniel took the other. Pattie drove our van and I returned to the Mercedes with Allie, LB and Preston. Flex drove the pickup truck with Hannah and two other women. Cat drove the Jeep. It wasn't until we were in the vehicles that the giant attacked the building. He used a long, wooden log, probably a telephone pole, like a battering ram. He hit the building's second-story windows and smashed right through them. The entire building shook with the impact.

I still wasn't sure what was going to happen and then Asher pulled up beside the Mercedes SUV in a restored 1975 Cadillac DeVille convertible. He had the top down, and in the passenger seat, Matthias held our shotgun with the barrel pointed straight up.

"Don't wait for us," Asher said with a cackling laugh.

"We've got one last adventure left in us," Matthias said.

Before I could reply, Asher gunned the old car's engine. It roared, the rear tires squealed on the slick concrete floor, then it shot forward and raced up the ramp. As soon as it cleared the entrance, I heard the shotgun go off. Three quick booms, then the engine roared again. Only this time it was joined by the wail of pain and fury from the giant. I didn't see what happened but, after nearly a full minute, I risked moving the Mercedes up the ramp. In the distance, I could see the giant. It was moving north and away from the Shiloh building and swinging the huge pole as it went. Rooftops were torn from buildings, and some even collapsed completely. Cars left in the streets that were covered with snow were flipped over and smashed flat by the raging giant. It was three times the size of an adult human, but much, much stronger.

Following behind the giant were a set of SUVs and a military-style Hummer painted flat black. It had a large public announcement speaker on top where normally a gun turret would be. They seemed to be trying to get the giant back under control. I wished at that moment that I had some way of contacting the two elderly Jewish men. We heard more gunfire in the distance, and it was clear we had to go before the NARA group returned and stopped us.

"Crazy old coots," LB said. "You gotta love 'em."

"I just hope they don't get caught," Allie said. "If they can't die for five months, they could suffer a lot if they're in enemy hands."

"They made the sacrifice for us to get away," I said, waving for the caravan of people behind us to follow me in the Mercedes. "We can't waste that opportunity."

"They wouldn't want us to," Preston said.

We pulled out of the Shiloh building and onto the street just as a loud crash was heard. I kept driving, but we all looked back. The upper floors were collapsing down onto the second story, where the damage had been done.

"Come on! Come on!" I shouted.

The Jeep was right behind us, and the pickup truck behind that. We were all out on the street when the building started to give way. One van made it out, then another. A huge plume of dust shot out of the garage and the noise of the building collapsing down onto itself was so loud we couldn't hear anything else. A second later, the third passenger van appeared out of the cloud and, as we sped away, the Shiloh building fell like the walls of Jericho.

22

I wish I could say that we celebrated our escape all the way down to Key West, but the truth is, we were all shaken by the sacrifice that Matthias and Asher had made.

"You think they got caught?" LB said when we made the turn onto Highway 1 and started for the ocean.

"Hard to imagine they didn't," I said.

"It still rocks my world a little to see supernatural stuff," Preston said. "I've never seen a giant before."

"Saw my first one before the rapture," I said. "It was dead and stuffed into a crate at Fairfield Air Base."

"A giant?" Preston asked.

"Yep, smelled horrible," I said.

"Tell him how you got a look inside the crate," Allie said with a giggle.

"It was an accident," I said.

"My boy crashed the forklift he was driving," LB said.

"That doesn't bode well," Preston remarked. "Whose idea was it to let him drive?"

"Very funny," I said. "Let's keep things in perspective. None of you are fit to drive."

"Speaking of driving," LB said. "Did you see Asher laying down that sick burn out in his old caddy?"

"Hard to miss that," Preston said.

"They were like a couple of old timers breaking out of their nursing home," Allie said.

"One last hurrah before they close their eyes," LB said. "Can't blame 'em for that."

I didn't blame them either. I appreciated what they did, even though I would never have thought to ask them to risk their lives in such a crazy scheme. But it had worked and fifty-three people were headed south to safety.

It was a relief to see that nothing had changed in Key West or the Casa Marina resort. Cat took Hanna, Patty and a few other ladies to the grocery store while the rest of us got everyone moved in. Flex was in charge of moving the heavier suitcases through the resort, while I went down and powered up the generator. We saw no locusts and heard none of them, either. I had no illusions that we would be safe from the plague of demonic creatures but, at least, we were able to get everyone moved before the danger overtook us.

The retirees were used to sharing space by that point, so it was only a matter of dividing up the rooms. Most of the older people wanted rooms on the ground floor so they didn't have to climb stairs. Cat and I ended up sharing a room with Flex and Hannah on the third floor. In addition to the Suite Wing, we turned on the power to the kitchen. There were no fresh meats, but we gathered canned goods from the grocery store. Several of the ladies worked together to bake bread and prepare meals for everyone. That night, we were warm and resting well when the swarm reached Key West.

The sound was like rolling thunder. I woke up thinking a thunderstorm was forming. In fact, as I woke Cat, I was just about to ask her when hurricane season started. But as my mind cleared, I realized the truth.

"What?" Cat asked in a husky voice.

"Wake up," I told her. "They're here."

It was warm enough in our room that I could have slept in a tee-shirt and shorts, but having been on the run and dealing with the unexpected as long as we had, I learned to sleep in my clothing. I remembered closing the light-blocking shades in our bedroom. But we had left the bathroom light on. It shone through the gap at the bottom of the door. I hurried over and switched it off.

"What are you doing?" Cat said.

"I don't want to do anything that might attract them."

We moved carefully from our room to the sitting area. We were in the big suites on the top floor that had a large area between the bedrooms. Our suite even had a baby grand piano on a pedestal between the sitting area with a couch, plus another sitting area beside a small wet bar.

There was just enough light from the appliances in the kitchen area that I could see the large obstacles in the room. I went around them to the bedroom that Flex and Hannah were sharing. Before I was even close, I heard them talking.

"Hey," I said. "Turn off all the lights in there."

"On it!" Flex said.

"Can they get in?" Hannah asked.

"If they want to, I'm sure it's possible," I said.

What we didn't want was for the locusts to bust through the windows. If that happened, we wouldn't be able to keep the rooms warm. Landlines were uncommon in most places, but hotels and resorts still offered them so that guests could easily reach the front desk. LB and I had tested them earlier that evening. With the power on in the Suite Wing of the resort, the phones were operational. I started dialing the other rooms.

Not surprisingly, I didn't wake anyone up. Before I was finished calling the rooms with non-Jewish people in them, there were light clinking sounds on the suite's big windows.

"They're landing," Cat whispered.

"That's okay," I whispered back.

Needless to say, there was no more sleep that night. Flex and Hannah joined us in the main room of the suite. The girls stayed on the couch, while Flex and I paced. It was hard not to worry. I prayed all night, but the sound of the locusts didn't go away. The sound of their wings was deep and loud. Even just one taking flight could be heard in our suite. Their feet on the glass almost sounded like they had hooves, but if that were the case, they wouldn't have been able to hang onto the smooth glass.

When morning came, I managed to peek around the heavy drapes and was thankful for them. The curtains in the resort, like in most hotels, were meant to help dampen sound and keep the light out so a person could sleep without being bothered by the sunlight. In our case, it hid us from the locusts and probably helped to keep us from being heard as well. When I looked out, all I could see were the hideous creatures. They covered every inch of the window, hundreds of them. Their carapaces were glossy in the morning sunlight. Their long hair hung in shades of blonde, brown, and dark black. Some even had braids in their hair that reminded me of Viking styles that had come into vogue for a short time before the rapture. The little golden, spiky bands were so bright you would have thought they were polished.

I moved slowly away from the window. The last thing I wanted was to draw attention to the fact that we were in the room. Even the curtain swaying slightly would have been enough to get the attention of the demonic creatures. Leaving the window, I tiptoed back through the dark room toward the door that opened into the hallway. We had opened it quietly and left it propped slightly open in case a speedy escape became necessary.

"There are thousands of them," I said. "I could barely see past them."

"What do we do?" Cat asked.

"There's nothing we can do," I said. "Stay quiet, pray that they go away and be ready to run if they start breaking in."

There were no windows in the hallway or the stairwell. We snuck out, careful not to let too much light from the hall into our room, and met up with LB and Allie.

"That was fast," LB said.

"At least we're settled," I said. "Maybe we can ride out the storm."

"Somehow I doubt that," LB said, flexing his hand.

It was still swollen, but not as badly as before. My own hand was mostly back to normal, but I had only been stung once. It was difficult not to be afraid. Just one locust had taken down LB, Allie, and Preston. Just one locust had attacked the soldiers outside the Shiloh building and gave me the chance to escape. There were so many more on the Casa Marina resort building that I couldn't imagine escaping if they tried to get inside. The Bible said people would pray for death, although it would not come; it was hard not to think that so many of the demonic creatures stinging a person wouldn't kill them. If they smashed through the resort windows, we would probably freeze to death. The anticipation of what was possible was so stressful I felt like I might throw up.

But the locusts didn't get in. As the hours passed, we returned to our rooms, even to our beds. I slept more that first day than I had in a long time. The next day, I was horrified to find the locusts were still there on our windows. In fact, even though I couldn't see it at the time, they were on every surface, the walls, the roof, the other buildings of the resort, the dead palm trees, the gazebos, essentially anything but the snowy ground.

On the second day, our Jewish friends who were believers took a courageous step to help us through the fifth trumpet judgment. Daniel led the expedition.

"We're going outside," he told me in the stairwell. It was the only part of the resort where I felt safe enough to talk in a normal voice.

"You can't," I said.

"The Bible says they won't harm us," Daniel persisted. "We have the seal of God on our forehead."

He had the seal; I had seen that when we first met. And since his fellow Jewish retirees had put their trust in Jesus, they too had been sealed. I was a gentile believer, which was different than being a Christian in the church age before the rapture. During that period of time, anyone who believed in Jesus was filled with the Holy Spirit as a guarantee of their salvation. We in the tribulation would have to face the temptation to take the mark of the beast. The Bible was clear that we would be hard pressed, persecuted, hunted and even martyred for our faith, but if we held on and endured to the end, or to death, we would be saved. And that meant we were susceptible to the punishments being poured out on the world for its unbelief.

"If you're wrong, we won't be able to go out and help you," I said.

"Do you think I'm wrong, Hank?" Daniel asked.

The truth was, I believed Daniel was probably right. But I also hated for anyone to put themselves at risk for me. The group thought highly of me but, in reality, I was just a selfish guy who put off God's wonderful, free offer for salvation until it was too late. It was a testament to his mercy and grace that he would even give me a second chance to be forgiven. While I believed that Daniel was right and that the locusts wouldn't sting him, I felt guilty that he had to take that chance on my behalf.

"No," I finally managed to say. "But Daniel, please, be careful."

"We will be," he assured me.

On the ground floor, the hallway to the suites also led outside. While there was a dark tint on the glass door that led out of the building, there was nothing that would have kept the locusts from seeing people moving around inside. Fortunately, all the people on the ground floor were Jewish believers ... and I wasn't the only person who didn't want to see Daniel go. To my astonishment, Liz joined us in the stairwell. I hadn't realized it, but she and Daniel were still living together as man and wife.

"Don't do this, you old fool," she chided him.

"I will be safe," he told her. "Hank agrees."

Liz gave me a withering stare. I wished Daniel had left me out of it, but he wasn't wrong.

"He doesn't know anything," Liz insisted. "You saw the others. You saw what those vile creatures did to them."

"I did," he said. "But the Bible says they aren't allowed—"

"Stuff your Bible!" she snapped. "What happened to your reason, Daniel? What happened to logic and clear thinking?"

"I was a fool for a long time," he said. "Blind too. Lorenzo urged me to believe. He showed me many times that the scriptures point to Jesus, who fulfilled the old prophecies, but I was too proud to see it."

"What does that have to do with anything?" Liz demanded.

"It is everything, my dear. We are God's people and we missed his anointed. Now, we have a second chance to embrace his work in our world."

"You're babbling like a madman."

"Lorenzo told me that the church would be raptured and I thought the same thing that you think now," Daniel said. "But when it happened, I couldn't deny it."

"There are reasons why people vanished," she said, but the conviction was fading from her voice.

"Now you have the same chance as I have," he said. "If I'm right, and these creatures are a judgment from God, they will either kill me or refuse to harm me."

"You're betting your life on a whim!"

"No, my love, I'm betting my eternal soul on the one person who has the power to save it. Jesus is our lord and the sooner you see that, the better."

"I don't want to see anything but you," she said. "Don't leave me, Daniel, please."

"I promise, I will return."

Liz and I were left in the stairwell. We were both shaken, both frightened that Daniel was wrong. But the older man went boldly out through the door that led into the long row of hotel-style rooms and then into the lobby of the resort. There, he reported, the locusts covered the floor-to-ceiling windows that were meant to give guests views of the beach and ocean. He went out the main door and looked around. The locusts were everywhere. Those on the door he opened twitched a little, but didn't take flight or jump toward him. In fact, they seemed oblivious to his presence. He even shouted a few times to attract their attention, but they didn't respond.

Daniel returned less than five minutes after he had left. That fact alone was astounding. Don't get me wrong, I believe what the Bible says, but all we had seen of the locusts were videos of them attacking people and the demented creatures shattering windows and chasing people through Miami. To know that there were thousands, maybe millions of the creatures all over the resort property, and yet, Daniel had gone outside and not been touched, which was shocking.

But Daniel didn't return alone. In his hand was a locust. He held it between his thumb and index finger, right below the stinger on the scorpion-like tail. Its wings thrummed angrily, but it couldn't escape. Nor could it twist itself around to use the lion-like teeth to attack the man holding it.

"I wasn't wrong," he said with a chuckle. "The Bible is proved true again!"

His delight was not shared by me or Liz. As he held the locust, it went crazy trying to get to us. I even heard its teeth clacking together as it lunched in our direction.

"Don't let that go," I said.

"Don't worry, Hank," Daniel said. "The tail is its weak spot. Don't ask me how I know that, but I just did. It came to me and I had to test my theory."

"They didn't attack you?" Liz asked.

"No, my dear. I am sealed by God Almighty. These nasty things were given strict instructions by Hashem not to harm anyone with his seal on their foreheads."

"There is nothing on your forehead but wrinkles!"

"You cannot see it because your lack of faith blinds you," he told her. "Jesus is the Messiah. Our ancestor John, son of Zebedee, wrote in his gospel of Jesus that to all who receive him, who believe in his name, he gives the right to become children of God. That means that Hank is our brother, not Jewish, but God's very own family. And my love, unless you put your faith in Jesus, you will be eternally separated from God and his family."

"You want me to believe the Christians?"

"I want you to believe in Christ," Daniel told her. "Jesus was God made flesh, the promised savior, the Root of David, who will soon come and set up his eternal kingdom on planet Earth. He was crucified for our sins."

"I have heard many people accuse us of this, as if I am somehow responsible."

"Our ancestors played a role in his death, my dear, that is undeniable, but the truth is, Jesus went willingly to die. That was God's plan from before the creation of the world."

"I don't understand," Liz said.

"Perhaps Hank can help," Daniel said.

I was happy to. I spent the next hour with Liz, sitting on the metal steps in the resort stairwell, showing her what the Bible said. She had never heard much scripture outside of the Jewish holidays, where reading certain passages was tradition. It was the first time I had ever spent much time with her. I learned that Liz had been a reporter for nearly a decade before she and Daniel had a son. She had given up her career to raise Ely, but at age fifteen, he was diagnosed with a heart condition. He lived nine more years before finally dying of his illness. I was relieved to know that Lorenzo had spent time with Ely and that he had put his faith in Christ before his death. But it was that series of events that pushed Liz away from God. She felt that Jesus couldn't be real if he had failed to heal her only son. Her family, observant Jews, had considered Ely's conversion an insult to their heritage and had not even attended his memorial service. That pain, combined with her feelings toward the God who had let her son die at such a young age, had pushed her away from religion altogether.

When Daniel had converted after the rapture, she felt that he had abandoned her. Had it not been for the fact that Daniel had gone outside among the locusts and even brought one back inside, she wouldn't have listened. But she was face-to-face with undeniable facts. LB, Allie, Preston, and I had been stung. Her husband had not. She opened her mind to the possibilities and I was astonished to see the spiteful woman who mocked us for our belief in Jesus come to faith. For the first time since her son died, she prayed, and not just to Hashem, but she prayed to Jesus.

When she finished, Liz looked ten years younger. She was smiling, beaming in fact. Her eyes were bright, the deep lines across her forehead had softened and among them I saw the glint of the seal of God upon her forehead. We embraced, and I cried tears of joy, as Liz rushed out to tell her friends the good news.

23

Daniel soon returned with more good news. He had a group of the retirees, including Nathan and Saul, who went out to gather supplies. They found an AT&T store and came back with enough new iPads for the entire group. Some of the other Jewish retirees discovered that the resort had satellite internet. They also hauled all sorts of gear and goods into the stairwell, which for the next several months became a sort of community space for those of us who couldn't risk being seen by the demonic locusts.

We spent our days studying Bible prophecy and keeping tabs on the rest of the world with our new iPads. And there was plenty of news, too. The most exciting was from the two witnesses still preaching in Jerusalem. Most people mocked the pair of men, who looked the part of Old Testament prophets. They wore simple tunics that hung to their knees and wide leather belts. They had long, gray hair and beards that were tangled into one big mane around their wrinkled faces. But their voices were strong, and occasionally a foolish person would attack them. There were videos of the pair of men breathing fire on the people who tried to harm them.

They also declared a drought on what they called Moab, but

which had been called Iraq all my life. All the land around New Babylon was without water. The Euphrates River was nearly dried up and the Tigris was just as bad. Nearly all the surrounding towns and villages had been abandoned. Iraq had become a wasteland, but New Babylon was thriving. Water pumps pulled in water from the gulf to keep the canals filled. Massive ships full of cargo from all around the world were constantly unloading at the main dock. It was as if while the rest of the world languished, New Babylon thrived.

But there was other interesting news as well. People weren't dying. Hospitals were full, but the morgues were empty. Of course, the government was taking all the credit for the sudden drop in the mortality rate. It wasn't flashy news, and most people didn't seem interested, but it was historic. No deaths had been reported in nearly three months since the fifth trumpet judgment began.

The most constant news story was the plague of locusts. While there were dozens, maybe hundreds of theories about the creatures, no one could really explain their existence. They needed neither food nor hydration. No crops were destroyed by the swarms of large insects, no structures knocked down. They moved in massive swarms from city to city. Every mainstream news outlet tracked them, warning people who were in their path, reminding those under siege by the locusts to remain hidden. In some of the larger cities, the locusts had never left. People did their best to avoid the danger. They often stayed hidden for days or weeks in whatever inner rooms of their homes they could find, some even barricading themselves in. But few people had the food to stay hidden for long. Some starved themselves, others went out in search of food, only to be overwhelmed by the locusts. There were videos of people, especially those in hot climates where very little clothing was worn, and what they did wear was made of thin material and meant to be worn loose, being covered with hundreds of locusts. They would scream until they passed out from the pain, only to wake up screaming a short time later.

There was no relief from the awful pain caused by the stings. All sorts of home remedies were tried, from covering oneself in mayonnaise or tomato paste, to various essential oils and creams. People tried hot compresses, cold packs, and poultices made from all sorts of food, from honey to mud. But none of it worked. Nor did the pharmaceutical creams, ointments and sprays, which flooded the market. Even painkillers did nothing to stop the suffering. Desperate people on the street took whatever they could get their hands on. There were reports of people injecting themselves with enough heroin to kill several people, but the drugs had lost all their potency. The same was true in hospitals where people were given morphine to stop the pain, but it was completely ineffective. People who were high on pain-blocking drugs, both legal and illegal, were shocked when the locust stings sobered them in mere seconds.

It was, without contest, one of the most unique times in human history. People were flinging themselves off buildings and bridges in the hopes that they could end the suffering, but no one died. No one was killed, either on purpose or by accident. No one's illnesses got worse, no one who tried to shoot themselves or slit their wrists, managed to succeed in their suicide attempts. The news covered it all, but it seemed there was less and less interest. It was impossible to keep up with the news and not see or hear people cursing God. I don't just mean using his name in vain or cussing. There was plenty of that, of course, but people shook their fists at the skies and mocked God Almighty. Despite the claims from the Apkallu that they had seeded Earth and modified our genetics to help humanity expand their intellect, people still cursed God. Despite the official world religion that encouraged people to worship everything but the God of the Bible, the people in pain cursed him anyway. Atheists and devout leaders of the new religion were seen screaming in hatred at God Almighty. The experts claimed it was instinct to cry for help or lash out in animosity to the idea of a singular God. It was a result of thousands of years of organized religions and meant nothing, they claimed. But I knew better (and you probably do too). When everything else is stripped away, we as a race know that God is above us, watching, waiting and, hopefully, listening to our cries.

The internet was closely regulated. AI and a host of officials banned all sorts of posts. Some people were arrested for speaking out against the global government. Others simply disappeared. To post anything that was critical of New Babylon was a felony. While it wasn't mainstream news, fringe sites were reporting that large, clandestine groups of law enforcement officials were forming. They hid their faces behind masks, a practice that became necessary during the roundup of illegal immigrants just before the rapture. Liberal protesters took video of and posted the names, even addresses, of border patrol agents, who, in an effort to protect themselves and their families, took to wearing masks. The global government had held onto the practice and sent their secret police to carry out all sorts of atrocities. In most regions, there were camps set up for dissidents. Those who had spoken out too directly bypassed the camps and were sent straight into mass, unmarked graves.

New Babylon had all the same problems as any other major city. In the gleaming towers, the rich and famous partied night and day, but on ground level, the service workers hardly slept. Goods were brought in around the clock. Anything and everything was readily available, even though the new world capital was far from the production sites where their goods were manufactured. Food, wine, designer drugs and the finest luxuries from all around the world were brought to New Babylon. Videos were made in secret by the people building, repairing and cleaning the lavish penthouses in the towering skyscrapers. Everything was brought right to their door, from clothing to household goods. For the wealthy, it was paradise; for the lowly, it was hard, relentless work in what had become the largest city on earth.

But the truth was, they had been hit with some of the worst locust swarms. Tri-regional Administrator Paul Eon did a masterful job of spinning the news, but even that had become suspect, with many people claiming the reports from New Babylon were produced by AI. I had no idea what to believe anymore. You simply couldn't trust your eyes or ears unless you were seeing things firsthand.

And then a storm hit. It was a tropical storm that surged up from the south and drove most of the locusts away from Key West. The warm front kept the rain in liquid form, which fell in heavy sheets, melting much of the snow in and around the resort. But as soon as the storm ended, the temperatures dropped and anything wet turned to ice. Some of the retirees fell and, while we somehow managed to avoid any broken bones, we all knew that if the elderly Jews continued going outside, someone would eventually get hurt.

"It's the logical thing," I said as LB, Cat, and I met with Daniel and Nathan. "Yes, there's a risk, but we know the locusts won't kill us."

LB gave me a pained look, but didn't disagree.

"And we need to round up some things," LB said. "Propane's down to a quarter of a tank. We run out of that, we all freeze."

"Not to mention the fact that we can't stay here," I said. "It's been nearly three months, and we're already getting low on supplies."

"I don't like it," Nathan said. "If you get stung, you could be inca-pacitated."

"But we won't die," I said. "And if anyone else falls, they could break a hip or crack their skull open."

"We are not worthless old men," Daniel said. "We've been taking care of business since we arrived."

"Yes," Cat said. "And we are so thankful for all you've done. You took care of us and now it's time that we take care of you."

The elderly Jewish believers had done more than fetch groceries and iPads. They had scoured the island for resources. It was because of their hard work that we even knew about the propane outlet. It was a small business that trucked in natural gas. We needed to get to that establishment, find a way inside, and, supposing they had what we needed, find a way to get it back to the resort.

The propane was the most urgent need, but not the only one.

There were a few ships still afloat at Key West's commercial docks. Pier B had some options we needed to look into. The sooner we could set sail, the better, but we couldn't rush out to sea in a ship that wasn't whole or was too complicated to operate.

My first supply run in nearly three months was for ice pellets and rock salt. There wasn't much of either, but there was a lot of pool salt in Key West, where many of the private swimming pools used it to create chlorine. We dropped entire bags on the ground at the entrance to the resort. The ice didn't melt entirely, but became slushy enough that we could shovel it up and move it to where it wouldn't endanger the elderly.

With that done, Daniel and Saul became our chauffeurs. They drove LB, Allie and me to the propane company. It was a medium-sized warehouse with a chain link fence around the property. We had to cut our way in and use the manual override to get the gate open. The warehouse had two big overhead doors and a smaller man door on one end that led to the offices. I had gotten pretty good at picking locks and the one on the door to the office was easy. Once we were inside, we made our way to the warehouse space. There were two giant propane tanks on either side. Next to one was a specialty truck with a five-hundred-gallon tank where the bed would normally be. While Allie got it running, LB and I filled the big tank and made sure it had enough hose length to reach all the way down to the resort basement.

We were nearly finished when the booming thrum of a locust was heard.

"Time to wrap this up," I said.

"Don't have to tell me twice," LB said, pulling the filler hose from the top of the tank and securing the cap.

"Allie, any luck?"

"I'll try it again," she said.

I followed her to the cab. She sat behind the wheel, then reached for the key just as the locust came flying into the warehouse. I had opened the doors to get more light into the dark space and we had known that running into a locust was possible. In fact, we could have run into several. No one knew how many were on the island, or when the entire swarm might come back. I slammed the truck door shut and waved my arms.

"Over here," I shouted. "LB, get her out of here."

He would have argued with me, but we had already made our plan for if the locusts came back. His job was to get Allie to safety. She was the only person who could fix engines and she would be indispensable if we managed to get a ship working. The last thing we could afford was to lose her and have engine troubles on the high seas.

I was waving my arms and calling for the locust. LB was easing around the back of the truck, moving slowly. I opened the door that led into the offices and kept shouting. The locust came at me with a fury. That was the other strange thing about the creature that no scientist or government spokesperson could explain. Why did the locusts who didn't eat or drink, who didn't harm any animal but humans, seem to hate us so much?

I knew. The Bible said they came from the abyss and that their king was a fallen angel whose name, Abbadon, meant Destroyer. They were his playthings. They reflected his hatred of God's beloved creation. Despite people's hatred for him all around the world and through time, God never stopped loving us. The rebellious angels hated him for loving us so much. I couldn't say why. It wasn't even clear why the angels had chosen to rebel. Some speculated that Satan had persuaded them. Others pointed to ancient texts like the book of Enoch that described the angels as desiring human wives and plotting together because they knew God's wrath would be terrible. Why they wanted human wives was still another topic of debate, but the Bible was clear about a few things: some angels left their celestial estate and took wives, they had children, which the Bible called Nephilim, and they were locked in chains of gloomy darkness for their sexual sins. Now one had been released and was sending out his demonic swarms to terrorize the entire planet.

24

My plan was simple: keep the locust away from LB and Allie. They had the gas we needed to keep the lights and the heat on in the resort. If they could just get the truck running, they would make good their escape. All I needed to do was distract the locust for a few minutes.

It raced into the office after me and I slammed the door behind it. It took me only a second to slam the door to the office closed and start for the tiny restroom. But the locust was much faster than I was. It hit the back of my shoulder with so much force that I didn't feel the sting at first. Probably because I was too busy being knocked over one of the desks. I plowed across the old papers and sent the computer monitor crashing to the floor. I followed, going headfirst, one shoulder crunching hard into the desk chair. It was a painful landing, but I was desperate to reach the bathroom and used my momentum to roll over. I rose to my knees, then threw myself toward the little, closet-sized bathroom. It was just big enough for a toilet and a sink. My fall and subsequent crash had sent the locust buzzing around the office again, but there was no doubt that it was coming back to attack me, probably just taking a second to build up more momentum. Before I could get into the bathroom, it hit my back, nearly knocking me off my feet again.

I had a thick coat on, as well as a scarf around my neck. Somehow, the locust found a gap and stung my neck. It was exquisitely painful and I'll admit that I screamed as I stumbled toward the bathroom door. Without much coordination, all I could do was turn and fall against the doorjamb. My head hit the frame hard enough to make me see tiny sparks of light, but it worked to get the locust off my back. I heard it buzz as I stepped into the bathroom and pulled the door shut. There was no light except a tiny glow at the bottom of the door. And in that gap a shadow appeared.

There are times when I have acted almost without any conscious thought. This was one of those times. My only motivation was fear. It's hard to explain how frightening the locusts were and how desperate I felt to keep the creature away from me. I stomped down hard right where the shadow was, and by the grace of God, my boot caught the locust's head. It was pinned, and I heard the tail striking in retaliation, only that part of the locust was on the far side of the door still. The tail and stinger hit the door with small, yet powerful impacts that sounded like a lumberjack chopping down a tree. In fact, the entire door, which was a flimsy hollow core material, shook. But I had the locust in the perfect trap. My mind wasn't parsing it all out in real time. In fact, all I could think about was the horrible pain in my neck. It felt like my head was on fire, not in an oven, but in a bonfire. The heat and electric shocking throbs made me nauseous. My entire body was shaking. One shoulder had the same electric fire, but it wasn't quite as intense. I would later figure out that the locust had stung through my coat and clothing, which kept the stinger from making a full penetration. Still, it was horrible. It was like burning oneself; the heat and throbbing pain were intense and didn't go away just because a person was no longer in contact with the flame.

But the locust was stuck, its head under my boot, the tail on the far side of the door, and though it had incredible strength, its legs and body were pinned under the door. For a moment, I had the creature trapped, but it didn't take long to feel it pushing inward. The thumping of its tail stopped, and I could feel the locust moving under my boot. I shoved my hand into my pocket, pulled out a folding knife, and with a flick of my wrist swung the blade open. It snapped into the locked position with a satisfying ~*Click!*~

Keeping all my weight on the foot pinning the locust down, I squatted and slashed. My knife barely fit in the gap between my boot and the door. I felt the blade, which I kept sharp, grinding against the locust's back, but it didn't cut through. I sawed the knife and pressed as hard as I could, screaming with the effort, but the locust kept pressing forward.

"No!" I shouted. "Die demon!"

It didn't die. In fact, I could hear it cursing me in its own language. The voice was tiny, but full of hate. All I could do was keep on trying, so I pushed down with the knife blade again. It was like trying to cut a metal pipe, or maybe like when you are cutting into a T-bone steak and your knife catches the bone. I knew what I was doing wasn't stopping the creature. It was too dark to see and I was still in great pain. My mind felt like shards of red-hot metal were stabbing through it. But, somehow I managed to keep hacking at the locust.

Perhaps it was God's blessing, but the demonic creature wouldn't give up. It pressed forward, and my knife found the joint where its horrific tail attached to the locust's body. For the first time, I felt the blade bite down. There was even a spurt of something hot onto my fingers, and the cursing of the tiny mouth turned into a savage roar of pain and fury. I didn't stop. I kept pressing and sawing until my knife cut completely through the creature, severing its deadly tail.

My hand shook as I pushed open the bathroom door. Light was coming into the office through a pair of small windows. On the floor, the locust's tail writhed like a serpent with its head cut off. And the part of its body that stuck out from under my boot was scraped from my knife's blade. The delicate wings were shredded. I scooted my boot across the floor and sent the creature sliding over the polished concrete. It was still alive and all I could think of was getting away.

I stepped high over the tail, then shut the door and staggered from the office. The stings had taken a heavy toll on my body. When I reached the office door, I hunched over and was sick. I had to lean against the door and wait for the heaving to die down, then I swiped my coat sleeve across my mouth and pulled the office door open. The wind had kicked up outside. It was a blur for a moment as I looked for LB and Allie. They were gone in the big propane delivery truck. That fact was both a relief and a terrible fear. I could hardly stand up. Walking back to the resort was out of the question. And it was still below freezing. The last thing I wanted was to go back into the office, but I couldn't stay exposed to the elements.

Then, from around the corner, the black Mercedes SUV came quietly rolling into the warehouse. Tears filled my eyes. I could feel the muscles between my shoulders and up my neck starting to cramp. I lumbered toward the SUV as the window slid down.

"Hurry," Daniel called from behind the wheel. "There are more."

I didn't need to ask who he was referring to. I pulled open the door and collapsed into the soft leather of the passenger seat. It was warm, and there was hot air pumping from the vents on my side of the vehicle.

"LB?" I asked, pulling the door closed. "Allie?"

"They got the truck running and are on their way back," Daniel said. "I'm sorry we didn't see the locust sooner."

"Isssss okaaay," I said, having trouble forming the words.

"How many times were you stung, Hank?"

"Twissssse, I thinnnngggg," I said.

"Don't worry, we'll get you home," the older man said. "Saul is with the others. If we hurry, maybe we can beat the swarm."

It was a good idea, but by the time we reached the resort, there were over a dozen locusts buzzing outside the entrance. Daniel didn't even bother stopping; he just kept driving. I wish I could say that I passed out in the passenger seat. For all intents and purposes, I was out of it, but my mind never shut down. It registered the terrible pain for a full hour, and then the electric burning shifted to the awful pins and needles sensation. All I could do was moan. My body felt as though I had run a marathon. I was so weak I couldn't lift my head off the seat rest.

Daniel wisely drove us to a carwash and settled the SUV in the open bay so that we had cover on either side and above us. It was also relatively ice-free since the melting snow and ice near the wash bay had run down the drainage grate that we were parked directly over. If he had needed to get out and do something, he wouldn't have had to worry about slipping on the ice.

Fortunately, the wind was kicking up. Daniel kept the SUV running but parked so that we had heat. A few times, small groups of locusts sped past us, but none stopped. It seemed that either the SUV cloaked my presence, or maybe it was the proximity of Daniel, who was immune to the demonic creatures. I suffered, he prayed, we endured for over three hours before I started to feel like myself again. The venom was dissipating, but the muscles in my neck were locked up in tension. I knew it would take hours for the effects on my body to wear off completely. I was looking forward to getting back to my room, but the prospect of climbing three flights of stairs was miserable.

"If you are feeling better," Daniel said. "I suggest we make another test run to the resort."

"Sure," I said. "Good idea."

We drove back, but the locusts hadn't left. They were perched on the glass doors.

"Maybe I can run them off," Daniel said, shifting the SUV to park.

"No," I told him. "You can't get out in this ice. If you fall, I can't help you."

We had cleared the area in front of the entrance of most of the ice, but the big gas truck was parked as close to the entrance as it could get, filling that space. For Daniel to get to the doors, he would have to navigate the icy snow.

"Hank, I'm sixty-seven years old. I've traveled the world. I've been to six of the seven continents. I've explored ice caves in Greenland and camped out in Norway to see the Aurora Borealis. Besides, I've got the truck to hold onto. Stay here, but get ready to move."

I wanted to argue, but he was already getting out of the SUV. He moved slowly, keeping hold of the vehicle at all times. Twice, he suffered small slips, but he never lost his balance. After moving around the front of the SUV, he reached out and took hold of the side of our Jeep and did the same balancing act around it. From there, he managed two steps with nothing to steady him until he reached the gas truck. I was relieved when he reached the far side, where the ice had been removed.

There was no way to keep my heart from thundering in my chest as the old man approached the locusts. They held a place of deep, hideous terror in my mind. I couldn't imagine walking toward them, but Daniel was fearless. As he approached the doors, he waved his hands and shouted at the locusts. They seemed not to see or hear him. None of them moved.

The breath caught in my throat as he reached up and grabbed one of the nasty creatures. He flung it away, and I heard the thrum of its wings as the creature took flight. Daniel picked up another and flung it away, too. One by one, he removed the locusts. They circled around the big truck but didn't land on the doors again. It was almost as if Daniel's presence kept them away. After he removed the last one, he turned and looked up. The group of locusts rose higher into the air and then disappeared from sight.

Daniel stayed where he was and I waited several minutes. When I finally did act, it took all my willpower to open the door. But the world was quiet. Only the gentle waves lapping along the icy shore made any sound. I moved slowly because of the ice and because my body was still tense from the locust stings. When I was all the way out of the SUV, I turned and gently pushed the door until it latched.

Then I hurried toward the entrance. Unlike Daniel, I slipped and fell, banging my knee hard enough to bruise it. But nothing mattered to me in that moment other than getting inside to safety.

"There," Daniel said, pulling open the door. "Get inside."

He followed me and helped me all the way to the doors of the Suite Wing. We passed the kitchens and I could hear people working, talking, even laughing. I couldn't imagine laughing. Not only was I hurting but I was traumatized. The fear had filled every inch of me with cortisol and I needed time to rest and recover.

LB met me inside the stairwell.

"They gone?" He asked.

"Daniel removed them," I said.

"How bad were you stung?"

"Not bad," I lied.

"Yeah, you look like the hunchback of Notre Dame, pal. Where'd they get you?"

I pointed to the back of my neck. "Once there. My shoulder too, but that was through my coat, so it wasn't as bad."

"How'd you get away?"

"I killed the little monster," I said. "Or wounded it, anyway."

I did my best to tell him the story as he helped me up the stairs to the third floor.

"Should have kept that tail as a souvenir," LB said. "Made a necklace of it or something."

"I wasn't going to touch it," I said. "It was thrashing around."

"Well, you did good. We got back with a few thousand gallons of propane, enough to refill the generator and a few spare tanks as well."

"Great," I said, genuinely happy that my friends had made it back to the resort without getting stung. But at the same time, all I really cared about was getting to my bed. My knee was starting to swell from my fall.

Cat met me just inside the room and helped me to bed. I stayed there for three entire days, only getting up to clean my body and use the restroom. The venom's effects lingered. I had trouble concentrating and even staying awake was a chore at times. When I slept, I suffered horrible nightmares of being chased through hell by swarms of demonic locusts. I sometimes woke up covered in sweat and screaming. Cat was always there, always ready to help me. I felt like I was losing my mind but, eventually, I recovered.

And then it was time to go back out into the world again.

25

Storms kept us locked down for nearly a month after my adventure. When they finally let up, we collected the last of the shelf-stable food from the grocery store. To my surprise, we saw no more locusts. They were still around and reports of the dreaded creatures still dominated the news, but on Key West, we had a respite. LB and I were determined to make the most of that opportunity.

We did so by taking a small boat with an outboard motor, which Allie got running, into the harbor near the Port of Key West. At anchor was the *Manna T*, a cruise-freighter. The ship looked like a long, low commercial ship, complete with a cargo crane and a large hull for loading supplies. But in addition to the cargo capacities was a wide tower, almost like someone had placed a small apartment building on top of the ship. It had big windows and was painted in festive colors.

I was no expert when it came to nautical ships. I was an Air Force man after all. LB was a Marine and had the experience of traveling on Navy ships. Allie was a natural with any kind of mechanical device, but other than the fishing ship we had taken from the Yucatan, we had no knowledge of operating a ship.

We rode out and boarded the vessel easily enough. The deck was wide, nearly forty feet, and extended over a hundred feet from the bow to the stern.

"Seems like she's floating just fine," LB said.

"Why don't you two check for problems below. I'll see if I can find the bridge."

"Aye, aye, Cap'n," LB said with a grin.

"You are such a dork," Allie said, but she was smiling too.

We went to the main structure. A small door with a wheel locking device was the obvious way inside. We opened the door, which was made of thick metal that shrieked on rusty hinges.

"Better get us some WD-40 before taking off in this rig," LB said.

Just inside the very narrow corridor, we came to a set of stairs. They went down and I went up. On the second level, I found the officer's quarters. There were three cabins, two small, one larger, and a lounge with a rectangular-shaped table and bench seats that were all bolted to the floor. It was very Spartan, although there was a wide cabinet with some small appliances like a toaster and microwave. A large coffee machine with two pots had center stage and beside it was a lazy-susan with sugar, cream, and a bottle of Bailey's Irish Cream Liqueur.

Opposite the lounge was the ship's bridge or control room. It was wide with big windows on three sides. There were two large chairs, almost like barber's chairs, that gave the occupants a view of the entire room. Slightly lower was a wide control panel. There were screens which I guessed showed some type of radar and computer monitors as well. Beside that was a low seat with two joysticks that were clearly marked as the **bow thrusters** and **stern thrusters**. A set of two parallel levers was labeled **engines**. And a third red lever was labeled as **auxiliary propulsion.**

I won't lie and say it all looked easy, but it didn't seem all that complicated to me. If we could restore power and get the engines running, I felt confident we could sail the vessel. Along with the ship's controls was a separate station that controlled the big crane. I was just about to leave when suddenly the lights came on, and all the screens in the ship's control console lit up. Even more welcome was the warm air that came blowing into the room from the HVAC system.

It didn't take us long to determine that the ship was seaworthy and perfect for us. It had sixty passenger cabins, a recreation space, as well as a galley big enough to feed the entire crew and passengers. When I met back up with LB and Allie, I learned that the engines were in good order.

"We had to hand crank the generator," Allie explained. "But once we had power to the starters, the big engines fired up."

"The fuel is topped off, too," LB said. "No damage down below. She's been sitting for all this time, and I didn't see a drop of water in the hull."

"It's almost too good to be true," I said.

"You might call it a miracle," LB said. "Guess what else we found?"

"What?"

"Big holding bins inside the hull," LB said. "The type used to haul raw materials like grain and fruit. I'm pretty sure this ship was moving raw sugar and coconuts, besides whatever they had stacked on the hull."

"The galley is pretty well stocked," I told them. "I can't think of a reason not to utilize this ship."

"You think we can sail her?" LB asked.

"The controls look pretty simple," I said. "Let me show you."

To our surprise, when we reached the Bridge, there was a plethora of information on the various screens. The ship was lined with sensors that showed how the vessel was sitting in the water. All the cargo had been unloaded, and the stern was riding lower than the bow. On top of the cabin structure was a variety of radar and satellite dish receivers. It had all been covered with snow and ice when we arrived, but once the power was restored to the ship heating plates had melted the wintery precipitation and allowed the sensors to come online. The radar showed every ship in the harbor, and another display was a long-range radar overlayed with a GPS. It showed the entire state of Florida, as well as Cuba, and the islands of the Caribbean. Any ship with power transmitted a transponder signal. There wasn't a lot of sea traffic, but what was there we saw on the display.

Another screen was a range finder to show the depth of the water under the ship. And on the computer was a list of the ship's many systems. It showed fuel reserves at ninety-seven percent, and the electric battery system at only four percent. But there was an arrow pointing up beside the battery display. Another line on the computer screen showed that the ship's water tanks were full and that the water filtration and desalination system were online. The list went on and on, but everything was listed green for good. It was almost as if someone had prepared the ship for us.

Finally, there were weather satellites that were still online. A storm was brewing in the north, but the south looked clear.

"I think she's ready for a voyage," LB said.

"The sooner the better," Allie said. "That storm might make for rough sailing if it continues down the coast."

"I was thinking about that," LB said. "What this ship really needs is some extra weight up front along either side."

"You have a plan to fix that?" I asked.

"Maybe," LB said with his trademark grin. "I noticed that there is a loading dock with a wide gate, the kind used for ferry boats at the port."

"This isn't a ferry," Alley said.

"No, but if we can get into that spot, we could probably drive our vehicles onto the ship and just parking them right where the added weight would do the most good."

"It's not a terrible idea," I confessed. "It won't hurt to drive most of our people onto the ship and minimize the risk of people slipping and falling."

We took the small boat back to the port and explored the loading area that LB had seen from the water. We didn't have a depth finder on the small, open craft, but we had an anchor tied to a nylon rope. We lowered it into the water several times to test the depth and were surprised to find that the area around the Port of Key West was very deep.

"Probably has to be for the big cruise ships," Allie said.

"That woman knows things, Hank," LB said. "Her mind is sharp."

"And what about yours?" I asked.

"Dull... I'm 'bout ready to be put out to pasture."

"There is no retirement in the tribulation," I said.

It took a full day to do everything that needed to be done, including getting a gas generator to the dock and powering the hydraulic ramp that could be raised and lowered.

We had to gather other supplies, too. Food, of course, but also medicines. There was a medical clinic and pharmacy on the island that hadn't been touched. We cleaned it out. Finally, we picked up metal ramps and wheel dollies that would allow us to move the vehicles sideways or spin them around if needed. We got wedges, chains and even a few wrenches. The ship had a lot of equipment for securing the big cargo containers that had become universal on ocean vessels, but we wanted to make sure we had what we needed for the trip and that included candles. There was still no other light available during the supernatural darkness.

I volunteered to stay on the ship overnight, both to keep tabs on the weather and to help get things ready. Most of the cabins were either prepared for guests or stripped bare. LB, Daniel and Saul joined me. We took the little boat out to the big ship, then settled in before darkness fell. When it did, all the ship's satellite and radar systems shut down, and the computer controls, too. Fortunately, the engine continued supplying power, but none of the lights worked inside the ship. We lit candles and ate a kosher meal of lentil soup and crackers.

The next day, just before dawn, the storm hit. And even though I had hoped to get our entire group moved that day, we were forced to postpone. The storm lasted an entire week, and by the time it cleared, there was only one month of the dreaded locust attack left.

"I won't miss 'em," LB said. "Not one little bit."

"But what comes after is worse," I said.

"Hard to believe it could be worse," LB responded.

"And such is the nature of judgment," Daniel said. "The more people reject Hashem, the worse his wrath becomes."

I spoke softly, "I heard a preacher once say that it isn't God's allowance of evil in the world that we should be concerned with, but the fact that he lets sinners like us continue to live, day after day, that is the greatest mystery."

"I know that's true," LB said. "I don't deserve nothin' but judgment."

"None of us do," I said.

"Especially, his chosen people," Saul said. "I know that I was blind for so long."

"We all were," Daniel said.

"But not any longer," I reminded them. "We have grace and hope in Christ Jesus."

After weighing anchor, which was done via the computer controls, I tested the controls on the ship. She was not nimble or fast, but in open water, she was simple to control. We went slowly toward the dock. By the time we were close, Allie, Cat, Preston, and Patty were there helping to guide us into place. The ship also had external thruster controls on small balconies just off either side of the Bridge. I was able to go out onto that balcony and look straight down at the side of the ship. The thruster controls allowed me to gently glide the huge ship right up next to the thick rubber pylons. LB and Saul threw heavy lines to the dock, and they were pulled tight and tied the ship in place.

Another hour passed before we had the ramp lowered from the pier to the ship, and the portable, metal ramps set in place. The *Manna T* was built for hauling cargo that was brought on board with the crane or loaded into the big containers in the hull using conveyors. There was no place along the sides of the ship that didn't have a waist-high, metal railing. So the ramp from the dock had to be set down over the railing. Fortunately, the loading station had a hydraulic lift built under the ramp so that it could be raised or lowered to accommodate just about any ship. What we couldn't do was get the ramp high enough that it could angle straight down to the main deck of the *Manna T*. Instead, we positioned it flat over the railing, then used the portable ramps to enable us to drive our vehicles onto the ship.

Then it was back to the resort, where we already had everything loaded except for the people. There was minimal melting of the snow and ice, and what did melt just refroze within hours. We took our time and pulled every vehicle right up to the resort doors in order for the people, most of whom were elderly, to get inside without having to slip and slide or risk falling. LB and I had spent hours shoveling the snow off the deck of the *Manna T,* and by noon, we were making the caravan to our new vessel. It was loaded with food. The frozen goods had been spoiled and removed, but there were pallets full of dried goods and drinking water in bottles. There were also large cans of salted meat, soups, sauces, and vegetables, along with large sacks of flour, oats, beans, rice, and dried pastas. Everything was in place as we approached in the first vehicle. I got out with LB, and we helped guide each vehicle onto the ship and showed them where to park. The SUVs had no trouble, and the truck from Solar Solutions did well, too. The vans were a little trickier, but we managed to get the first one on board. But two were still on the dock, full of Jewish refugees waiting to come on board, when the thrum of locusts was heard.

"Dang, we're so close," LB lamented.

"Get inside!" Daniel urged us.

"We have to get the other two vans on the ship," I argued.

"Saul and I will handle that," Daniel said. "Go! Go!"

The good thing about the *Manna T* was that the superstructure sealed. It was designed to keep water out, but it worked to keep the locusts out, too. Myself and the other Gentile believers got safely inside while Daniel and Saul took over guiding the vans onto the ship. And we were shocked to see the sky turn dark with a swarm of locusts. From the Bridge, it looked almost like a storm front, but the roaring sound of millions of wings was unmistakable.

I wish I could say that with my friends all safe inside, that we escaped the wrath of the trumpet judgment, but that's not what happened. The truth is much, much worse.

26

The swarm, or actually just a fraction of the total swarm, bore down on our ship. I've seen movies where armies fire so many arrows toward their enemies that it darkens the sun. That's certainly what happened to us, only instead of arrows, they were locusts with scorpion tails.

Daniel and the other Jews who had believed in Christ as the Messiah were sealed with a mark on their forehead. They were safe from the flying demons. Saul and Daniel had to move slowly, carefully guiding Nathan and Liz, who were driving the other two vehicles respectively. The locusts didn't sting the two Jewish retirees, but they landed on the ship, covering every surface. That included the deck. Thousands were crushed by the wheels of the van as it was driven into place.

All the Jews had trusted in Jesus as their Messiah except for one. Oscar Silverstine had been a commodities broker. He made a fortune trading currencies and speculating on oil. But a series of setbacks in the market had turned his social drinking into a real problem. To make matters worse, his wife of twenty years divorced him. He found himself fresh out of rehab with no family and no place left to call home. He left New York City during the COVID madness and settled in Miami. Throughout his life, his Jewish heritage had been far on the back burner. He was neither an observant Jew nor an atheist. He believed that God was possible, and probably the best explanation for how the universe came into existence, although he struggled with the concept of an almighty deity who had the time to care about him. It all seemed a bit too convenient. In his journey to sobriety, he had learned to face the hard truths in life head-on. Religion seemed like escapism to Oscar, and even after hearing me share how the Bible had predicted everything the world was suffering through far in advance, he still refused to believe.

I had been in his shoes. Life had been hard for me from a very young age, when I lost both my parents to a car accident that I somehow managed to survive unscathed. Going to live with strangers, I accepted the lie that life had no meaning. Fortunately, God hadn't given up on me. I knew the truth, but there was a difference between knowing it and believing it. I had heard Lorenzo teach on the truth about God's love and how Christ came to be the sacrifice for our sins. But it took the shock of seeing my good friend and mentor taken in the rapture to shake me out of my malaise. I didn't deserve God's mercy. Nothing in my life was good. And yet, despite it all, the moment I cried out to him, God answered me.

Oscar was about to learn his lesson the hard way.

There was no way to keep everyone in the vans. A group huddled around Oscar, who wasn't sure what to think. He didn't really put much faith in his Jewishness, and yet, he had seen his companions going outside in the swarms that were attacking people all over the world. If anything, I think he believed they had been spared because they were Jews. Maybe his people had some sort of physical trait that made them immune and the world just hadn't discovered it yet. So, when the van emptied, he went without complaint.

He made it two steps out of the vehicle before the first locust landed on him. He was wearing a thick coat with a hood, but that didn't stop the locust. It landed lightly on his chest, crawled up, and stung him in the throat. Oscar panicked. Not that I can blame him. The locusts are horrible creatures; just the memory of them fills me with fear. When they sting you, the pain is so sudden, so severe, every instinct in your body is to get away from the creature.

Oscar knocked down the three women closest to him in his mad scramble to escape. He was wailing in pain and people were shouting for him to stop, but as he broke free from the group, he was instantly swarmed. It was as horrible as anything I had seen on the internet. The locusts seemed to understand that they could do the most damage if they got inside his coat, which they did. Several dozen ran down the front collar, while even more raced up from the bottom. How he stayed on his feet is a mystery to me. But he ran for the hatch. LB and I saw him, and we ran for the hatch too, but we couldn't get there before he yanked open the door.

And that's when all hell broke loose on the *Manna T*.

To be perfectly honest, we had been blessed. Most of our group hadn't been stung in the four months the locusts had been tormenting mankind. We knew of places where surge after surge of the swarming creatures had invaded and that in between those waves of locusts, stragglers persisted in stinging the unfortunate people. But none of us were prepared for what happened when the hatch opened.

Thousands of locusts rushed inside. LB and I were bowled over. The ship's passenger section was five stories. The top deck was divided into a recreation space with access to the roof and a few small restaurants. The ship was nothing like a cruise liner. It wasn't a floating city, and certainly didn't have bars and buffets on every level. There were just staterooms, a small gym, the main galley, a movie theater that also served as an auditorium, and the recreation space on the top floor. There were two stairwells, both with heavy metal doors that sealed off at the top and bottom when closed. There was a working elevator, too, and a flight of stairs that gave the crew on the second level quick access to the deck. The door at the top of that set of stairs was like the one leading out onto the deck, heavy metal with a locking wheel.

"They're in!" I managed to scream before I was bowled over.

I can tell you what happened, but not because I was aware of it in the moment. LB and I were immediately swarmed by the locusts. And when I say we were swarmed, I mean covered from head to toe. They crawled inside my tightly laced boots, and crawled under me as I writhed on the deck of the ship between the stairs leading up to the Bridge, and the hallway that opened to the galley and a dozen staterooms. I was stung everywhere, from the top of my head to the soles of my feet. The only exception was my face. We had seen enough tutorials online of what to do when you're overwhelmed by the locusts. There wasn't much that could be done, but we managed to get our hands over our faces before the locusts stung us there. All we could really do was try to protect our eyes. But you have to understand that the locusts were stronger than we were. They pressed hard against our hands, trying to pry them up and give them space to sting us underneath. And to make matters worse, they stung all over our hands. In fact, we were stung so much, over every part of our bodies, including our genitals, that our minds disengaged. It was like the lights had been turned out; only the pain existed in my mind.

LB, Oscar, and I were incapacitated, but the locusts flooded inside. Fortunately, Cat and Allie were on the Bridge. When I shouted out, Cat dashed to the interior door and slammed it shut just before the first of the locusts to reach it could get inside. At the same time, Allie used the ship's computers to lock down the elevator and close off the HVAC system. It wasn't a perfect fix, but it helped. There was no way to stop the locusts from crawling into the vents, but they were slowed by the grates that covered the heating and cooling ducts.

Meanwhile, Nathan and Liz had dashed inside and thrown

themselves against the heavy door. The locusts could have pushed back, but they were too focused on getting inside. They flew around the door until it was nearly closed, then Liz was forced to turn her back against the door and put one foot on the wall. They shoved hard, got the door closed, and spun the lock. But already thousands of locusts had gotten inside.

You have to understand that these weren't normal insects. They couldn't be killed by swatting them with a newspaper or by a toxic spray. They were powerful creatures with few weaknesses. The junction where their tails joined the body was one; the strangely human faces were another. But their bodies were armored and killing them was difficult, even under perfect conditions.

Nor did they fear the Jewish believers. It was more like they ignored them, trying to avoid them altogether. They were thick in the main hallway and even into the galley. There was no way for Nathan and Liz to stop them. But what they could do was move our bodies. The locusts, having swarmed us already, had mostly moved on after the first sixty seconds of the attack. Liz and Nathan moved LB first. He was the biggest and weighed the most. They half-carried, half-dragged him into the nearest stateroom, and somehow managed to drop him onto the nearest bed. That stateroom had two double beds and looked like a nautically themed hotel room. They carried me in next and put me on the bed next to my best friend. That's where I woke up, at any rate.

Oscar was placed on the other bed just before the sprinkler system went off. Cold water came spraying from the overhead spouts. The locusts weren't killed by water, but they didn't like it. Their wings didn't work once they were soaked. Turning the sprinklers on in the galley was Allie's brilliant idea, even though it ruined all the food that wasn't sealed in plastic bags or metal cans. Within minutes, the deck was filled with almost two inches of water and thousands of locusts. Nathan and Liz began the tedious work of collecting them all. Of course, some found shelter under the tables in the galley and in the vent-a-hood over the stove.

Soaked, shivering and our bodies swelling from the toxic venom, we struggled to breathe. Under any other circumstance, the attack would have killed us. But unable to die, we fought for air through constricted airways and chest cavities that were stretched to the breaking point by the swelling. I'm not sure how I noticed anything other than the burning fire that had consumed me. I felt as though I had been dropped in a pool of lava. But somehow, as I struggled to breathe, panic filled my incapacitated mind. You wouldn't have known it if you had been with me. I could no longer move and could scarcely suck in a breath. As the swelling somehow got worse, I began to feel as if my bones would snap and shatter under the pressure. For three straight hours, I endured the worst torture I could imagine, and when the searing pain shifted to the raging numbness, I nearly lost my mind.

During our hours of suffering, Daniel and Saul untied the long ropes that held us to the pier. Cat took the controls and moved the ship into deeper waters. It was still pretty warm inside the ship's upper decks, and the rest of our group spent the time stuffing whatever they could find in the vents to keep the locusts from breaking through. In the end, it was a futile effort.

Daniel and Saul stood guard at the hatch leading into the upper section of the ship. Their presence there kept the locusts from swarming in. As Nathan and Liz filled stock pots with the locusts, they were able to pass them out the hatch where they were dumped over the side of the ship and the process was repeated. Eventually, all the Jewish believers got inside and helped with the cleanup. Once the incapacitated locusts were disposed of, the water had to be removed. The kitchen had a drain, yet the other areas of the ship had to have the water syphoned out. Fortunately, the ship had tubes with syringe-type plungers inside that could suck up the water.

The group did their best to round up all the locusts, but it was inevitable that some would slip through the defenses. Those that broke into the venting shafts, for instance. They had to pry apart the metal flanges on the gates, then squeeze through, but several managed it, Once night fell, the ship grew very cold, forcing the passengers to clear the heat vents and turn the system back on. I came back to my senses in the supernatural darkness. Normally, a locust sting hurts for three hours, then becomes numb for two or three more hours. The swelling associated with a sting often lasted twenty-four hours, unless it was severe ... and the swelling didn't get any more severe than ours.

As the ship weighed anchor somewhere south of Key West and north of Havana, I tried to open my eyes. Unfortunately, my face was so swollen that my eyes were mere slits. Not that there was any light to see. We were alone in the room, our bodies swollen so big there were tears in our skin. The feeling that I was being devoured by a million tiny bugs was gone, but I still hurt all over. Despite my wet clothes and the wet bedding I was lying on, I felt like I was burning up with fever.

LB moaned beside me and we lay in agony, unable to do anything else, even sleep. Sometime during that long stretch of supernatural gloom, Cat and Allie came in with candles. The light was good. They filled us in on the situation, which wasn't as bad as it could have been, but wasn't great either. The pair of women did their best to comfort us, including cutting off our clothing, which, in our swollen state, only made the pain worse. Eventually, I fell asleep.

When I woke up, the sun was rising, and I could turn my head. It would be a few days before I could walk on my own, but with some help, I managed to get to my feet and up to the second floor, where I could get into some dry clothes and settle into one of the big captain chairs on the Bridge.

"How's LB?" I asked.

"The same as you," Cat said. "Miserable, but alive. He had some tearing in the skin around his toes. It might be a few days before he feels like walking."

I had tears under my arms and along the insides of my thighs where my legs joined my body. They made it hard to sit still, but I was glad to be upright. My face was still round and puffy, but my eyes were open, and I could breathe a lot easier.

The sun rose over the cold waters, which were dark blue and calm. We weighed anchor and turned southwest. Sailing with the global positioning system made it easy. It wasn't like being on the fishing boat, where we had guessed at where things were. On the screens, we could see everything, even if the land masses were out of sight. The *Manna T* was averaging fifteen knots, which was equivalent to seventeen miles per hour. It took us all eight hours of daylight to slide around the western end of Cuba. I had no desire to be spotted by the NARA officials on land. They were surely aware of us via their own radar systems, but I feared that just as they had stolen everything from us in Miami, they would do the same with the *Manna T*.

Throughout the day, people were stung by the remaining locusts in the ship. Fortunately, the Jewish believers stayed close. When the demonic creatures attacked, the Jews could snatch them up by their tails. We kept covered pots nearly full of water to dunk and drown the creatures in. Still, nearly half of the non-Jewish believers were suffering by the time the supernatural darkness fell.

We could have kept sailing, but eight full hours with no way to spot land or tell where we were going was too big a risk. We dropped anchor and tried to sleep, but that was difficult for me. It was impossible to get comfortable with my body still swollen and sore. When I did manage to fall asleep, I was plagued with nightmares. I saw the swarms coming for me whenever I closed my eyes. The only relief was in prayer. I could close my eyes in prayer with my mind turned toward God and find peace. But if I stopped praying, the horrors came back.

We set sail again when the darkness passed. The sky was full of stars. We relied on our radar and GPS to guide us south through the Yucatan Basin, and then southeast toward the Cayman Islands and into the Greater Antilles. By morning, we were south of Jamaica, but within sight of the famous island. It was green and inviting. Perhaps more importantly, the locusts on the hull of the ship had left us. I hated thinking that they were drawn to the people on the islands, but there was nothing I could do for them. We were paying the price for our stubbornness, and our calling during the seven years of Tribulation was to endure.

I took the chance of stepping outside onto the Bridge wing balcony. The warm, humid air rushing over my sore body felt intoxicating. There were still three weeks of danger from the locusts, but I felt more free in those few moments than I had in a long, long time.

We stopped that night near Isla Alto Velo, an uninhabited island south of the Dominican Republic. I slept better that night, and we stayed put until dawn. Life on the *Manna T* wasn't bad. The big ship was steady in the water and easy to operate. It had been a long time since any of us had enjoyed any real warmth, and so we took a chance. LB and I stayed on the ship, both to keep watch over the radar and because we weren't well enough to do much more than sit all day long. But the rest of the passengers took our small boat to the island. It was a huge risk for the non-Jewish members of our group, but the chance to walk on the beach and swim in the crystal clear waters was too good to pass up. Besides, we understood that water was the locusts' weakness. If a swarm came around, the Gentile believers would jump into the water and hope the demonic creatures passed them by.

The next day, we set sail again, traveling southeast in hopes of shooting the gap between the Lower Antilles and Trinidad. We caught sight of the Venezuelan coast just before the darkness fell. Even from a distance, we could see large swaths of land that had been burned up by the fire and hail of the first trumpet judgment. The blackened soil had been cultivated and crops planted. Large farm equipment was also visible as we dropped anchor and settled in.

"Can you believe it?" LB asked me. "They're probably growing enough food for the whole world."

"The fires probably dumped a lot of minerals into the soil," Allie said.

"It's got to be more than what the locals need," Cat said.

"All the governments are connected now," I spoke up. "I think LB is probably right, they're probably shipping their produce all over."

"And lining the pockets of the politicians," LB said.

Cat sighed in frustration. "Even at the end of the world, some things never change."

27

There were still two weeks left of the fifth trumpet judgment when we sailed into the Georgetown harbor. Guyana had become an important area within the South American Regional Administration. Goods were being stockpiled in the Georgetown warehouses for shipping across the Atlantic. Little did I know how important that would become.

When we arrived in the harbor, everything was shut down by a massive swarm of locusts. We could see the new buildings and continuing construction of the city, including a large temple where the St. George Cathedral once stood.

"We're here now," LB pointed out. "What's the plan?"

"I don't really know," I told him. "We couldn't stay where the government knew we were Christians."

"You don't think they share that kind of information?" Cat asked.

"I think they want to," I said. "But our identities are not in their network yet. We can be whoever we want here."

We stayed on the ship in the harbor for two whole weeks. On day ten, the locusts started dying. Not all at once, but several that had landed on the glass of the Bridge windows turned ashy gray and fell off the glass. By day fourteen, they were all dead, and we could see people moving about the city.

Up until then, we had remained inside; even the Jewish believers who had no fear of the locusts didn't venture out. I didn't want to draw any undue attention. Once the town realized the threat of the locusts was over, they flooded the streets. We could see them dancing with long ribbons and large SARA flags.

Going outside was wonderful for the first five minutes. But the sun was bright, and the temperature was high. Within minutes, I was sweating. Back inside the ship, the massive radio, which was way more technical than I was used to, crackled to life.

"*Manna T, Manna T*, this is harbor control. Stand by for customs agents to board and inspect. Harbor control, out."

"I guess we got company," LB said.

"Better gather up everyone and let them know," I said.

Ten minutes later, everyone was gathered in the ship's galley while LB and I met the customs agents at the side of the ship. It was a pair of men in lightweight uniforms. Their skin was dark brown and they showed no sign of being affected by the heat as they scrambled up to our deck.

"Welcome," I said. "How can we assist you?"

"Where are you from?"

"North America, most recently Key West," I said.

"Cargo?"

"Just some vehicles," I said.

"Passengers?" the agent asked.

"Yes, sir, forty-seven passengers, six crew."

We had determined that LB, Allie, Cat, Preston, Patty, and I would act as the ship's crew. There were protocols for large ships and if we were going to be in trouble, I didn't want the retirees to have to shoulder that burden.

The customs agents split up. One went inside with LB, the other stayed out on the deck. He was thin with a receding hairline and sinewy forearms. After giving us a few instructions, he went straight to the Mercedes.

"Whose vehicle is this?" he said.

It wasn't a demand for information. He was obviously very wowed by the luxury vehicle. Before I could answer, he opened the driver's door.

"It's ours," I said. "We brought it on board before sailing south."

"To escape the cold," he said, which I found to be reassuring. We were obviously not the only people moving away from the areas of the planet affected by the supernatural darkness and the global cooling it caused. "It is very nice."

"Thank you," I said, even though I had nothing to do with the G-Wagon or the upgrades it had gotten in Miami.

"That Jeep is nice too. I must call them in."

He stepped away and pulled a small radio from his pocket. I didn't know what was happening. The man chattered away in Guyanese Creole for a few moments, then another voice chattered back.

"You are the captain of this vessel?" he asked me.

No one had elected me to be the captain. It could just as easily have been LB, or Cat, for that matter. But I was there and so I nodded.

"The mayor wants to see you."

He waved toward the small boat he had come aboard in and started walking toward it.

"What about your companion?" I asked.

"He will be along when he is finished. This will not take long."

I hated to leave without telling anyone, but I didn't seem to have a choice. I followed the customs agent into his little boat, and he started the outboard motor while I untied the line that held the small craft to the side of the *Manna T.* We zipped across the harbor and went directly into a newly built structure only a couple of blocks from the port. I was sweating freely by the time we reached the building, but inside it was cool and clean. The building was simple-looking from the outside, but the interior was all fine woods and golden fixtures. There were exotic-looking rugs on the floors, and large, ornate pots with bright flowers growing in them.

I was taken straight to the main office, which had a huge, wooden desk and heavy, leather sofas in the ample space. Against one wall was a small bar and above that a large map of the city with new construction penciled in and labeled. The other wall had several tinted windows that showed the city's main street. The celebration was still going strong. Hundreds of people were dancing to music being played by musicians who paraded through the throng. I saw lots of disposable cups in the hands of the revelers and guessed that alcohol was being consumed in vast quantities.

There was no one in the office. The customs agent and I waited several minutes before a man in a business suit appeared. He was black, with broad shoulders and a scar on his right cheek. He extended a broad hand to me, which I shook.

"Welcome to Georgetown," he said. "I am Mayor Nazar. Won't you have a seat, Captain?"

"Oh, thank you," I said.

"Drink?"

I would have enjoyed some cool water, but I didn't want alcohol. "No, sir, thank you."

"Sir, you hear that Azruddin? Ah, such respect, I am grateful for it. My agent tells me you have a fine car aboard your ship. Is this correct?"

"Yes, sir, a Mercedes G-Wagon," I said.

"And you are bringing it here?"

"We weren't sure what we might need," I said "We brought enough vehicles for the passengers."

"And you will continue moving goods in your vessel, Captain? I know, I am asking you many questions, but as you know, much of the shipping capacity was lost and we are in need of your services."

"We're not opposed to that," I said.

"Excellent. I have warehouses full of goods waiting to be taken east. But there are still many ships that can accommodate these needs. What I am looking for is a vessel that can ferry automobiles. We have many luxury vehicles that are in high demand in New Babylon. You can take them for us, yes?"

"Once I've settled the passengers, I can do that, yes, sir."

"Outstanding. Your passengers can stay here, in Georgetown. We have new apartments available every day. And there is no shortage of jobs here. Yes, it is a good thing. As you can see, the city is celebrating the wonderful news that the terrible locusts are finally dying off. There are similar reports from around the world."

"That is good news," I said, ignoring the lump in my stomach as I thought about the next judgment that God would unleash.

"It is. And we have excellent communication, so I will know if the automobiles do not arrive where they are supposed to. And should that happen, we would be forced to hold your passengers responsible. I think you understand what I am telling you, Captain."

It was the nicest threat I had ever received.

"I do," I said. "We won't disappoint you, but we will need to take on fuel, fresh water, and food."

"Of course," he responded.

"And we don't really have anything to pay with," I said.

"We will provide what you need in exchange for your cooperation with our luxury vehicles. The Mercedes must stay on board, of course. Fine cars like that must be shared with those in need. I'm sure you understand."

I did. He was stealing our G-Wagon and turning it over to the government in New Babylon. I also understood that it wasn't the needy who would get the cars, it was the politically powerful. But I didn't argue. My goal was to keep as many of the people who looked to me for leadership alive. If that meant I had to sail around the world and deliver a load of cars, that's exactly what I would do.

"He has a very nice Jeep Wrangler as well," the customs agent said.

"Very good!" the Mayor exclaimed. "You can begin offloading

your passengers. Azruddin will show you where to dock your ship so that we can transfer our vehicles to your ship. And Bharrat will escort your people to the Grangar complex here on the north side of town."

He tapped on the map with a long finger. I stood up and nodded as Azruddin opened the door.

"Thank you, Mr. Mayor, sir," I said.

"It has been a pleasure, Captain. I will be in touch soon. Stay close to your ship."

I nodded again and followed the customs agent out of the building. By that point, the crowds had reached the municipal building. A drink was shoved into my hand as people danced around me. I pretended to take a drink, but didn't. The cup had strong liquor inside. The smell of it burned my nasal passages, and I couldn't imagine what it would do to my tongue and throat. Azruddin was pushing his way through the throng and I followed close behind him. It was a bit frightening, if I'm being honest. The smell of liquor and sweat was strong in the crowd as people danced, their bodies rubbing against one another. Hands touched my shoulders and chest. I was pinched and groped until we broke through the crowd. All around, the people were convulsing and wailing, some in pleasure, some in pain. Worse still, I could feel a sense of oppression in the city. It's hard to explain, but there was something unseen in that town that exuded a sense of evil malevolence. I couldn't wait to get away from it.

28

The customs agent had a smaller, less posh office near the pier. He left me just outside with the instructions not to leave. All I wanted to do was get back to the *Manna T*. Part of me wanted to hide there. To get away from the evil and the danger that I knew was coming. For five months, no one on planet Earth had died. There were, according to reports, six billion people spread all over the world. But with the second woe, which was the sixth trumpet judgment described in Revelation chapter nine, a third of them would be killed. Was it wrong to want to escape that carnage?

To be honest, death didn't frighten me. I believed that when I died, I would be united with Jesus in a celestial paradise. I was actually looking forward to that, but I knew God had a purpose for me here and now. What I wanted more than anything in all the world was to hear him say to me, *Well done, my good and faithful servant.* I didn't deserve it, although I longed for it. It was why I fought against the rising tide of despair around me. And why I wasn't surprised when a familiar face appeared around the corner.

"Praise God in Heaven!"

"Jonathan!" I said. "What are you doing here?"

"Looking for you!"

He was laughing, and we hugged. Dr. Jonathan Weinblatt was a Jewish believer who came to the faith after seeing Lorenzo's videos that I posted online shortly after the rapture. He was the first Jewish believer I met and an answer to prayer after LB and Allie were hurt in the great earthquake. I don't know what we'd have done if God hadn't brought him to us on the old farm in central Texas.

"How'd you know I was here?"

He pointed up and grinned. "I had a little help. But to be honest, I had no idea it would be you. I was told to go to the pier and that help would be waiting and here you are, Hank. I'm so glad to see you again."

"I'm glad to see you too," I said, tears welling up in my eyes.

The door behind me opened, and Azrubbin stepped out. I can't say what prompted me to do what I did. There are times when it feels like the Holy Spirit just takes over. I suddenly had a desire to speak and simply couldn't keep the words in.

"Sorry, I'm new to town. I can't help you. I captain the *Manna T,*" I said, pointing toward the flex/cargo ship sitting in the harbor.

"Who is this?" Azrubbin asked suspiciously.

Maybe I was being paranoid, but I was suddenly reminded of the NARA government people. They were suspicious, too, always looking to catch a person in a lie. Or maybe I'm just not a good liar, but either way, it was not a pleasant feeling.

"Dr. Weinblatt," Jonathan said, extending a hand to the customs agent. "I was looking for a bathroom."

I felt bad for Jonathan, but also happy that he understood what I was doing. We both knew the dangers of our faith, not to mention the fact that any dissenter or vocal opponent of the government had a tendency to disappear in a nefarious manner.

"Try the harbor master's office," Azrubbin said. "It's the big white one."

"Ah, yes, thank you. That's very helpful."

Jonathan left us. I glanced at him before following the customs agent back to the boat, which we took out to the ship. When I got on board, the other agent was waiting.

"Well?" He asked.

"Mayor wants them in dock C," Azrubbin said. "Do you want to pilot then, or shall I?"

"You do it," the other man remarked.

LB looked at me with big eyes and I nodded from behind Azrubbin. It was all I could do to reassure him.

Half an hour later, we were docked and the vans had been removed. Cars seemed rare in Georgetown, not that they could have gone far with the people flooding the streets. I had just enough time to tell everyone that I had seen Jonathan. The Jewish retirees didn't know our friend but the rest of the group did. No one was surprised when, halfway through the period of darkness, a lone man with a tiny candle approached the ship.

"Been waiting for you," I said as I helped Jonathan onto the *Manna T.* "Come inside. There are people anxious to see you."

"And I am anxious to see them."

Jonathan had formed the group of believers in the Yucatan. He was one of the evangelists who was supernaturally gifted by the Holy Spirit to win people to Christ. Even though he felt called to the Jews spread across the world, he was happy to share the gospel with anyone who was interested.

He went in and celebrated with old friends. Soon, he was making new ones. He was friendly and encouraging to everyone he met, but thrilled to find nearly thirty Jewish believers. Oscar was still the lone holdout in the group of retirees. The swarming attack from the locusts had traumatized him and he spent most of his time alone in his cabin since he recovered. Just getting him to eat had become difficult. If not for the moratorium on death, I think he might have committed suicide.

In the town, the supernatural darkness did nothing to slow the hedonistic celebrations taking place. Candles, torches and bonfires were lit. In the lurid glare of the wavering flames, what little inhibitions the people of Georgetown felt were cast aside. Most went completely naked through the streets and many engaged in whatever intimate acts they desired in the open with no qualms about who saw them.

We retreated to the officer's lounge. It had portholes but not the big windows like the bridge. Cat and I had moved into the captain's berth nearby and LB and Allie had moved in across from us. If we weren't on the Bridge or in the galley eating, we often hung out in the lounge. When the rest of the passengers had gone to bed, Jonathan joined us.

"Welcome to Guyana," he said to us. "We're a long way from Texas, my friends."

"Gonna get farther," LB said.

"We've been commandeered," I told Jonathan. "The Mayor wants us to transport some vehicles to New Babylon."

"Oh, praise God above," the evangelist said. "He is faithful, always faithful."

"You'll have to catch us up," Cat said.

"I've been traveling," Jonathan explained. "Driven south almost by the Holy Spirit. There was a community of Jewish people here, most of them transplants from Argentina. They made a long, harrowing journey north shortly after the rapture of the church."

"I'm guessing Argentina is under a sheet of ice about now," LB said.

"Yes," Jonathan said. "And the interior of Brazil has become a dangerous wasteland of tribal fighting, murder, and worse. Over half their number was killed during the journey."

"How horrible," Allie said.

"What can we do to help them?" Cat asked.

"You have a sweet spirit," Jonathan said as tears filled his eyes. "To be surrounded by believers like you four touches my heart more than you know." He wiped his face, then looked up at me. "Believe it or not, we have for the past month felt an intense call of the Spirit to return to the promised land."

"You want to go to Israel?" I asked.

Jonathan nodded. "Want is not strong enough a word. We must go. As you know, travel is strictly limited. What was once as simple as boarding a flight has become almost impossible. Especially for those who aren't registered."

"You mean the mark of the beast?" Cat asked.

"It is not that invasive, not yet. But the registry is close to it. The authorities here are more focused on putting everyone to work. Construction or farming labor seems to be the greatest need. And the government is implementing a socialist style division of roles. In exchange for housing and food allowance, one must work in a job approved by the government officials."

"It's the same back home," I said. "It's why we had to flee North America."

"You won't find it any easier here, my friend. And the Prince of this place is very strong, very violent. People die here every day by human sacrifice. Newborns are the preferred offering, but as there aren't many of those, the elderly and those with mental deficiencies or physical handicaps are slaughtered in the temple."

"Maybe leaving ain't such a bad idea," LB said.

"The sooner the better," Allie agreed.

"We have to take on provisions and the cargo," I said. "But that could be completed as soon as tomorrow afternoon. How many people are with you, Jonathan?"

"Two hundred," he said softly, sounding almost apologetic.

"Oh," Cat said.

"I know that is no small number," Jonathan said. "But we must go to the promised land before the midway point. When my people are run out of Jerusalem to the place God is preparing for them, we must be ready to care for them."

"I hear you," I said, "but we don't have room for two hundred people."

"Well," Allie said. "We don't have cabins for that many."

"What are you saying?" LB asked.

She shrugged. "We could double up. Some people will have to sleep up on the fifth floor, share bathrooms, and eat in shifts. We could make it work."

"We'll have to clear it with the others," I said. "I'm not even sure if we've got enough food for that many people."

"God will provide," Jonathan said. "If you are willing, he will ensure that we have everything we need."

I thought for a moment. There was no question of willingness. It didn't matter to me if we sailed with just my closest friends or with hundreds of strangers as long as they didn't interfere with the operation of the ship. The *Manna T* was itself a gift from God. I did wish at that moment that so much food hadn't been spoiled when we were forced to turn on the sprinkler system on the main deck, but I also knew Jonathan was right.

"We'll need to move people onto the ship without attracting attention," I said. "I have a feeling that the authorities won't want us taking people out of their region."

"And taking on more people than the ship is rated for," Allie said.

"We can hide them in the hull, if comes down to that," LB said. "Plenty of space down there."

We sent Jonathan away with instructions to bring people back the next night. Only the following day didn't play the way we hoped, not for the Jews in Georgetown, and not for the passengers on the *Manna T.* If God was at work, it was for sure in a mysterious way.

29

The cars arrived on a truck. There were eight in total, all high-end exotic cars that surely cost a fortune to import to the small South American country.

"How much you want to bet those all got impounded when the new Administrator took charge?" LB said as we watched the truck approaching the dock.

"No bet," I said.

The cars were driven off the semi-truck and then over the ramp and onto the ship. The port's ramp was a lot like the one in Key West, so we were prepared. Flex pitched in to help, and then a man with an orange vest and a ball cap with the title Harbor Master embroidered on it approached.

"You gotta get them all secured," he barked. "And covered. I don't have to tell you what the salt will do to the finish."

"We're on it," LB told him.

The deck was lined with a pair of Lamborghinis, three Ferraris, a Porsche, three Mercedes, including our G-Wagon, two Bentleys, a Rolls-Royce, and our Jeep, which looked clunky and utilitarian in comparison to the other vehicles. There were five on each side of the deck, which left the middle portion open with movable plates so that the bins in the hull could be filled. I was surprised when the Harbor Master ordered his people to start loading our bins with produce.

"I wasn't told we were carrying anything but the cars," I told him.

"I've got the orders right here," he said, waving a clipboard at me. "We're topping off the fuel and fresh water tanks, then filling the hull bins with wheat, corn, and beans. You got a problem with that, you can go see the Mayor, but you gotta move this ship out of my dock today."

I didn't argue. We just went to work. A massive hose was moved into position, but the Harbor Master didn't want to load anything until the protective covers were over the cars. We put in the wheel wedges, then used yellow cargo straps that went over the front and rear axles of each car. When we had them secured, the specialty covers were slid over the vehicles. They were made from a soft, microfiber cloth on the interior and waterproof vinyl on the outside. They even cinched at the bottom. Once we got all the covers on the vehicles, the big hose belched the produce into the huge bins inside our hull. The process took a couple of hours, then our fresh water tank was refilled and Allie set about the process of adding a few tablets to kill any local microbes that might have an adverse effect on our digestive systems.

The fuel tanks were filled while several pallets of food were moved on. We hurried to move all the food off the pier and into the galley. The Jewish retirees took charge of it from there. And then Azrubbin showed up with a pair of men in police uniforms with assault style automatic rifles.

"I'm here for your passengers," he told me.

"Actually, they have decided to stay on board," I told him.

"No, they will come with me," he said.

It wasn't a suggestion. I was about to argue with him, but then Preston appeared at my side.

"We're ready," he said.

I wasn't sure what was happening, but I didn't argue. Hannah led the group, each one with a bag of clothes and personal belongings. We didn't have much else, and the group didn't complain.

"What's going on?" I asked Preston.

"God told us to stay," he said.

"What?"

"We had dreams," he said. "I thought I was the only one, but then Patty mentioned hers. By the time we finished, all of us from Mérida realized we had the same dream."

"I didn't," I said.

"It's no wonder," Preston said, his voice thick with emotion. "Jesus met us and told us to stay in Georgetown. But you'll need to pick everyone else up down the coast."

"Where?" I asked.

Preston shrugged, then he threw his arms around me. I felt a little worried that Azruddin might get suspicious, but when I looked over, he was busy talking to the other passengers.

"You've done so much for us, Hank. You and Cat are family. We love you."

Patty appeared at my side and took my hand. "We will be praying for you every day."

"Thanks," I said, suddenly fighting my own emotions.

"This isn't goodbye," Preston said, swiping a tear from his cheek. "We'll see you again."

"I'm already looking forward to it," I said, meaning every word.

Flex was the last to go. He shook my hand. "Wish I was going with you, bro."

"Me too," I said.

"But Jesus has something for us here."

"Just be careful," I said. "Take care of Hannah. The enemy is strong here."

"Greater is he who is in me..."

"Than he who is in the world," I said. "Specifically, Guyana, South America."

"It's going to be an adventure, my man. Thanks for everything, Hank."

I watched him walk over the pier and then I turned to see Cat and Allie in the doorway. They were crying too. That wrecked me. Fortunately, I was also sweating in the sweltering heat and no one on the shore noticed or paid us any attention. LB and I secured the ropes holding us in place, while Cat gently bumped the thrusters to get us moving. By the time I got my ropes coiled neatly on the deck and made it up to the Bridge, we were turning toward the mouth of the harbor.

"How much time do we have left?" I asked.

"Before what?" Allie asked.

"Before dark," I said.

"Maybe an hour and a half," LB said.

"Once we're out of the harbor, head due east until we're out of sight of land."

"Then we turn back?" Cat asked. "In the dark?"

"I think so," I said, silently asking God to give me wisdom.

We sailed east at half speed. The water outside the Caribbean was different. There were larger swells and the wind seemed stronger. When the supernatural darkness fell, we turned back toward South America and sailed south slowly, hoping we didn't hit anything in the dark.

"Hank?" Allie said as I came inside from the starboard Bridge wing.

"Yeah?"

"There's something on the radar."

"What?" I asked, since nothing with light worked during the eight hours when things went supernaturally dark all over the planet.

"I'm looking right at it," she said.

There was a green glow on her face. I had thought she had lit a candle at first, but then it hit me that no candles emitted green light.

"It's just one thing," she said. "Not even the coastline or anything like that is showing up. Just a single blip on the radar."

I was silently praying, *God, is this our sign? Should we go toward the light on the radar?* There was no answer, but no check in my spirit either. That was the way things often worked. God rarely repeated himself. But when something was wrong, I often felt it deep inside. My feelings and emotions were messy and often made it hard for me to discern what God was saying to me, but in the supernatural darkness, it seemed intuitive to follow the light.

And follow we did, because as we turned toward the light, it moved. We sailed in the darkness for six hours and the entire time we got no closer to the light. I was starting to fear that the radar was glitching, but then it shouldn't be working at all.

"I think we should go out onto the deck," LB said.

"We still won't be able to see anything," I told him.

"True, but we can hear," he replied.

I couldn't argue with that. We had slowed to a crawl as we approached the object on the radar. Allie took the controls and Cat helped her keep tabs on us as LB and I took candles down to the deck. The water was surprisingly calm and there was absolutely no wind. LB and I went out and stood by the railing at midships and then I went out to the bow.

Several minutes passed. Fears of sea monsters flooded my mind. What might be drawn to the light I was holding? As the fear assailed me, I did my best to pray while keeping an iron grip on the railing. The fear of falling into the ocean and getting attacked by sharks was booming through my mind as if I was standing next to a public address loudspeaker.

And then I saw it. At first, I thought my eyes were playing tricks on me. It wasn't a ship, just a tiny light, like a spark. It appeared, disappeared, then reappeared and stayed steady.

"Do you see that?" I called to LB.

"Sure do," he said.

We stood, waiting, as the tiny spark of light seemed to get closer. And then a voice carried over the waves.

"Ahoy, *Manna T*!"

I raised my candle in response. "Ahoy! LB, go stop the ship."

"Got it," he said, hurrying away from the railing.

A few minutes later, the first of several small fishing boats, the kind used by villagers, came rowing up beside us. Jonathan's face appeared in the light of his own candle.

"His wonders never cease," the doctor shouted to me.

Soon, we had a dozen Jewish believers on board, and more boats were coming. The entire fleet of a tiny fishing village was rowing out the Jews who had come from Argentina and those who had come from Miami, too. They came packed in the wooden boats rowed by the fishermen who I learned later had made a historic catch earlier that day, after Jonathan told them they would. The villagers came to faith in Jesus and happily rowed them out into the total darkness.

We got everyone on board safely, another miracle considering the odds. If the wind had kicked up or the sea had been anything but totally calm, the overcrowded fishing boats might have swamped, or we might have dropped someone scrambling up the rope ladder onto the *Manna T*.

As soon as we were all safe inside the passenger section of the ship, Allie turned back toward the open sea and pushed the throttles to their stoppers. When the supernatural darkness ended an hour later, we were heading due east at top speed.

You might expect that the former passengers might lay claim to the staterooms they had occupied before, or balk at the idea of sharing their space. But just the opposite happened, they invited the newcomers in. They came from opposite hemispheres and widely divergent cultures, but they were all Jews and they were all sealed with the Holy Spirit. We had a long, long voyage ahead and kept the ship running through the night. LB and I took turns on the bridge and, the next morning, Jonathan joined us there with Cat and Allie.

He told us what happened and we all gave thanks to God just as the sixth trumpet judgment was unleashed.

30

Along with the other satellite receivers on the roof of the *Manna T's* five-story superstructure, there was a Starlink commercial internet setup. The signal was strong enough to power the wifi across the entire ship. As the passengers shared the cabins and set up sleeping pallets in the common areas, it was inevitable that people got online. We had over thirty iPads and there were desktop computers in the recreation space on the fifth floor. The latter were set up for games, but they also had internet access. Across hundreds of live feeds, from social media, to news sites, and even on YouTube there were images of the horsemen coming out of the mountains in eastern Turkey.

Word passed through the ship quickly and soon everyone was watching. Even on the Bridge, which was where I spent most of my time, we had the footage pulled up on an iPad. Daniel and Jonathan were with Cat, Allie, LB, and me as we watched the troops coming down an icy clearing from the thick, tree-covered mountain. Like much of North America, there was snow and ice everywhere, but the mounted troops didn't seem bothered by it. Probably because the warriors were riding monsters.

"Knew this was coming," LB said. "And I still can't believe it."

"They are real," Jonathan said. "Born from four angels that were reserved for this day and hour."

The troops were in armor that included helmets that covered their faces. The armor wasn't steel or any kind of metal I had seen before. It looked more like ceramic, a kind of heavy armor with a high gloss. It was bright red, brilliant blue and a dark yellow. The colors were cheery, but somehow looked menacing on the mysterious riders.

"What are they?" Cat asked.

"Manifestations of evil," Jonathan said.

"The sixth trumpet judgment," Daniel said. "Set loose to kill a third of the people on earth."

"A third is about two billion people," LB said grimly.

We already knew what the Bible predicted, but seeing it coming to fruition before our eyes was shocking. We were heading northeast toward the Mediterranean Sea and the Atlantic was wide open. Occasionally, we saw another ship far in the distance, but nothing was close to us. The ship was running flawlessly and we had nothing to do but keep tabs on things. Most of our attention that morning was riveted to the iPad.

The most shocking sight was the troops' mounts. They had bodies and legs like horses, the big kind, Clydesdales, or Shire horses with thick, powerful legs that had the distinctive feathering above their massive hooves. But what drew the eye to these creatures was their head. Instead of an equine head, they had wide, black manes surrounding a lion's head. Their mouths were open and breathed out black smoke. Occasionally, fire could be seen flickering from between their massive fangs.

Speaking of fangs, the heads weren't the only strange part of the animal. For a tail, they had snakes. Most were coiled up on the big horse's hindquarters, but a few stretched out. There was no denying what they were, thick-bodied, scaly snakes. Just like the riders, their scales were glossy. They hissed and bore deadly-looking fangs as their forked tongues licked the air.

"I... I've got to sit down," LB said. "It's like a bad dream."

"Long has it been thought that the fallen angel Watchers and their Nephilim offspring carried out genetic crossbreeding," Jonathan said. "You have read first Enoch, Hank?"

I nodded. "They sinned against the birds, the beasts, the reptiles and fish."

"Yes, that is what we read. What it means exactly, we do not know. It is within a passage talking about their monstrous appetites. They ate all the food that humans could provide and when that ran out... they ate people."

"Cannibals," Cat said softly.

"But it goes on," Jonathan said, "claiming they turned against one another, eating their own flesh and drinking the blood. It is heinous, but perhaps this reference is simply that they ate animals. There are many other chimeras in our holy scriptures. Many of the holy angels are beings with the features of different animals."

"Still, hard to believe my own eyes," LB said.

We kept tabs on the growing army. Experts were guessing they numbered in the hundreds of millions, but we knew the exact number from scripture. Twice ten thousand times ten thousand is two hundred million. It was the largest army the world had ever seen and we didn't have to wait long to see what they intended. The closest village to where they came out of the mountains was still inhabited by several dozen people. The mounted troops charged in and set everything ablaze. Their mounts didn't just breathe smoke; they spewed fire from their mouths like dragons.

I know, it seems crazy. How can an animal breathe fire? I don't know, but what we knew for certain was that the chimeras weren't normal animals. They were supernatural beings. The villagers were slaughtered. Those who were brave enough to try to fight the horsemen were struck by their snake tails, which didn't seem to kill them. I know some types of snake venom are paralytic, which is what the tails of the chimeras seemed to possess. Those bit staggered back, wailing in pain, before they stiffened and toppled to the ground. You might expect that they were then trampled to death, but the chimeras never wasted a chance to burn a person up. They spewed not only fire, but a strange burning liquid. It ran and pooled in a way that reminded me of mercury, but I knew from scripture that it was sulfur. The liquid stuck to whatever it touched and burned a bright, blue flame that burned anything it touched. The buildings of the village, the snow-covered vehicles and even the metal roofs burned up. It was a horrific sight.

"So, this is it," LB said. "War against the monsters. Can we kill them?"

"The Bible doesn't say that," I explained.

"We shall have to wait and see," Jonathan said. "How long until we reach Israel?"

"Two weeks, give or take," I told him. "It depends on how much traffic there is in the Med and if we have to stop for inspections along the way."

"Two weeks, oh, my," Jonathan said.

I understood his anxious desire to get to his people. The world was a frightening place and getting scarier by the day. But Jonathan didn't want to hide. He was going to Israel to help his people survive the horrors that were coming in the latter half of the Tribulation period, what was commonly referred to as the Day of Jacob's Trouble, or the Great Tribulation.

I enjoyed seeing the way the American Jews mingled with the Argentinian Jews. The latter spoke Spanish, but most had gained a basic understanding of English from their time in Guyana, where English was still the official language. We made space for Jonathan in the crew's lounge, hanging a blanket for privacy. He slept on one of the sofas and spent several hours a day alone in his makeshift cabin, praying.

Daniel and Liz moved into another of the tiny crew berths on the second floor. Unlike the rooms on the other floors, the crew cabins were very utilitarian with shared bathrooms. But no one complained. I felt a little guilty in the captain's more spacious quarters, but no one would trade with me. Cat and I served the same sixteen hours of the day so that we could have a block of private time together. We took our meals on the Bridge and, occasionally joined Allie in the basic maintenance tasks required to keep the ship's engine running smoothly. As we sailed north toward the Strait of Gibraltar, it grew colder. Fortunately, and I think providentially, we avoided any storms, although at times snow fell in soft flakes that seemed almost magical. I often spent hours just staring out at the dark blue water we passed over, as snow fell, and I could almost forget about the horrors happening across the world.

Eight days after leaving Guyana, we came within sight of the north African coast. The Moroccan coast had become a lush, flourishing land. It was cold, but not snow-covered. Yet what drew our eye wasn't the expansive beaches, or tree-lined fields of green, or even the Atlas Mountains in the distance. Instead, we were drawn to the thick columns of billowing black smoke. It wasn't surprising really, since we had been following the news online and knew the mounted warriors had attacked in all directions. Satellite imagery showed the marching troops who didn't seem to need sleep or respite of any kind. They didn't trail supply lines or pillage the towns they came to for food. They simply marched and killed, burning everything in their path.

The global government had responded. They labeled the demonic warriors as militias from the mountains of Turkey, Georgia, Armenia and Azerbaijan. But their narrative, parroted by all the mainstream news outlets, fell apart when those countries were ravaged by the horsemen who rode north. Half of the demonic army moved east, swooping down across northern Iran, then spreading through Afghanistan and Pakistan, before invading India. The other half of that dreaded army split again, some going north to destroy Europe, and others going south to attack Egypt, Libya, Algeria, and Morocco.

The horsemen didn't seem to care about conquest. They weren't moving in coordination toward strategic targets, but rather moving in general directions and killing everyone in their path. The global government fought back... or tried to. Bombers and missile strikes were utilized in numbers that had never before been unleashed at one time. But the horsemen were fast and could avoid the blasts. In the same manner, fire didn't seem to hurt them at all. Fuel-air bombs, sometimes called Vacuum bombs, that filled the air above an enemy position with combustible mist that was then burned up quickly and in the process consumed all the available oxygen a person, or animal, needed to breathe, was found to be completely useless against the riders. It seemed that they were impervious to fire and needed no air to breathe.

That's not to say that some weren't killed. Tanks were rolled out, but the riders displayed no fear. When an enemy force came against them, they charged, spreading out and utilizing great strength. The chimeras were as fast as war horses, yet they didn't get tired. The supernatural creatures could gallop for hours with no need for rest or even to drink anything. They spread through desert regions and swarmed over military installations. Each day, the supernatural darkness fell, forcing humans to take shelter and hope the riders wouldn't come for them in the inky blackness. But the demonic creatures had no trouble seeing their way through the darkness and continued their killing spree day and night. The death toll was so high that news agencies couldn't keep up.

Nor were the riders bothered by the cold. Millions of them rode north and crossed the Arctic regions where ice had covered the oceans in thick sheets and connected Europe to North America. Eventually, they would make their way down through Mexico, Central America, and into South America. I worried about my friends we had left in Guyana, but I also worried about us.

On day nine of our voyage, we passed through the Strait of Gibraltar. Spain had fared no better than Morocco. Towns and villages were burned indiscriminately. We saw what had once been lavish coastal cities that were razed to the ground. There was very little rubble, just mounds of sulfur that continued to burn for days, melting and spreading over the concrete and steel of the more modern cities.

It was warmer in the south, and we hugged the African coast, passing devastated communities in Tunisia. Cold winds blew clouds of ash out into the ocean. It soon covered the deck of the ship and smeared across the big windows of the Bridge. All we could do was keep going and pray that people came to their senses. Along with news reports, there were anonymous videos that proclaimed the truth. People read from Revelation nine that described the demonic horsemen with their fiery breath. They showed videos of the two witnesses in Jerusalem pleading with people to repent of their sin, call out to God, and believe in his Anointed One.

The videos were quickly flagged and removed, but even quicker were the people who managed to save the videos and repost them over and over again. With hours to fill each day and very little work to do, people studied God's word. Jonathan taught studies in the galley between mealtimes. We were forced to slow down in the busier Mediterranean Sea, even stopping during the supernatural dark period every afternoon. I continue to say it was supernatural because it fell within the same time frame each day, no matter what time zone a person was in, and because it somehow affected every kind of light but flame. Flashlights, emergency lights, and even night vision equipment were ineffective during the eight hours of darkness. Often, Jonathan joined us on the Bridge, which was surprisingly spacious considering all the important controls found there. We read scripture together, prayed and shared a meal that the volunteers in the kitchens graciously brought up to us.

"Any idea how long the riders will be around?" LB asked.

"The Bible is not clear on that point," Jonathan said. "I have theories, but that is all they are."

"Tell us," Cat urged.

"Keep in mind, this is just my ideas," he said. "But here is what we know is coming: the world does not repent. It says at the end of Revelation chapter nine that they continue in their worship of demons and idols. They do not repent of their murders, sorceries, sexual immorality and theft. I take that to mean that things go back to a sense of normalcy. Then in chapter ten, it describes an angel that descends on both the land and the sea."

"The seven thunders," I said.

"Yes, we do not get to know what the apostle John heard, but something is happening," Jonathan said. "And then he is instructed to eat the scroll that is in the angel's hand. He does, and it is sweet in his mouth, but turns bitter in his stomach."

"Which means what?" Allie asked.

"Yeah, we get caught and lost in the weeds with all that," LB said.

"We cannot say for certain," Jonathan said. "But, my guess is that we will see a short respite. Think of it like a boxer who steps back to catch his breath before launching into the next barrage."

"It's been almost three and a half years," I said. "I can't believe we made it this far."

"It wasn't easy," Cat said.

"Yeah, I wouldn't want to do it again," LB said. "But then, if it wasn't so bad, I wouldn't have realized how much I need God."

Allie nodded, blinking back tears.

"That is true for all of us," Jonathan said. "I was raised to believe in Hashem and follow his commands, but other than observing a few holidays, I did nothing. I was a hotshot doctor in New York and then the world I knew dissolved before my eyes. Somehow, I escaped New York before the nukes fell, but like so many survivors, I was shattered. Then, one day, I overheard a man talking online. He was saying that the holy scriptures predicted what was happening in the world, from the seven-year peace covenant with Israel, to the widespread wars and overwhelming inflation that followed.

"I asked for the name of the man in the video. When I typed in his name, what came up were a series of videos of Lorenzo Maltza teaching about things no one had ever told me about. He showed from the Old Testament right through to the New Testament how God had foretold what was to befall our world. And he also showed how often the book of Revelation points back to and outright quotes the Old Testament scriptures. Suddenly, things began to click in my mind. I found a Bible and started reading the New Testament. It was like the truth had been staring me in the face, all my life, and I had never seen it. Jesus was the Messiah, of that there could be no doubt. I was on the road in Tennessee, trying to get away from the nuclear winter and avoid the radiation fallout. Then and there, I called out to Jesus, confessed that I believed he was the Messiah and that he died for me. It was my sins that held him to the cross and his love for me that moved him to make that sacrifice.

"So, while I mourn for those who have died and hope that more people will come to faith in Jesus, I do not regret these judgments. Our God is mighty and just. His discipline always has meaning and purpose. No one living these days can say that God does not exist. I believe that proof will only become more and more clear."

We spent hours that evening talking about Bible prophecy. There was so much more to come and we had a front row seat to what God was doing.

31

As we sailed past Tripoli and made our way toward Egypt, the carnage across the world continued. To be honest, I wasn't in a hurry to reach our destination. The two-week voyage had been like a vacation. Sure, there was work to be done. We swept salt and ash from the car covers and off the deck. We shut down the main engine every fourth day for almost two hours, running the ship on the auxiliary engine so that Allie could check the fluids, add oil, test the belts and electrical connections. The cooling system needed to be flushed on the eighth day of our trip and we all took our turns cleaning various areas of the ship's superstructure. Having so many passengers wasn't easy, but it felt like a holiday to me. I'm an only child and an orphan. I was adopted by my foster parents because I had no other family. The Sotos were kind, but different. They tried to adopt American customs, but things were always a bit odd and never like I imagined they would be if I was with my mom and dad. Having a crowded ship full of excited believers was a bit like being in a crowded house with aunts, uncles, cousins, and grandparents. Part of me didn't want it to end.

I had grown close to Nathan, Daniel and Saul. They were strong believers and encouraged my faith every single day. Liz, too, had become a friend I knew I would miss terribly. She had radically changed since we first met in the Shiloh building in Miami. She had gone from skeptical, cynical, and cold to warm, excited, and overflowing with kindness. I saw her working in various places on the ship every day. The *Manna T* had a large laundry. Having extra blankets, pillows, towels, and bed sheets was very handy with over two hundred passengers on board. Liz spent hours every day washing, drying, folding, and even ironing clothes, towels, and bed sheets.

But after eighteen days at sea, the coast of Israel came into view. I wish I could say it had been spared from the fiery wrath of the demonic riders, but it had suffered the effects of the sixth trumpet judgment just like the rest of the world. Gaza's towering coastal hotels and resorts were gone. Palm and date trees were blackened husks. A wide swath of fire and destruction had been blasted through the middle of Tel Aviv. Ashdod was no more. The Jewish passengers wept over the destruction, but from all the reports we had heard, Jerusalem had been spared.

We dropped anchor outside Haifa and requested boats to take the passengers to shore. When the harbor master heard that I had over two hundred Jews from Argentina and the United States, he asked no further questions. Boats were launched, and people disembarked with their belongings. It was bittersweet. Of course, I wanted to go with them, but Israel was not my homeland. Nor had God called me to go there. Besides, if I didn't deliver the luxury cars to New Babylon, it would be the community of believers in Georgetown that would pay for our failure.

"Once again, we must bid farewell, my friend," Jonathan said. "I cannot thank you enough for what you have done, Hank. God is using you in a mighty way."

"I don't know about that," I said.

"Look at you, look where you are," he replied. "Captain of a ship, no less. I'm betting you didn't see that coming."

"No," I told him.

"And look at what you have done for your brothers and sisters in Christ. They told me the stories, Hank. You kept them alive. You found a way to get them to safety. You stood up for them against the authorities and sacrificed yourself more than once when the locusts attacked. God is with you, which is why I am certain we will meet again. Keep tabs on your email, my friend. I will be in touch soon."

"I look forward to that," I told him.

He embraced me and kissed Cat on the cheek. We all cried, even LB, as we embraced our friends. We stood on the deck and watched him climb over the side and down into the last of the passenger boats.

"What now?" LB asked.

"Now we go back to the Suez Canal and make our way to New Babylon," I said.

It was true, but the harbor master had a surprise for me. When I got to the Bridge, the radio was chattering.

"This is the *Manna T*," I said. "Go ahead, Haifa Port."

"*Manna T*, what is your departure port?"

Fortunately, I had studied up on my nautical lingo and knew that he meant my destination.

"Haifa, we are sailing out of Georgetown, Guyana, en route to New Babylon. This wasn't an official stop, but we had precious cargo."

"That's what I thought," the harbor worker said. "I have passengers seeking passage to New Babylon. How many can you take on?"

I turned and looked at my friends. There were just four of us left on board: LB, Allie, Cat, and me. We could sail the ship to New Babylon. If I'm being honest, the computers did most of the work. All we had to do was keep the *Manna T* following the yellow line on the GPS navigation screen and try not to run into any other ships. But taking on passengers would require people to cook, clean, and look after the passengers.

"Haifa, we're running a skeleton crew here. We have no personnel to work the passenger cabins."

"Stand by, *Manna T*."

"We can't really take passengers, can we?" Cat asked. "I don't think I can handle cooking and cleaning for sixty people."

"How about two hundred?" LB said. "That may be what we're looking at after all the passengers we just let off."

"There's no way," I said. "But we better get our ducks in a row. Cat, will you check the laundry? Allie, can you check the galley? I'm sure we don't have enough food for that many people."

They both hurried off. It didn't take them long to come back with good reports.

"The laundry is clean, and all the linens are stocked," Cat said. "The rooms I passed along the way were made up and clean too."

"Galley's in great shape, but we're down to about a quarter of the rations. The cooks left us with half a dozen loaves of Challah bread."

"God bless 'em!" LB said.

"Did you hear from the harbor master yet?"

"No," I said, still waiting.

It was nearly ten more minutes before the radio sounded again. A warning beep went off, then the Harbor Master's voice came over the speaker.

"*Manna T*, this is Haifa. We want to show our appreciation for your delivery of precious cargo. We have located half a dozen Gentiles willing to trade work for passage to New Babylon. And we have fifty-five passengers, all vetted with hard currency, willing to pay for passage. Would that situation work for you?"

I looked around. Cat shrugged, and LB nodded.

"Hard currency?" Allie asked.

"Probably gold and silver," LB said. "Paper money is worthless."

"We could probably use it," Cat said. "I say we agree."

"Me too," Allie said.

I was nervous about the prospect of taking on strangers, but the ship was built with division between the ship's crew and passengers in mind. I prayed a silent prayer and asked Jesus if we should take on the passengers. Almost before I finished asking my question, the word *yes* popped into my head.

"Haifa, we appreciate your generosity," I said into the microphone. "We'll take the passengers."

"That's great news, *Manna T.* We will transmit your passenger manifest and then begin ferrying passengers, starting with those set to join your crew."

A minute later, the list showed up on the ship's computer screen. None of the names meant anything to me, but the amounts of their fare were staggering.

"Is that gold?" LB asked. "Like, real gold?"

"That's what it says," I was surprised myself.

"What's a Gold Dinar?" Cat asked.

None of us knew, but a quick internet search revealed that the Islamic Dinar is a coin made of 4.25 grams of 22k gold. Another search told us how much gold was trading for. The world had moved to digital currency, but physical assets like gold bullion were still being traded, and the value of gold was higher than at any time in human history.

"They're all paying us a fortune in gold," Allie said with a giggle.

"Is that right?" Cat asked when I checked what gold was trading for. "Ten thousand digital dollars an ounce?"

"These fools must be stupid rich," LB said.

Next to each name on the manifest was the sum of one hundred Gold Dinars. It made me feel a little weak in the knees. Each passenger was paying us four point two million in gold. Given that it was twenty-two karat, not twenty-four karat, the value was probably less, but we were still looking at over two-hundred million in currency that wouldn't lose its value. I wasn't sure it was legal to take the gold in payment, but I was willing to take that chance. We were still operating off the grid, in a manner of speaking, and having trade goods was smart.

We made a full inspection of the passenger cabins. Most were clean, but a few needed touch-ups. We also checked the recreation space. The sleeping pallets had been removed and the furniture returned to the way it had been before the Jewish believers came on board. On the top floor, across from the recreation space, were two café-style spaces. Both had full bars with liquor on the shelves. We hadn't bothered locking it up before, but I thought it was probably for the best with strangers coming on board.

We also took the time to move some things to the crew lounge and checked the rooms the new workers would occupy. Everything was ready when the first boat reached the *Manna T*. Cat and I met the workers. They were mostly girls. All of them were teenagers. I felt sorry for them and yet the way they talked and the way they dressed told me they weren't children.

"Do you all speak English?" I asked.

They nodded. A few already looked bored. Cat took over the supervisor duties. She asked the girls a series of questions and then divided them into groups. One pair would be in charge of the galley, another pair would be in charge of the laundry, and the rest would be housekeeping.

After a quick tour, the girls were settled into their cabins and given a strict warning that for the duration of the trip, they would need to refrain from fraternizing with the passengers.

"What about him?" One of the girls asked. "Can we fraternize with him?"

"I'm spoken for," I said, feeling my face flush with embarrassment, which was probably what the girl was aiming for to begin with.

"You'll survive the next two weeks without it," Cat said. "Anyone caught breaking the rules will be returned to Haifa."

It was an empty threat, but the girls didn't know that. There were no uniforms, but Allie found enough red bandanas for all twelve girls. They were thin with no design, and Cat told the girls to wear them around their necks so the passengers would recognize them. And they had about an hour before the first passengers arrived.

They came in suits and designer dresses. All of them had dark complexions and more luggage than expected. Yet it was clear at a glance that they were used to the finer things in life. More than a few had clear signs of cosmetic augmentation work. It wasn't my place to judge them, but we took their money and showed them to the cabins. Most spoke English, and I was quick to let them know we didn't have trained staff or a culinary specialist on board. None of them seemed to care. Getting to New Babylon was all that mattered and travel by land was too dangerous with the riders still running rampant across the world. We didn't know it yet, but the neat ranks had been released to go marauding as each demonic creature saw fit. That meant that no one was safe. Even one of the riders was enough to terrorize an entire town and set every structure ablaze. Even in the Haifa harbor, I could see a dozen plumes of smoke in the distance. And it was no surprise that the only place that seemed safe was New Babylon. That wasn't true either, just more propaganda from Paul Eon's communications department. It seemed that truth was almost anathema to the people who worked for the globe's most powerful administrator. Whatever other lies they pedaled, the common folk were expected to believe.

We stayed in the harbor until the supernatural darkness ended. The girls in the galley managed to make enough spaghetti for the entire ship. It was boiled pasta and canned sauce, but it was warm and there was plenty of it. We sailed south and got in the queue to pass through the Suez Canal. Cargo ships were no longer charged tolls for passage through the canal. Any ship with cargo that was headed for New Babylon was sent right through. By morning, we were in the Red Sea.

LB brought me a cup of coffee that morning and we looked at the body of water that Moses and the Israelites had crossed on dry ground.

"Hard to believe," he said. "Least it was before the world was plunged into a horror movie."

"Did you ever think you'd be cruising around the world, seeing things you can't explain?"

"Not in my wildest dreams," LB said with his characteristic, deep chuckle. "I was planning a quiet retirement outside St. Louis. Maybe get season tickets to the Cardinals and watch my hair turn gray."

"Do you ever regret not having a family?"

"Always thought there would be time," he said. "Then the clock sped up. I feel like it's overtime ever since the rapture. It's like I got a second chance. And Allie, oh man, she is everything to me. Absolutely everything and I'm not lying. I just hope that I can be what she needs till Jesus comes back."

"I know that feeling," I said.

That first day wasn't bad. The passengers slept late and the girls took care of their tasks without too much complaining. It was pretty obvious right from the start that our group of workers was from a different world. Many had spent the three years since the rapture partying. Nothing was off limits anymore. They did what they needed to in order to survive. We all took turns walking through the passenger spaces. It wasn't our goal to give the passengers a top-shelf cruise experience, but they had paid a small fortune to be traveling with us and I didn't want people to complain.

It would have been faster, easier, and much cheaper to fly to New Babylon. A massive airport had been one of the first construction projects the Apkallu built as they constructed the new world capital. But there were no more airlines allowed to operate while the military was trying to fight the demonic riders. And while it would have been quicker to travel by car or bus, it wasn't safe on the ground. Sea travel was not just the only remaining option, but it was perhaps the safest place to be while the riders roamed the Earth.

We took our time. Traffic in the Red Sea was much higher than anywhere else we had been. We sailed sixteen hours a day and dropped anchor when the supernatural darkness fell. Meanwhile, we did our best to show kindness to the passengers and staff on the ship. Most of the passengers stayed in their cabins. I set a limit on alcoholic beverages, but the wealthy passengers had all sorts of drugs and liquor among their personal effects.

By the time we reached the Arabian Sea, it was clear that of all the new people on the ship, only one was open to the gospel. She was one of the workers, a young Jordanian named Misha. Cat took the girl under her wing and encouraged her, being careful not to give her the easiest assignments, but somehow managing to spend the most time with her. If the other workers noticed, they didn't seem to care.

Reports came in that the riders had reached South America. Like every other place, the North American Regional Administration had tried and failed to stop them. In South America, the demonic troops were attacking villages and towns. Meanwhile, news from New Babylon revealed that the Apkallu, appalled by mankind's warmongering, was finally willing to get involved, although there were no clear reports on how or where they were working to stop the threat.

When we reached the Strait of Hormuz, we began to feel antsy. It seemed impossible to me that we could actually just sail into New Babylon and leave the Antichrist's capital city unscathed. We had no mark on our forehead, but I felt like my allegiance to Christ was plain to see. As we joined the throng of ships delivering goods to the opulent world capital, we began to pray like never before. We were going into the lion's den and there was no guarantee that we wouldn't be devoured.

32

I'm going to tell this next part of the story exactly the way it happened. I won't lie, either by exaggeration or by omission. It may be hard for you to believe if you didn't see it with your own eyes; in fact, I still sometimes doubt my own memories of New Babylon and what happened there. But I have learned that not everything is as it seems. Lorenzo's mantra that we are living in a world at war was never more true to me than as we sailed into the Great Babylonian Canal.

If you have ever been to a major city, you know that it is often visible from a great distance, both by day and by night. New Babylon was no different. We could see it before we entered the canal that led up from the Persian Gulf to the massive docks that serviced the new world capital. And it wasn't all gleaming skyscrapers either. First, we saw the familiar plumes of black smoke. New Babylon wasn't like Dubai, which had been hit by the demonic riders of the sixth trumpet judgment so hard that nothing was left. The high rise building weren't just knocked down, they were covered with sulfur that continued to burn. The magnificent yachts were sunk, the piers left in charred ruins, and the great auditoriums and grand venues of one of the world's richest cities were completely destroyed.

There were fires in New Babylon, too, but no signs of major destruction. In fact, the city was an awe-inspiring sight, starting with the massive alien ship that hovered over it. The ship was huge, a great saucer-shaped vessel that gleamed in the sky like a second sun. In fact, it reflected so much light that the area around New Babylon was noticeably warmer than it had been further south.

The next thing we saw was the massive main gate. New Babylon reflected many of the former Babylonian wonders, including a big wall around the main city, which was painted dark green, and a huge gate structure that was brilliant blue. The doors of the gate stood at least a hundred feet tall and were open wide. Through the gate, much of the city could be seen, but what initially captivated us were the two giant guardians on either side of the gate. It may be difficult to fathom, but I am not lying when I tell you that the giant guardians were three hundred feet tall, taller than the city walls. They were dressed in Roman-style armor, with dark red cloaks and massive swords hung from their belts. At first, we thought they were statues. But they moved, turning their heads, looking directly at our ship, sometimes shifting their incredible weight from one foot to the other. They looked like men, but their faces were terrible to behold. They had flaming red hair and milky white skin with livid scars and bright blue tattoos on their necks and the sides of their faces. Their cheekbones and forehead brows stood out so much that they looked like skulls with facial features painted on them. Thick, wiry beards covered their wide jaws, and even though their mouths were closed, it was as if they were full of so many teeth they could hardly be contained.

Neither of the giants spoke, but the sound of their breathing could be heard as we approached. Because the *Manna T* carried passengers, we were directed into a dock not far from the city's main gate. There, our passengers were transferred to land. Cat and I wished them well after the ship was secured at the pier. They ignored us and hurried off the ship, anxious to explore the gleaming capital city. New Babylon was not just the home to the world's regional government; it was the home to the global religion and the world's digital banking system.

It was also home to the most evil spiritual beings at large in our world. The Bible says there are principalities among the fallen celestial beings. In other words, geographic rulers that have direct authority over a given place. In Deuteronomy 32, it says that God divided mankind and fixed the borders of the nations, according to the sons of God. In other words, he divided up the world and assigned angelic beings to watch over certain areas. But in Psalm 82, it says that these same celestial rulers were judged and found wanting. They showed partiality in their judgments, favoring the wicked. In Daniel it says that the Prince of Persia fought against God's angel for two weeks and that the heavenly messenger only reached Daniel after the Prince of Israel, Michael, came to his aid. It also, in that same passage, refers to the Prince of Greece. So, there can be no doubt that there are fallen angels with authority over certain places. There was a presence of great evil at New Babylon. My friends and I felt it, while the passengers on the ship and the staff working their way to the global capital seemed oblivious.

We didn't leave the ship at the passenger pier, but we could see the gleam of the buildings through the massive gates. Polished chrome, glass and steel glittered in the Arabian sunlight. The streets were bright white and spotlessly clean. Throngs of people moved about the city streets and, around them, were the tallest buildings in the world. The skyscrapers in New Babylon rose up much higher than the city walls. They weren't just boxy towers either, but ornately designed wonders. Some were arches, others were like trees with a wide central trunk, but also branches that extended out and up. There were spirals, ovals, and enormous globe-shaped buildings. Even more fantastic were buildings that appeared to be floating in the air. It was so spectacular and, yet, there was also a feeling of make-believe about it. It was like visiting a movie set or how I imagine visiting a movie set would feel. When you're on the street looking up at the buildings to either side, they seem real; although seen from above or behind and you realize it's just painted set pieces designed to look like buildings from a singular point of view.

The passengers were swept up in the grandeur. Most of them had been trying to get to New Babylon for months. Once they all disembarked, our lines were cast off by surly looking dock workers. I imagine that it is hard to be the hired help in a vacation destination where all the people you meet are having the time of their lives, but you are left slaving away, day after day.

LB and I coiled up the lines as Allie gently feathered the thruster controls and got us moving back into line for the cargo docks. It was nearly dark when we got pulled into place, and a ramp was lowered to allow us to move the vehicles. The staff workers who had traded their labor for passage into the grand city were formally dismissed by Cat, who, with our approval, gave each of the girls two gold Dinars.

"Hang onto these," she told them. "If you find yourself in trouble, this can get you the help you need."

It was pretty clear that most of the girls would be exchanging the gold bullion the first chance they got. Their priorities were fun and fashion. The idea of being prepared for tomorrow never even entered their minds. But they had done what they were asked to do on the *Manna T,* so even though we weren't obligated to give them anything, we all felt better making sure the girls had some way of escaping what we knew would be a hard, dangerous future.

Misha was the lone exception. Cat begged her to stay. We had all shared our testimony with her and encouraged her to put her faith in Jesus at some point along our journey. But she had been hesitant. In that regard, she reminded me of the way I had held off when Lorenzo showed me the truth. I had balked. I had used the distractions of other things, even other people, to put off the decision until it was too late. I hoped that Misha wouldn't do the same thing. We had all thought that she would stay and join our tiny crew, but when she saw New Babylon, the lure of the exotic city was too great. She left with the others and Cat was heartbroken.

It's one thing to have friends move on. We all go through different chapters of our lives at different times. Some friends remain, others move on, drift away or grow cold. But Misha's leaving wasn't just about a friend moving on. We were all very much aware that her eternal soul was hanging in the balance. She had no family, no one to look after her, and yet she found herself caught up in the excitement that every young person craves, with no concept of the danger around her. Yes, New Babylon was full of rich, handsome men, but I knew those men were in league with evil spirits that hated humanity. The true love and acceptance we all seek isn't found in excitement or hedonism. It isn't the absence of judgment, but rather the grace God offers us despite the reality that we all deserve judgment. We've all sinned and fallen short of God's standard. It is only by his grace and mercy that we have hope.

"I can't believe she's gone," Cat said as we began to uncover the luxury vehicles on the deck of our ship."

"You did all you could for her," I said.

"It wasn't enough."

"You don't know that," I said. "We don't know how her story ends. What I do know is the truth that you shared with her will never be forgotten."

"I hope you're right," Cat said.

"We all had to come to realize the truth in our own way," I reminded her. "I'm very proud of how you loved Misha. And how you managed all the staff."

Cat smiled, and then darkness fell like the curtain at the end of a play. It was as if God had flipped the light switch.

"Oh, dang," LB said. "I was hoping we could get this done before the dark."

"Let's just all be careful," Allie said.

We were slowly working our way back to the ship's main structure in the darkness when men with torches came toward the ship. We stopped and waited for them.

"Hey, what the hell are you lot doing?"

"Can't do nothing in the dark," LB pointed out.

"Americans," the dock worker said with disgust. "You lazy lot aren't slowing down my work quota. Take these torches and get your vehicles off that tub."

I took a torch, and Cat took another. We didn't mind doing the work, but it was a bit strange trying to move the vehicles in almost total darkness. The torches were bright, but the darkness seemed to override their light, confining it to a small circle barely enough to see your next step. Still, we did what we could. Allie and Cat held the torches and helped us remove the obstacles. Fortunately for us, the dock at New Babylon had hinges so that the end that came over the railing of our ship rested on the deck. We didn't need our portable ramps, which would have been harder to navigate in the darkness. One by one, we got the vehicles off the ship. They all started easily enough, but the gauges wouldn't work, and the digital displays were all dark. In the Mercedes G-Wagon, even the neon cabin lights failed to work. But the engines ran, and we crept the vehicles off the ship. We were nearly done when everyone's worst fear appeared.

The dock was a wide, concrete area that was actually just outside the city walls on the eastern side. Beyond them, before the supernatural darkness fell, I had seen rough, arid terrain stretching toward craggy mountains in the distance. There were stacks upon stacks of cargo containers, many being moved by cranes. Of course, that stopped when the darkness fell, but the ship workers were given torches and forced to continue working.

I had taken the last vehicle, the custom-fitted Jeep Wrangler with it's over-sized tires, snorkel exhaust, heavy-duty cargo rack, and fuel canister on its custom-machined platform on the back, over to where the other exotic vehicles were lined up. I left the keys fob on the dash, which I couldn't really see, and made my way over to the dock foreman.

"Sorry to bother you, but we need to resupply our fuel and fresh water," I said.

"Can't do that here," he snapped.

"Oh, okay, is there another dock where I can get what we need?"

"You Americans," he said as if our nationality was a curse word. "You always expect everyone to do your work for you. Learn what the hell you're doing, *ahbal!* I learned later that he was calling me an idiot. "Refitting is in Kuwait City."

"Oh, okay," I said. "Thank you."

I was afraid we wouldn't be able to get what we needed. And, truth be told, we had no clue what our next destination would be. How would we get more cargo and how long could we keep up the charade that we were merchantmen? I didn't know. Even though we had a ship and we had gold, I felt the sting of fear. It was almost like a voice in my head was taunting me with the concept of failure. I didn't want to let my friends down, but I didn't know what we should do. I started to pray, but there was such a sense of oppression in that place. It reminded me of the terrible demon that tormented and attempted to possess me before I put my faith in Jesus. I felt weak and helpless as thoughts invaded my mind that I didn't want to think. For instance, I knew that I could have slipped past the dock workers in the darkness. I felt a pull to go into the city, as if all my most lavish fantasies could be fulfilled. Images and memories filled my mind of things in my past that I'm ashamed of and I was suddenly filled with a desire to kill myself. I could easily just dive into the water of the canal and drown myself. The temptation to just end all my worries and suffering was so strong, I didn't think I could resist it.

But then the riders came. They were huge, much larger than I had thought. There were three of them. We heard the hooves of their terrible steeds before we saw them, but that sound was enough to cause people to start screaming and running. The dock wasn't that crowded, but it was very gloomy. Suddenly, the brightest light was a plume of fire, and it was billowing straight toward me. All I could do was turn and run.

I probably would have been killed if not for LB. He started shouting for me.

"Hank! Hank! Over here!"

I turned, suddenly feeling lost. There were maybe a dozen torches being utilized on the dock, but to the south, where the ships were located in the wide canal, there was only darkness. Human nature has trouble running blindly into the dark. Cat had wisely extinguished her torch, and Allie was holding hers low, hiding the light behind the *Manna T's* railing. More fiery blasts from the demonic horses with heads like lions and snakes for tails lit the area. I saw LB and Cat feverishly trying to untie the thick ropes from the pylons that held the vessel onto the pier. I raced toward them, knowing we needed to get away, but feeling a growing sense of hopelessness like I had never felt before.

And then, out of the darkness, near where LB was hunched over wrestling with the bowline, I saw a rider. It reared on its massive steed. The horse was easily fifteen feet tall. The rider on its back was like the Nazgûl, or ring wraiths from *The Lord of the Rings* stories. He didn't have a sword, but he didn't need one. Fire was flashing in the mouth of his mount, and from its light I saw the serpentine tail thrashing behind him.

Then it came back down on four hooves, and fire billowed from its mouth. LB leaped back, but he wasn't fast enough. The fire hit the mooring line, which burst into flames that flared high and hot. I heard him scream as he drew back his hands and fell backward. Before I knew it, I found myself running toward my friend. Cat was right beside me. In that moment, no conscious thought entered my mind save one. It was like a spark, small, silent, just a flicker of an idea. I felt stupid for even thinking it. But I knew I had to do some-thing. I wasn't going to let my friend die.

We reached LB just as the rider's mount roared. It sounded deep and terrifying. The sound vibrated through my body and turned my insides into water. I could hardly stand, I was so afraid, and barely felt Cat's hands on my back. Then suddenly her hand came up around my side. She was holding a pistol. I hadn't realized she was carrying it, but she raised the semi-automatic .45 caliber weapon and fired. Not just once, but all eight rounds just as fast as she could pull the trigger. Back in the days before the rapture, she had been a survivalist and hunter, living off the grid in the rugged wilderness of central Idaho. It's one of the largest wilderness areas in the Contiguous United States and only accessible by bush plane or by boat up the River of No Return. She had become a tender, loving person, that no one would ever suspect of being so tough and capable in a dire situation, but that was my Wildcat. She wouldn't have missed even if we hadn't been less than ten feet away from the roaring, lion-headed chimera. But the bullets did no damage. I didn't hear them ricochet off the creature and I didn't see any wounds. All I saw was fire springing forth from the open maw and I knew that it was the last thing I would ever see.

<h1 style="text-align:center">33</h1>

"Stop in the name of Jesus!" I shouted.

I was holding one hand up, palm out, like a beat cop on traffic duty. I can't say why I stood like that, and I can't say what I expected. But the spark of the idea to command the rider to stop had flashed through my brain. I felt stupid and weak and silly before I did it, but I was filled with a supernatural courage when the words came out of my mouth.

The chimera's mouth, full of fire, snapped closed, and it actually took a step backward. I still wasn't thinking. Everything was happening fast. Call it instinct, but I believe the Holy Spirit came over me in that moment.

"In the name of Jesus, be gone!"

The rider reared, the mount roaring again. Its massive hooves pawed the air. Being so close to it was terrifying. I could feel the wind from its hooves and was shaking all over. The creature was huge and ferocious. Fire billowed over my head. I couldn't take my eyes off it, but I heard LB moaning in pain. It was a pitiful sound.

"Hank, he's hurt bad," Cat said. "We have to get him out of here."

I agreed, but the rider came crashing back down onto all four of it's mount's legs. The front hooves hit so hard they cracked the cement pier. As the fire rolled through the air above us, I felt the heat from it. Sweat broke out all over my body from the overhead barrage and I saw the rider spin around. It was incredibly fast and agile for such a huge creature.

"Jesus! Help us!" I cried to God.

The serpent tail lashed out. Somehow, in the lurid light from nearby fires, I saw the unblinking eyes of the snake just before its mouth opened wide, revealing long, curved fangs. They were flying straight toward my face. Frozen in fear, I didn't move a muscle. The snake's mouth snapped closed right in front of me, then continued to swing in an arc away from me. I felt so weak I nearly fell down. But the chimera kept turning, its head was low to the ground, trying to avoid me and reach LB. I stepped over my friend.

"You cannot have him!" I shouted. "He belongs to Christ. Jesus will not lose even one of those his father has given him."

The beast rose back up and snarled at me. The rider on its back pointed at me and spoke in a voice that was high-pitched and terrible. I couldn't understand the language it spoke, but I recognized that it was cursing me.

"No weapon formed against God's elect shall stand," I said loudly. "You cannot hurt us."

If it had been solely based on my faith in what I was proclaiming, I would have died. The words felt hollow in my throat. My entire body was trembling in dread. It was hard to believe the demonic rider wasn't just toying with me. The big chimera pranced sideways, and in the wavering light, I saw the other two riders charging at us.

I held up my other hand toward the approaching riders. "In the name of Jesus, stop!"

Their hooves slid across the pavement. Fire was flooding up around the faces of the chimeras, and the riders were like demonic shadows. They twisted, moving sideways and trying to lunge in, but it was as if some invisible shield had sprung up between us and the terrible creatures.

"In the name of Jesus of Nazareth, Almighty Lord of this world, you must leave us! Go now!" I screamed.

And to my utter amazement, they obeyed. It was shocking. I was barely able to stand, but the riders turned away from us and chased after other people. By that point, several fires had been started. Even metal cargo containers were no match for the sulfur the riders spewed. As the port began to burn, I looked down at my friend. Tears flooded my eyes and I fell to my knees. LB was burned. His hands, arms to the elbow, and most of his face was burned. Most of his hair was gone, and there were fluids oozing where the skin had cracked and split open. He was unrecognizable and I felt my heart drop. Third-degree burns weren't always life-threatening, even though I had no doubt in that moment that LB was dying.

"Han..." he managed to say. "Geth me... home."

"I will," I said. "Don't worry, brother. I'm here."

"Tell... Al...eee...lov...er..."

"You are going to tell her yourself," I said. "Just hang in there. It's going to be okay."

I straightened up and had to wipe the tears from my eyes to see. The demonic riders were gone. That was good, but the dock workers were all gone too. Not that I wanted to take LB to a hospital in New Babylon.

"What should we do?" Cat asked. "He's dying, Hank."

"No," I said as more tears ran down my face. "He's not dying. Stay here."

I sprinted off. I was still shaky and weak, but it felt good to run and get my pent-up fears out of my body. It was still very dim and hard to see, but I knew where I was going. The cars we had delivered were lined up in a row. I ran straight to the Jeep and jumped behind the wheel. The push-to-start button wasn't glowing, but I knew where it was and pushed it. No lights came on, but the engine started with a steady growl. I pulled the gear select lever into Drive and hit the gas.

Within seconds, I was pulling to a stop beside where LB lay. Cat was hunched over him. I jumped out, opened the back and laid down the rear seats.

"Let's get him inside," I said.

I slid my arms under his shoulders. LB moaned in pain. I couldn't imagine what he was feeling. With a heave, I got him up and Cat did the same with his legs. We could only get him halfway into the Jeep. From there, Cat had to go around and get inside. She pulled, I pushed, and we got his long body into the vehicle. I didn't even bother closing the back gate. As I ran around to the driver's side of the Jeep, the *Manna T* started to drift away from the dock. The sound of the dock scraping across our deck plates was like fingernails scratching a chalkboard, but a thousand times worse. I drove quickly to the ramp, made it up and over. I drove the Jeep right up to the ship's superstructure. There was no time to clamp it down or wedge it in place. I hit the emergency brake, put it in park, then shut down the engine.

"What now?" Cat asked.

"Just stay there!" I shouted as I sprinted back over the ramp. It was already flexing up over the railing.

Deep in my mind, I knew I didn't have much time. I sprinted to the mooring line at the stern of the ship. It was still tied to the pylon. The ship was moving, pulling it tight. My hands tore at the ropes that were thicker than my wrist, but they wouldn't budge. If I couldn't get the rope untied, the ship would slap back and forth against the pier and probably sink.

"Oh, God, please help me," I said. "Give me strength."

That time I felt the Holy Spirit come on me. It was like the heat from the chimera's fiery breath, only instead of burning me, it filled me with a sense of calm. Suddenly, the rope seemed light as a feather and I easily unwound it from the pylon. I should have thrown the end of it onto the ship, but there was no one to catch it and pull it in. So, I pushed it into the water. The ship was floating freely and moving both forward and out from the dock. I sprinted back to the ramp. It was sliding off the railing of our ship, but I had just enough time to dash across and jump on board.

Only I didn't expect the end that was past the hinge to drop out from under me when it pulled free from the ship. The same handy feature that allowed us to do our job so easily before nearly cost me my life. The ramp dropped out from under me without warning, and I fell. My side hit the railing of the ship so hard it snapped three ribs and caused me to lose my grip on the railing.

The water was shockingly cold. I fell between the pier and the huge ship. If it had shifted back toward the dock, I would have been crushed. As it was, I struggled just to get my head above water and take a breath. When I did, pain shot down my side. I tried to call for help, but I couldn't breathe deep enough to shout. The boat was moving away from me. I reached out for something to take hold of, but the hull was smooth. There was nothing to grab onto.

What little light was from the fires on the pier above me. My body was growing numb from the cold and I was struggling to stay above the water. But then I saw the rear of the ship slide past me and I realized that I was going to drown in the canal. It was a bittersweet moment. To be honest, dying didn't seem so bad, but leaving Cat, with LB so badly hurt, seemed wrong.

Then I jerked in the water as something touched me. I guess I've seen too many movies about sharks and underwater creatures. I tried to twist away, but that sent spasms of pain shooting through my chest and down my back. I groaned, slipped under the water, came up sputtering, then felt the gentle bump again. Slashing in the water in a vain attempt to swim, my hand brushed down a long, hairy thing that was floating near me. Finally, my brain realized it was the mooring line. I had just enough sense to grab it. Fortunately, the big ship wasn't moving too fast through the water. I was able to pull myself back to the ship. Climbing on board was the hardest thing I've ever done. But my friends were depending on me, and I knew that I had to get back on board. So I ignored the pain from my broken ribs. That agony was nothing compared to what LB was feeling. I climbed up the side of the ship, which, fortunately for me, rode low in the water.

I staggered around the big superstructure where the passenger quarters and Bridge was located. When I got to the front, I found Cat and Allie at the back of the Jeep. Allie had stuffed the handle of the torch through the metal spare wheel holder on the back gate. She was sobbing, and Cat had one arm around her and one on LB's leg. I heard his raspy breathing as I approached.

"What happened?" Cat asked.

"Nothing," I lied. "How's he doing?"

Cat didn't reply; she just looked at me. The truth was plain on her face. My best friend was dying. I knew enough about burn victims to know that one of the deadliest things that can happen is for a person to breathe in the flames. The intense heat sears the lungs and makes it impossible to transfer oxygen into the bloodstream. And it sounded just then like LB was struggling to breathe.

I dropped to my knees and covered my face with my hands.

"Oh, God, please don't let him die," I whispered. "I need him. We all need him. Please, I know you can heal him if you just will. Let him stay with us. Take away the burns and heal him. I beg you, please, in the name of Jesus my Lord, please heal LB."

When I fell silent, all I could do was listen to LB's raspy breathing. Tears flooded my eyes, and I was shaking all over, partly from being wet and cold, and partly from grief. I would have traded places with LB if that were possible. Then his breathing stopped.

I've lost a lot of people in my life. My parents were killed when I was young. Lorenzo was taken in the Rapture. But those losses didn't prepare me for the grief of losing my best friend. I felt like a part of me had died and there was nothing I could do.

"Are we moving?" LB's familiar voice said.

My head snapped up, and I jumped to my feet. My face must have contorted in the wave of pain that wracked my body, but I didn't care.

"You're alive!" I said.

He was alive. In fact, his hands were no longer burned, and his face was normal. Even his hair was back.

"Yeah, somebody up there loves me," LB said. "I don't know what happened."

Allie, who had been frozen in shock, suddenly threw herself onto LB. He laughed as she pulled him forward and kissed him all over his face. Cat was laughing, but there were tears still running down her cheeks. It was an incredible moment, but then LB's question hit me hard. We were moving. The ship was drifting through the dark with no one at the controls.

"See you in a bit!" I told him, turning and lurching for the hatch. I staggered in and then climbed up the narrow set of stairs. Every step with my right foot sent pain surging through my body, up my neck, and down my hip. It was like someone had smashed a glass bottle on my insides, and the shards were grinding in my joints and around my bones. Every breath hurt. I turned, stepping up with my left foot so that I didn't have to put too much weight on my right foot. I was near the top of the stairs when Cat came through the hatch below me.

"What's wrong, Hank?" she called, hurrying to catch up to me.

"The ship's adrift," I said.

"No, what's wrong with you?"

"I fell," I said, as if that was explanation enough.

When I stepped into the Bridge, I expected the workspace to be pitch black, but instead, there was a faint, green glow. Moving over to the controls, I saw that just like the night when we had found the Jewish refugees, the radar showed a single blip. It was just ahead of us. I wasn't sure if I was supposed to steer around that blip or follow it. But there wasn't time. The engines weren't engaged. I couldn't get them spun up fast enough to turn the ship away, but I did my best. And to my relief, just like before, the blip remained the same distance ahead of us.

"You're soaked," Cat said.

"It's a bit of a story," I said.

"Get out of those clothes, and I'll bring you some towels," she said.

I didn't have time to do anything else. The blip on the screen was turning and I had to work the thrusters to follow it. When I got the chance, I pulled off my jacket and then my shirt. They fell with a wet flop at my feet. Cat returned with towels and a candle. She wrapped one around my shoulders and carefully draped one over my head.

A few minutes later, LB and Allie joined us. In a few minutes, we had candles lit around the Bridge and Allie took charge of the controls. LB pulled me aside and said, "Let me take a look at you, Hank."

"I can't stop looking at you," I said. "You seem completely normal."

"I am," he said.

"I thought you died."

"I did," he said. "And I met Jesus."

"What?" I said loudly, then grimaced in pain.

"You, my friend, have cracked ribs," he said, his hand moving gently down my side. I still grunted as he touched the area that had smacked into the ship's railing.

"You saw Jesus?"

"I did ... and when we get into safer waters, I'll tell you all about it."

34

Cat helped me out of the rest of my wet clothes. I rinsed the saltwater from my very bruised and swollen body, then I put on sweatpants and a sweatshirt. As I settled into one of the captain's chairs on the bridge with a blanket, LB brought me coffee and some ibuprofen. Cat got a cold pack and shook it to activate the chemicals. It felt good on my side, even though I couldn't seem to get warm.

"Tell us what happened?" I said as the supernatural darkness ended.

Lights came on, and the radar showed nearly a dozen ships nearby. We were out of the New Babylon canal and in the Persian Gulf proper. I was just about to suggest we turn west toward Kuwait City to get more fuel and supplies.

"First of all, we're not to go to Kuwait," LB said. "Head south."

Allie glanced at me and I nodded.

"I was in a lot of pain," LB said. "But when Allie showed up, I felt myself leave my body. I just drifted upward and I was looking down at my body. I didn't like seeing Allie cry, but I felt a strange sense of detachment. There was a warmth and a sense of peace. It's hard to explain. I was no longer hurting, no longer scared, just everything felt right."

"Were you dreaming?" Allie asked.

She was still at the controls, but she was turned toward us. I was in one chair, LB was in the other. Cat stood by me, her hands on my shoulders.

"No, it wasn't like a dream. It was more real than anything I've ever experienced. More real than this conversation we're having."

"And you saw Jesus?"

"I saw a light above me. I looked up and I was moving toward it, just sort of flying or drifting without really thinking about moving at all. I felt drawn to that light. You know when it's cold out and you step into the sun and feel the warmth of it. It was like that, only much, much better. I wanted to be in that light, that's for sure.

"But then a man appeared in the light ahead of me. I couldn't see his face, but I could see him, sort of like in silhouette. Only, instead of casting a shadow, this guy was shining brighter than the warm golden light."

"Wow," Cat said.

"Yeah, it was really something. Strange thing was, I knew him. Can't say how, but I knew it was Jesus. And I could feel the love coming off him in waves. They were strong, sort of like ocean waves rolling into me over and over. I just fell down, if that's possible. I had been floating up toward the light, then Jesus appeared, and I fell at his feet, you know."

"That's amazing," Allie said. "I'm so jealous."

"Me too," Cat confessed.

"Me three," I said.

"He taps me on the shoulder and says, 'LB, it's not time for you yet.' Now let me tell you, as much as I love you guys and I never want to leave you in the lurch, that was some hard words to hear. It was like every cell in my body was drinking in that light and the love of

Jesus. I didn't want to leave, that's for sure. Then he said, 'You are not to go to Kuwait. I need you to take the ship back to the Red Sea. There I will show you where to go and what to do.' Suddenly, I felt myself flying backward, or falling, maybe. I sort of landed in my body and that made me take a deep breath. You know the rest."

"That's incredible," I said.

"Well, I'm not going to argue with Jesus," Allie said. "And we've seen plenty of things I can't explain, but you're a walking, talking miracle, babe."

"Yes, I am," LB said.

"But we're down to a quarter of our fuel," she said. "If we don't top that off soon, we could run out."

"We've got the gold," I said.

"Is there another place to get fuel?" Cat asked.

"There have to be more ports we could stop in," Allie said.

"No, we can't do that," LB said. "We have to go to the Red Sea. God will show us what to do and how to do it. That much is for sure."

Allie looked at Cat and me. "Obeying God always requires faith," Cat said.

I remembered how I felt when the spark of what to do with the demonic riders on their fire-breathing chimeras flashed in my mind. It was like I knew that it was God telling me what to do, but I still felt foolish thinking that I could command the terrifying beasts to leave us alone. Of course, it wasn't me, it was all Jesus. My point is, in that moment of decision, we all had our doubts, despite the fact that we had just seen LB hideously burned one moment and completely healed the next as if nothing had ever happened.

"If Jesus has something for us, I don't want to miss it," I said.

"Good," Allie breathed a sigh of relief. "I feel the same way."

So we headed south, trusting God and wondering what was next. It was something big and I'm so glad we obeyed. There's nothing like seeing God at work and realizing he let you be part of his story. I'm looking forward to telling you all about it, but that will have to wait for another book.

.   .   .

"The second woe has passed; behold, the third woe is soon to come." —
Revelation 11:14

AUTHOR'S NOTE

There is so much I could say about this book. I've been wanting to write it for a long time, but I didn't feel like God wanted me to until now. And I'm excited to say that I'm already making good progress on book five. If you'd like to read an unedited sample I've included it immediately following this note.

There is a lot in this book that was speculation, but here is what we know for certain, at some point during the seven year tribulation period (most theologians agree the Trumpet Judgments will take place in the first half) there will be a shift from ecological disasters to supernatural events that will bend humanity's understanding of what is possible. While it could be argued that the locusts that come up out of the Abyss are simply a strange species that has never been identified before, no one can make that claim with the chimeras the two-hundred million man army will ride. Perhaps gene splicing and cross species hybridization is further along than we know, but I doubt it. And I personally believe that these supernatural judgments will be physically seen and experienced by the people still alive during that part of the Tribulation period.

My books are explorations of what the Bible talks about. Did you know that nearly a third of the Bible is prophecy? And we are seeing more Bible prophecy coming true than at any other time of human history. People tend to focus on things they consider to be main points, or those that are difficult to imagine how they might come about like the forthcoming mark of the beast that will be required to buy and sell starting at the halfway point of the Tribulation period. But as I write this the United States and Israel are attacking Iran, and specifically targeting Iran's missile launching capabilities. In Jeremiah 49:35 it says, "Thus says the Lord of hosts: "Behold, I will break the bow of Elam, the mainstay of their might." (ESV) Many prophecy commentators and theologians are saying that we are seeing this prophecy fulfilled. Elam is the ancient name of the people from that part of the world, before they were absorbed into Persia in the sixth century BC. Perhaps more telling is the building of alliances between Iran, Turkey, and Russia which is predicted in one of the most dramatic prophecies of scripture often called the Gog-Magog war.

But while I am basing these stories from scripture, they are not a commentary. If you want to really dig in there are a lot of great resources to choose from. I would highly recommend that you take advantage of some great Bible teachers who have given us wonderful written and video lessons on the times we are living in, such as this video podcast by Pastor Jack Hibbs that covers the entire book of Revelation in one episode. Or, if you prefer more depth, the late Dr. Chuck Missler has a 24 episode commentary on the Revelation that you can find here. Of course there's much more to Bible prophecy than just Revelation. The book of Daniel is essential reading, and it's prophecies (specifically regarding the empires set to rise in and after his life, and the specifics of the conflicts between the Poltomy and Selucid kingdoms during the Greek Empire) are so clear and accurate that people argue it had to be written during the current era, not over five hundred years before the birth of Christ.

Personally, I just discovered that the little book of Joel (just three chapters) gives prophecies that match what we have just covered in *Three Woes*. For instance, Joel 1:2-4 I believe is a reference to the fifth trumpet judgment: "*Hear this, you elders; give ear, all inhabitants of the land! Has such a thing happened in your days, or in the days of your fathers? Tell your children of it, and let your children tell their children, and their children to another generation. What the cutting locust left, the swarming locust has eaten. What the swarming locust left, the hopping locust has eaten, and what the hopping locust left, the destroying locust has eaten.*" (ESV). And in verse six we have a reference to the demon riders of the sixth trumpet judgment, "*For a nation has come up against my land, powerful and beyond number; its teeth are lions' teeth, and it has the fangs of a lioness.*" (ESV).

These wonderful prophecies not only educate us as to what will happen in the future, but they are the proof that God's word is true. As Chuck Missler used to say, it is a self-authenticating message system from outside of time. God has not only given us his word to reveal himself, his love, his purpose to redeem mankind, and the path to his salvation, but also to show beyond doubt that he is real and trustworthy. If you have trouble seeing the Bible as a whole, might I recommend my own pastor's book, *Called to be Free: A Study in Dispensationalism.* It is a short, simple outline of the scriptures (historically presented) with an explanation of how God was interacting with mankind in each phase. We are currently in the Church Age, a time of grace for anyone who wants to know God. When you believe that Jesus is who he said he was, God made flesh, and put your faith in his death on the cross for your sins, you will be reconnected with God and given the gift of his Holy Spirit that will reside within you and lead you to truth. But after this age comes a time of God's wrath upon the earth for the failure of mankind, and specifically the Jews, to recognize Jesus as the Messiah. Every judgment and supernatural event is intended to help people recognize the truth. But there will be a great delusion that will blind many people and it will be an incredibly dangerous period of history. Jesus said that if it wasn't kept short that no one would survive. For those of us who have believed in Jesus, we are promised that he will come to call us home before it begins in an event called the Rapture (Latin *ratura*, a translation of the Greek *Harpazō* meaning to sieze, catch away, pluck, pull, take by force, occurs thirteen times in the New Testment). If you want to know more about how you can know God personally, or any of the topics covered in this book, you can send me a message here and I'll be glad to get in touch with you.

I absolutely love being a storyteller. And the End Times Biblical Prophecy books are very dear to me. I hope you are enjoying them as much as I am. Thanks again for reading, and many happy adventures.

BITTER SCROLL 1

It's hard to believe we're still here. Three years after the church was raptured, what the world calls the Vanishings, I find myself on a ship in the Persian Gulf. I'm still a little shaken by the close encounter we had with the demonic soldiers riding fire-breathing chimeras with the head of a lion, the body of a horse, and a serpent for a tail. As I write these words, those demonic riders are in the process of killing two billion people.

By the grace and power of God, we escaped the port at New Babylon, sailed out of the canal in complete darkness without crashing the *Manna T,* and now we're heading south, out of the gulf and toward the Arabian Sea. I'll be honest, I never saw myself here. Out the little window in the cabin I share with my wife, Cat, I can see endless ocean waves. I'm at the captain's desk contemplating the days and dangers that lie ahead. In case you aren't familiar with what the Bible reveals regarding these seven years, you should know that we're experiencing a series of judgments. There were seven seal judgments that started with Paul Eon brokering the historic peace deal. The seal judgments led to seven trumpet judgments, the first of which was the fiery hail that burned up a third of the planet's flora and caused massive damage across the globe. The second trumpet judgment was the asteroid that hit the ocean, and the third resulted in the contamination of the world's fresh water supply. Then the fourth judgment, which is still in effect, is the loss of light from the sun, moon, and stars for a third of the day and a third of the night. As you can probably guess, the lack of light isn't just physical darkness. It has warped the climate all around the world. Worse still, in the supernatural darkness, the beings who love evil have free rein. My friends and I have seen everything from terrible visions to ghosts in that daily eight-hour stretch.

The last three judgments are also called the three woes. The first was the opening of a shaft leading down to what the Bible calls the Abyss. Again, forgive me if you know all this, but a lot of people don't realize that there is more to the *afterlife* than heaven and hell. The Bible mentions a place where the fallen angels were locked up in gloomy chains of darkness. It's called various things: the abyss, the bottomless pit, and Tartarus. Out of that shaft came the demonic locusts with tails like scorpions. They attacked people for five full months, and during that time, people couldn't die. It was a difficult time, and certainly the most frightening, until the second woe or sixth trumpet judgment. I'll be honest and say that I don't understand it completely. The Bible says four angels were unleashed, I'm guessing in the spirit realm. In the physical world, they manifested as two hundred million demonic warriors riding chimeras with the power to kill people by spewing fire and sulfur from their mouths.

Up close and personal, the riders are huge beings that clearly have a deep, burning hatred of humanity. They have the authority to kill a third of mankind, which is around two billion people. And they're still at work. I've found that writing my story helps me cope with what we're going through. If you haven't read my other books, then allow me to catch you up.

I'm a Christian, but I didn't come to my faith until after the church was raptured. I know some of you were taught that the rapture was just a false doctrine by hard-headed dispensationalists and preachers who taught Bible prophecy as if it were really going to happen. It's pretty hard to deny that now, as we see supernatural events taking place all around the world as described in the Bible. Me and my friends are doing our best to survive and get the word out about what's really taking place. Most recently, we were in the Miami, Florida area when the plague of stinging locusts was unleashed from the shaft leading down to the Abyss. It's the same place that the Greeks called Tartarus, where their supposed gods imprisoned their forebears, the Titans. Go back and read my first book, and you'll get a good idea that all the so-called gods of what we were taught was mythology are actually real, although the Bible calls them fallen angels or more accurately the *Bene ha'Elohim*, the sons of God. These celestial entities aren't children, nor are they the same as Jesus, who is God the Son, part of Almighty God's triune nature. No, these are powerful created beings who rebelled against God's rule and sought the worship of mankind. And many of them have been released as part of God's judgment on planet Earth.

The Bible says that the terrible locusts that came out of the shaft to the Abyss are ruled by one such being, a powerful entity in the spirit realm called *Abbadon*, or Destroyer. Well, if you haven't closed my book by this point, I'll give you points for your courage. Most of the world absolutely rejects the truth about God and the cosmic war that has been raging since creation. I rejected it too until the truth smacked me hard in the face. That's when I fell on my knees and cried out to Jesus to save me. I didn't deserve it, but none of us do. We're all sinners, even the best of us fall short of God's glorious standard every single day. And that means we need help. Jesus was that help. He died as a perfect, unblemished sacrifice to pay the penalty for all our sins. Then he rose from the dead three days later to defeat death, too. Now, all we have to do is believe in him, and he will give us his perfect righteousness. Jesus said it best, *For God so loved the world that he gave his one and only son, that whoever believes in him will not perish, but receive eternal life.* And let me tell you, friend, you for sure want eternal life. The alternative is eternal death, and well... it's bad... really bad.

Because of the supernatural darkness that blacks out the sun for four hours and the stars for four hours each day, planet Earth has entered into a new ice age. And with the new Global Government looking to register everyone and persecute anyone who doesn't subscribe to their new global religion, we knew we had to leave Miami. We found a ship that is considered a flex-freighter. In other words, it's a cargo ship with rooms for up to sixty passengers. It's called the *Manna-T,* and my friends and I just dropped off a load of cargo and passengers in New Babylon. While we were there, we were attacked by the demonic riders, and my best friend, Lester Barski who we all call LB, was nearly killed. In fact, he saw Jesus, who told him not to go to Kuait for refueling and resupplying the ship. Which is why we're cruising south and I'm here in my cabin writing this book. I know it's a bit scattered, but there's a lot going on in the world, and I'm just trying to wrap my head around it. I'll write more in a bit, but first I need to go and check out our fuel situation.

BITTER SCROLL 2

"It's bad," Allie said.

Allie is LB's wife and a wiz with mechanical stuff. We met in a government camp outside of Abilene, TX. Allie, suffering from the loss of her children in the Rapture, blamed Christians like me for their disappearance. She reported me, and I was pretty close to getting killed for my faith, but the camp was attacked by Abilene locals who were starving. During the raid on the government camp, only a few of us managed to escape. LB and Allie were with us, and soon after, they came to believe in Jesus just like me and my wife, Cat.

It's just the four of us on the *Manna-T*. Fortunately, the big ship is really easy to operate. Unfortunately, we were just about out of fuel and food.

"How bad?" I asked.

"Less than an eighth of a tank," she said. "We maybe have enough to keep going for a day, but I can't guarantee it."

"God will provide," I said without much conviction.

Don't get me wrong, I believed that God was our provider. But I also understood that we were in the middle of what the Bible calls the Tribulation period, a seven-year span when God judges the world for its disbelief. In other words, we weren't guaranteed a happy ending. I knew good people, strong believers in Jesus, who had died for their faith. The global government liked to live-stream the executions. Facing danger is part of the cross we have to bear as we follow Christ. Not that there was ever really a time when Christians didn't face danger for their faith. And I wasn't completely convinced that we weren't going to crash the *Manna-T* or run out of food, or both.

"He'll have to," Allie said. "I've got one five-gallon can of fuel that is for the outboard motor on the inflatable, but that's hardly a drop in the bucket considering how the main engine goes through fuel."

We shut off the lights and made our way back up to the ship's superstructure. Being a flex/freighter, the *Manna T* had a long main deck with reinforced supports for stacking cargo containers. She also had massive bins inside the hull, which were filled with produce from South America. It was supposed to have gone to New Babylon, but with the demon riders attacking, the dock workers all ran away, and we certainly weren't going to stick around to finish the delivery. On the back half of the main deck was the five story super structure with space for the passengers and crew. It wasn't nearly as lavish as a cruise ship, but it was still a comfortable vessel. The best part was being on the water, since it didn't seem like the demon riders could swim. In that regard, we were safe, but once the *Manna T* ran out of fuel, we would have no choice but to go ashore and take our chances at surviving until the sixth trumpet judgment ended.

"How bad is it?" Cat asked. Her real name is Mira, but before we met, she was a survivalist and primitive skills expert going by the nickname Wildcat. She had a pretty big following on YouTube before the rapture.

"Worse than I thought," Allie said. "We need to head for shore now."

"No," LB said. He was a tall, black man with traces of gray in his dark hair. A former Marine Officer, he and Allie had fallen in love and gotten married. "We can't do that."

"Listen, I know you have a feeling about this, LB," she told him. "But we could get stuck out here."

"We're out of food, too," Cat said. "I just did an inventory. We'll be eating the last of the food tomorrow."

"If we get stuck out here without food, we could starve before anyone comes to help us," I said.

"God isn't going to let that happen," LB said. "I know it sounds a little off, but do y'all remember that story about Elijah and the widow woman?"

"The one with her only son," Allie said softly. "They had no food."

LB put his big arm around her. "That's it. You remember, she had just enough for one last meal, then she expected that she and her son would die. And Elijah tells her to make him some food. That was a tough thing for him to ask of her, because if she fed him, there wouldn't be anything left for her and her boy."

"But God," Cat said.

"Best two words in the English language, but God," LB said with a chuckle. "Elijah tells her that she'd be able to cook for herself and her son after she obeyed him because God wouldn't let the flour and oil run out until the famine ended."

"I know you're trying to make a point," I said.

"That's right, I am," LB said. "I've been thinking and praying this whole time, and I'm pretty sure we need to pour the last of the fuel into the tank."

"That's the fuel for the dinghy, babe," Allie said. "It's not enough to keep the main engines going even half an hour."

"Plus, if we use that, we won't have any way to get to shore when we run out of fuel," I pointed out. "We'll be stranded on the ship with no food, man."

LB looked pained at our response, but then Cat spoke up. "Did any of you ever read Prince Caspian?"

"What?" I asked.

"It's a children's book, but C.S. Lewis, part of the Chronicles of Narnia."

"I think I saw the movie once," Allie said. "I don't remember it, though."

"It's the only one I read," Cat said. "And I'm not an expert on literature or anything, but there's a scene in the story where Lucy, that's the youngest of the children in the story, sees Aslan."

"He represents Christ," I said. "Lorenzo used to talk about that."

"Right, and so Lucy knows she should go to him, but he's higher up the mountain, and her siblings are trying to find a way down. When she tells him that she saw Aslan, they complain that they haven't seen him. And when she tries to convince them to go up the mountain, they refuse. They're tired and frustrated and just trying to figure things out."

For a full minute, we all just stared at each other. LB had seen Jesus in a vision, or an out-of-body experience, after he had been burned pretty badly by the demon riders. God healed him. That's a moment I won't ever forget, and he led us through the New Babylon canal in total darkness. And yet, for some reason, taking LB's advice was a hard pill to swallow.

"What happens in the story?" LB asked.

"Eventually, Lucy disobeys her brother and goes into the woods where she has seen Aslan. She finds him," Cat said with a smile. "But then he sends her back to convince the others. It's no easy task, but eventually she succeeds."

I looked at LB, "You really think this is what God is telling you to do?"

"Yeah, man, I do."

"Alright," I said, my heart pounding in my ears, "I'm in."

"Me too," Cat said.

Allie nodded, then she and LB went back down to the engine room. They were gone for almost an hour. I was about to go and check on them when they reappeared.

"You guys okay?" I asked.

"Better than okay," LB said. "Tell him."

"Where's Cat?" Allie asked.

"Preparing our final meal," I said. "She's opening those cans of spam no one else would eat. What happened in the engine room? We've still got power."

"Got it and gonna keep it," LB said.

"We used the fuel from the outboard engine can," Allie said. "Remember I told you it was five gallons?"

"Yeah," I said, feeling a tingle rush across my skin.

"Well, we poured it into the main engine tank... and filled it up."

"What?" I said, hardly believing what I was hearing.

"That's a five-thousand-gallon tank," Allie said.

"She started pouring, and it just kept on coming," LB jumped in. "I saw it, and I still can't hardly believe it. But we are full on fuel, my man. No problems there."

"There's even more fuel left in the spare can!" Allie said. "It was a miracle. I'll never doubt God again."

"We celebrated with fried spam and saltine crackers. Everyone was excited. At least until that afternoon, as we approached the Strait of Hormuz, only to discover it was clogged with human bodies.

BITTER SCROLL 3

I don't enjoy writing macabre scenes, but I can't skip over them. The Strait of Hormuz is a narrow point in the Persian Gulf between the United Arab Emirates and Iran. It's also very close to Dubai, which, unlike some places, lost very little of its population in the rapture. In fact, there were nearly five million people living there before the demon riders were unleashed. We had seen the destruction of the modern city in the desert on our way to New Babylon. On the way out, we found the bodies of the dead.

"Good God Almighty," LB said softly.

Cat was asleep, and soon the supernatural darkness would fall. We thought of it as supernatural because it didn't merely get dark; it somehow rendered all forms of light other than fire inert. I had hoped to get through the narrow Strait before that, but there were thousands, probably tens if not hundreds of thousands of charred human bodies floating in the water like driftwood.

"What do we do?" Allie asked.

"Can we keep going?" LB wondered aloud.

"I think we have to," I said.

The Strait of Hormuz isn't straight at all. It curves east, then back to the west around a peninsula that juts out from the UAE into a pie shaped indention along the Iranian coastline. On the map, they looked like puzzle pieces that would fit together. But the *Manna T* couldn't merely plow through the bodies. We had to guide the ship through the strait, and we didn't have a lot of time. When darkness fell, we would have to weigh anchor. Sailing without our radar and GPS was too dangerous.

"Let's see how it goes," I said.

We didn't leave the Bridge, but still we could hear the bodies as the *Manna T* plowed into the corpses. The ship had a pointed bow. On the deck was a storage area with a mooring cleat. We normally kept one of the thick ropes used to hold the ship in place when docked at the bow of the ship, but it had been burned up during the attack at New Babylon. That edge moved through the bodies, pushing them to one side or the other. At first, it was simply a matter of steering. I couldn't see the bodies in the water up close to the ship, so I kept us on the heading for southbound vessels as projected by the ship's GPS navigation system. Because the Strait of Hormuz was so busy, sea lanes had been established. There were buoys in the water, but they were lost among the blackened bodies.

Looking back on it, I'm really glad of two things. The first is that even though it looked like the strait was clogged with bodies, there was actually enough space here and there that our ship could push through. We had to increase power to the engines, but we never got bogged down or stuck in the glut of corpses. I was also glad that none of the bodies got sucked under the ship and chopped up by the propeller.

Once we made it through the bodies, I stepped out onto the Bridge wing and looked behind us. The trail through the macabre cluster of corpses was closing back together, but in the gap I saw several shark fins. The carnivorous sea creatures were feasting on the bodies of people who had been slaughtered by demonic riders. You might wonder how the bodies ended up in the water, but I remember seeing pictures of Dubai. There had been towering apartment buildings erected right on the edge of the water, many with their own docks for private yachts. Those structures were all gone, but if they had toppled into the sea, it wouldn't take long for the bodies inside to come floating to the surface.

I hurried back inside, trying not to remember the burned faces and gnarled limbs that stuck up out of the water.

We made it through the Strait and into the Gulf of Oman before the supernatural darkness fell. That night, after weighing anchor, the four of us went down to the galley. Cat had already searched it top to bottom. The only things left were dry pasta and crackers. But we were all hungry, and with nothing better to do, we carried our candles down to the storage area and gave it another look. The dining area was empty, and as we usually did during the daily period of strange darkness, we saw shadows moving at the edges of the candlelight. The empty ship was creepy in the dark. Normally, we stayed together on the Bridge, or close to it. The galley seemed especially haunted, as any large, dark space usually was.

When we reached the pantry, we expected nothing. It was a rectangular room with large shelves on three sides. At one point, all the bins and shelves had been full. But we had gotten very few extra rations since leaving Key West, and during the journey across the Atlantic Ocean, our two hundred and thirty passengers made short work of what we had. The passengers from Haifa had done the rest. We were hoping to find some salt and maybe a few dried spices that might make plain pasta a bit more palatable. What we found was shocking.

"This... no... it's not possible," Cat said as we stepped into the pantry.

LB started chuckling. Allie and I were speechless. All the way in the back of the pantry, on a single row of shelves, were fruit and produce baskets overflowing with perfectly ripe, seemingly fresh picked goods. There were oranges, lemons, and limes in one basket. Another had dividers with all sorts of ripe berries inside. Still another had apples, bananas, peaches, and pears. There wasn't a bruise or spot on any of them. There were clusters of asparagus, sweet onions, red, yellow, and orange bell peppers, heads of broccoli, cauliflower, and lettuce. Another basket had bundles of fresh herbs. There were potatoes, squash, zucchini, tomatoes, avocado, and yams.

"This is amazing," Allie finally said.

"I can't believe it," Cat said.

"The Lord will provide," LB said, picking up an apple and smelling it.

"Guys," I said, my voice trembling and tears flooding my eyes.

It was all that needed to be said. You might find it strange that we went to our knees right there in that pantry, held hands, and gave thanks to God in prayer. But it wasn't strange to us. The world around us had become strange. Everything happening in our lives was like we were living in a Hollywood movie that was a strange mashup of genres. And yet, despite the craziness, terror, and pain so many people were enduring, despite our lack of safety and the knowledge that we probably would not live long enough to see Christ's triumphant return to Earth, we felt loved. That word almost seems too trite for what we were feeling. You have to understand, we had been living on the verge of desperate for years, and suddenly we had been blessed with a gift of such kindness it took my breath away. God didn't have to feed us. Plenty of people went without, and yet, he was supplying all our needs.

After our prayer, we gathered food to make a meal. And when we got to the prep area in the kitchen, I turned and opened the over-sized, commercial-grade refrigerator. The interior lights didn't come on, but by the light of my candle, I discovered the pantry wasn't the only place where food had miraculously disappeared. I could have told the others, but instead, I reached out, picked up a cold can of Dr.

Pepper, and pulled back the tab. It opened with a hiss and pop that just about anyone would recognize.

"What?" LB said, his voice a full octave too high.

I took a drink and turned toward my friends. They were all staring at me wide-eyed. In the darkness beyond the candlelight, I saw movement. It wasn't the usual shadowy displays that made your skin crawl. It was the looming figure of an angel. It's hard to describe exactly. I couldn't make out the features of his face. It had long hair that hung down either side. It was so tall it had to kneel. It wore a kind of robe, but I could see the handle of a huge sword. Its hands were lost in the darkness. What was clearest of all were the angel's wings. They were massive. I could tell what they were, but not what they were made of. And the angel didn't just have two, but four wings. Two were wrapped around us, and two more covered us.

"We're not alone," I said.

My friends turned, and for a moment, they too could see our protector. I can't say what was happening exactly. But I was certain that God had shown us the angel as a way of confirming that he had a task for us.

"Was that... an angel?" Cat asked.

"Had to be," LB replied.

"We're safe," I said. "And come take a look in here."

They came to where I stood. Inside the refrigerator, there were all sorts of goodies. Milk, eggs, cheese, soft drinks, fruit juice in tall containers, and even a row of bottles of beer.

"Did God give us beer?" LB asked.

"I don't think he's against alcohol," Allie said.

"The Son of Man came eating and drinking," I said, quoting Jesus in Luke 7:34.

"He drank wine," Cat said.

"Well then, I don't mind if I do," LB said, taking a bottle of beer and twisting off the cap. He sniffed it, sighed, then took a drink. "Oh, I've missed this."

Along with the other goodies in the refrigerator was a tray with meat of various kinds. They were separated with little dividers, thick steaks, lamb kabobs, and two whole chickens. In a nearby cabinet, we found sugar, flour, oil, and wine. For the next hour, we cooked together and feasted like we hadn't done in a long time, probably since before the rapture. It was wonderful. We had fun and felt safe. It's a memory that I will never forget.

ALSO BY TOBY NEIGHBORS

End Times

The Four Horsemen

Surviving Wormwood

Wizard Rising

Magic Awakening

Hidden Fire

Crying Havoc

Fierce Loyalty

Evil Tide

Wizard Falling

Chaos Descending

Into Chaos

Chaos Reigning

Chaos Raging

Controlling Chaos

Killing Chaos

Elder Wizard

Lorik

Lorik the Protector

Lorik the Defender

We Are The Wolf

Welcome To The Wolfpack

Embracing Oblivion

Joined In Battle

The Abyss Of Savagery

The Vault Of Mysteries

Lords Of Ascension

The Elusive Executioner

Gryphon Warriors

Regulators Revealed

Avondale

Draggah

Balestone

Arcanius

Avondale V

Third Prince

Royal Destiny

The Other Side

The New World

Luck Holds

Zompocalypse

Spartan Company

Spartan Valor

Spartan Guile

Dragon Team Seven

Uncommon Loyalty

Total Allegiance

Kestrel Class

Jump Point

Gravity Flux

Modulus Echo

Zero Friction

Planet Fall

Charter

Jack & Roxie

My Lady Sorceress

The Man With No Hands

ARC Angel

Battle ARC

Broken Crucible

Hidden Kingdom

War INC

Carthage Prime

Cronus Team

Skandia Seven

Mercurial

Magnificus Prime

Incursio

Merlin Appears

Runners

Survivors

Infiltrators

Resistance

Conquest

Occupation

Extraction

The Signal

Battle Orders

Base Of Fire

Hard Site

Recall

Evade

Assault

Space Fever

Staying Alive

Fractal Cut

Blast Zone

Action Zone

Covert Infil

Armor Brigade

Havoc Squad

Thunderbird

Ghost Tactics

Quantum Combat

Infinite Threat

Shadow Threat

Evolving Threat

Lingering Threat

Latent Prowess

Gravity Masters

Gravity Storm

Daughter of the Night

Supernova

Artifact

Blood Moon

Renegade

Juggernaut

Retribution

Independence

Sons of Perdition

Iron Man

Brutal Planet

Hell Flyers

Foray

Conspire

Siege

Colossus

Dead Space

With Pete Garcia

Apocalypse One Percenters